THE LODGER

VALERIE KEOGH

Boldwood

First published in Great Britain in 2022 by Boldwood Books Ltd.

Copyright © Valerie Keogh, 2022

Cover Design by Head Design

Cover Photography: Shutterstock

A CIP catalogue record for this book is available from the British Library.

Paperback ISBN 978-1-80415-454-0

Large Print ISBN 978-1-80415-450-2

Hardback ISBN 978-1-80415-449-6

Ebook ISBN 978-1-80415-447-2

Kindle ISBN 978-1-80415-448-9

Audio CD ISBN 978-1-80415-455-7

MP3 CD ISBN 978-1-80415-452-6

Digital audio download ISBN 978-1-80415-446-5

Boldwood Books Ltd
23 Bowerdean Street
London SW6 3TN
www.boldwoodbooks.com

For my nephew, Stephen Doyle, with love.

1

Mostly, a decision we make has few consequences, and often we can do a three-sixty, reversing it with a shrug and a smile. Sometimes, though, that decision is irreversible, and we must live with what we've done.

We can look back and analyse what led to our choice. The path we took. The very moment we turned the corner, put a foot on that slippery slope and were swept away. For years, Leigh had wondered exactly which point had been the one of no return, when she'd lost her balance and went careering towards a destination she'd never, ever, *ever* contemplated.

Finally, after going over and over every word of every conversation she could remember, or thought she could remember, she'd chosen... not the moment she'd lost control and lashed out at her manager... but a rare spontaneous act of kindness to a young woman who'd said she was in need. Such a simple thing to have led to such a catastrophic outcome. To this day, five years later, Leigh couldn't remember it without a feeling of despair.

Perhaps if she could have spoken about what she'd done... and why... it might not eat away at her and colour every day in shades of darkness. But she couldn't talk about it. *Ever*.

Only one other person knew the truth.

And Leigh didn't know who she was.

2

FIVE YEARS EARLIER

Leigh Simon pushed open the door of the café that sat halfway between King's Cross station and her office on Harrison Street. A cappuccino was an essential part of her morning routine. Usually, she took it to go and drank it as she speed-walked the rest of the way to work. That morning, having woken at the ungodly hour of four, she'd time to spare.

The usual barista was behind the counter. Leigh, a slim five foot six, always felt like a giant beside the petite woman whose heavy, pale foundation was a canvas for implausibly thick eyebrows and bright red lips. Her auburn hair, striking on its own, was streaked with pink and twisted into two thick plaits that hung down her back almost to her waist. It was hard to tell if she was beautiful or even attractive under all the make-up, but she was undoubtably striking and made the classically good-looking Leigh, and probably every other female who frequented the café, pale into insignificance.

Leigh was too tired to feel the usual glimmer of envy. 'Morning, Gina. I'll have the usual, but I'll have it here and can you add an extra shot, please. I'm going to need more caffeine today.'

'Sure thing.'

It was an unusually subdued reply from a woman whose manner generally reflected her appearance. Words of concern hung unsaid on Leigh's lips. She wanted to get her coffee, sit at the window to watch the world rush by, and wait for the caffeine to reach the parts that hadn't quite managed to wake up that morning. But although the excellent coffee was one of the reasons she frequented the café, the other was Gina's smile and friendly effervescent enthusiasm.

'Is everything okay?' Leigh finally asked.

'I've been better.' Gina put the brimming cup of coffee on the counter with a smile so forced it immediately wobbled and died. 'You don't need to hear my woes.'

Leigh didn't; she'd troubles of her own. And she was tired. But she was also a pushover for a sad face. She waved to a table near the window. 'Why don't you leave Isobel to manage for a while and take a break with me? A trouble shared is a trouble halved and all that, eh?' Leigh took her coffee to the table and sat with a sigh. It was shaping up to be a long tiresome day. She looked up with what she hoped was a welcoming expression and not a grimace when Gina sank onto the chair opposite.

'This is kind of you.'

'It's little repayment for the cheery smile and welcome you give me every time I come in. Honestly, you're as good as a tonic.' Leigh wondered if that made her sound pathetic... a sad and lonely overworked professional. She used to think she had it all, but recently she wasn't so sure. Her fingers tightened around the coffee cup. Gina was speaking; Leigh needed to focus.

'The friend I'm living with is getting married. She hasn't said as much, not yet anyway, but I know she's hoping I'll find something else and move out.' She huffed a laugh. 'On a barista's wage, around here, that isn't happening. I did think about looking for something further out, but commuting would be an expensive nightmare. Plus, you know the hours I work.'

Leigh did. They'd often had a collective moan about their long hours when she called in for a coffee on her way home from work in the evening. It would be a shame if Gina left. Sometimes her cheerful enthusiasm reminded Leigh of the woman she used to be, before the stress of her job and the passing of years had chipped away at the softer edges, a time when she was kinder, nicer. She smoothed a hand over the lapel of her sensible navy M&S suit jacket. Sensible, suitable and incredibly dull. She used to be more colourful, more spontaneous, up for anything. That woman had vanished with age and responsibility. But she missed her. It was this thought that made her open her mouth without thinking. 'I have a spare room. You could move in with me.'

She caught the flicker of surprised disbelief on Gina's face and hurried to add, 'At the same rent you're paying your friend.'

There was no hesitation. With a squeal loud enough to draw every eye in the café, Gina jumped to her feet, rushed around the table and wrapped both arms around Leigh. 'Thank you, thank you!'

'I can't breathe!'

'Sorry!' Gina released her. 'You've no idea! What a relief!' With her breasts and bottom jiggling in the tight-fitting café uniform, she danced across the café, negotiated tables and chairs and hopped over extended legs and dropped bags, her face glowing with pleasure.

Her antics drew a smile from most of the other customers. Leigh kept hers in place with difficulty. Too late, she wondered what Matt was going to say.

Matt, her Friday evening to Sunday afternoon boyfriend. They'd been together a year and the longest they'd spent together was a two-week holiday in Portugal earlier that summer. He was a teacher in a school in Salisbury where the incumbent principal was expected to retire soon. Matt had his eye on the position, so wasn't interested in moving to London despite there being equally good schools with similar opportunities.

As a commodity trader, Leigh's work was always going to be in the capital, and with her long hours, commuting was out of the question. Recently, she'd felt more stressed and tired but whether this was due to the job she'd started almost three months before, which was proving more difficult than she'd expected, or worry about how long this relationship could last when neither seemed able to compromise, she wasn't sure.

Gina danced back and dropped noisily onto the chair opposite, dragging Leigh back to the present. 'You don't know how much this means to me.' The barista clasped her hands together. 'How soon can I move in?'

It was impossible not to be infected by her excitement. 'As soon as you like. I keep the room ready for visitors so there's nothing I need to do, apart from moving a few clothes from the wardrobe.'

'Brilliant! I'll finish early and be over tonight then, if that's okay?'

That night! Leigh picked up her cup to hide the doubt shivering through her. What had she done?

3

When Leigh arrived home that evening, tiredness weighing her down and stooping her shoulders, Gina was sitting on her doorstep surrounded by her belongings. Leigh wanted to cry. The day had been hellish, her manager, Bernard Ledbetter, more obnoxious than usual. One of these days she'd have to do something about the lecherous misogynist. But the pale-skinned man with the strawberry-blond hair and skinny caterpillar-like moustache creeping along his top lip was sneaky and careful. She didn't think anyone noticed his behaviour towards her: the slight brushes against her, the leering looks, the ever-so-slightly unacceptable words he used when he spoke to her.

Wanting to cry, to tell Gina she hadn't meant it and knowing she couldn't, Leigh pushed the corners of her mouth up into some semblance of a smile. 'Hi!'

'This is so exciting.' Gina jumped to her feet. 'Your house is amazing!'

Inside, some of Leigh's tiredness and bad mood lifted as she showed Gina around.

'Amazing!' Gina enthused of everything, even the main bathroom she'd be using with its dated avocado green suite and bizarre green and brown wall and floor tiles.

'I use my en suite so you'll have this to yourself. Mostly anyway. Matt likes to have a bath now and then when he's here at the weekend.' Leigh saw the quizzical raised eyebrow. 'Matt, my partner; he lives in Salisbury but stays here most weekends.' She opened the shower door. 'Despite looking like something the eighties forgot, it all works well. Someday when money and time allow, I'll have it updated.'

'It's fab,' Gina insisted. 'And I love the colour.'

It had been a while since Leigh had looked around the bathroom without thinking of the cost of replacing the suite. She did now, seeing the space, the art deco mirror over the wash handbasin, remembering when she'd seen it in an antique shop and known she had to have it. It had been expensive, but she'd handed over the money without hesitation and had carried it home and hung it the same day. When had she last looked at it with the same delight? It was good to see things through Gina's eyes, to reclaim the pleasure.

'Let's get your stuff inside.' Leigh helped Gina bring the collection of black plastic bags, holdalls, and boxes containing her belongings up to the bedroom.

'My friend dropped me off,' Gina explained as she dropped a box on the floor. 'I think she was afraid I might change my mind.'

More likely she was afraid Leigh would. She dismissed the cynical thought and waved to the wardrobe and chest of drawers. 'I just need to remove a few things and it's all yours.'

Gina was opening and closing drawers, looking at everything with an air of contentment.

Her enthusiasm was infectious. Leigh, who was used to a solitary dinner five days a week, found herself saying, 'I was about to take a lasagne from the freezer for dinner. I can take another out for you, if you'd like?'

'I love lasagne! That would be great, thank you.'

'Right.' Leigh nodded and left her to her unpacking. Twenty minutes later, when Gina pushed open the kitchen door and looked nervously around the edge of it, she waved a bottle of Merlot in her direction. 'You drink red?'

'Sounds great, thank you.'

'A celebration. I don't normally drink during the week.' Leigh twisted the cap from the bottle and poured the wine into the glasses she'd set on the counter.

'This is nice.' Gina wandered around the extended kitchen diner, picking up photographs to peer closer, lifting ornaments, and to Leigh's amusement, turning them over to see their provenance. Something she'd often wanted to do herself in friends' homes, and had done on occasion when she could get away with it. Gina's frank appraisal was far more honest, and admirable.

'Here you go.' Leigh put the plates of lasagne on the table and sat. 'It's from the deli on Kentish Town Road, a good place to shop if you want to stock up for meals for yourself.' The comment wasn't exactly subtle, but there was no point in misleading her new lodger. This shared dinner was an exception, not the rule. She pointed to one of the kitchen cupboards. 'I'll clear out that one and you can have it for your things, and I'll leave a shelf in the fridge and the freezer empty for your use.'

'Great.' Gina lifted her wine glass. 'Here's to happy days!'

'Happy days!' Leigh clinked her glass. This had been a good decision. Gina's constant exuberance might become wearing after a while, but Leigh had been rattling around the house feeling lonely for too many nights. It would be nice to know there was someone else around.

Gina tucked into the lasagne, asking the occasional question between mouthfuls. Finally, she pushed the empty plate away. 'That was really good, I'll have to investigate that deli.' She accepted a refill of wine and sipped it, her eyes sliding around the room. 'You were lucky to inherit such a fabulous house, weren't you?'

Leigh, still eating, held the fork poised at her lips and looked across the table, eyes wide. She dropped the laden fork to the plate and pushed it away. 'How did you know I had?'

'You mentioned it in the café. Don't you remember?' Gina took a large and noisy gulp of wine. 'I think it wasn't long after I started working there. I made some comment about how expensive it was to buy property in the area, and you said how lucky you were because you'd inherited.'

'Oh yes, of course, I remember now.' Leigh stood and took both plates to the sink. She kept her head down as she scraped the remains of her meal into the bin, hiding her face and the worried expression she knew was there. When her mother's younger sister had died suddenly after a short illness, Leigh had been stunned to discover the house had been left to her. But she'd rarely discussed her personal circumstances with anyone.

Certainly not with a stranger.

So how did a woman she'd invited to share her home know something so private about her?

4

_____

When Leigh turned back to the table, her new lodger was sipping her wine, oblivious to having said something wrong. Looking so completely innocent, in fact, that Leigh wondered if perhaps she had, at one time, mentioned her good luck.

She finished tidying up. 'Okay, I'm going to make a few calls then head to bed. I hope you've a good night.'

'I know I will.' Gina tilted her glass. 'And thank you again, you're a life saver.'

Upstairs, Leigh shut her bedroom door, then, something she'd never done before, turned the key in the lock. Frowning at this new foolishness, she undressed and readied herself for bed, then picked up her phone to ring Matt.

He answered on the first ring. But then, unless she was away, she always rang on the dot of nine. Such a boring creature of habit she'd become. It made her invitation to Gina all the more out of character.

Matt, when she told him, was horrified. 'You did what?'

'I invit—'

'Yes,' he snapped, 'I heard you! What possessed you to do something so crazy? You don't know her; she could be an axe-murderer.'

'Very unlikely, Matt.' She didn't mention feeling uneasy about Gina's presence following her remark about inheriting the house. There was now no doubt in Leigh's mind... she'd never have said anything about it. Nobody knew about the inheritance apart from Matt, her parents and one old friend who lived in Glasgow. 'Anyway, it's done now. If it works out, it'll be company for me.' She let that soak in. 'And if it doesn't, I can ask her to find something else.' She changed the topic of conversation, suggesting they try a new Italian restaurant at the weekend. 'I'll book a table for Saturday, shall I?'

'Sure.' His sigh drifted down the line. 'We're not going to have to eat with her when I come up on Friday, are we? I don't want to have to make small talk with a stranger; I want to be with you, Leigh.'

She knew there was no point in suggesting they go out to eat on that night too; he'd cite exhaustion from his busy week, and the tiring train journey to London. 'Don't worry, she works long hours so she won't be here.' The lie appeased him and stressed her. She'd have to find out what hours Gina was working over the weekend, and maybe subtly hint about wanting the place to herself on Friday evening.

'You could at least have waited till after half-term,' Matt said.

Leigh was about to snap and ask what difference it would make when she stopped herself with a swallowed groan that verged on despair. It was the school's half-term holiday; he was off for a few days and had planned to stay in London for most of the following week. 'It doesn't matter; we'll be out every day, won't we.' Visiting the art galleries and museums Matt had insisted he'd wanted to see that week. Not the relaxing break in a spa hotel she'd have preferred. He got his way; he usually did.

Mentioning their plans was the perfect antidote to Matt's irritation; he spoke of the museums they'd visit, the exhibitions he'd read about, the ones he was certain she'd find as exciting as he did.

Trawling around galleries and exhibitions didn't float Leigh's boat, but she smiled at his enthusiasm. 'I'm looking forward to it.' What an accomplished liar she'd become. 'I'll see you on Friday.' A final *love you* and she hung up and sank back against the pillows with a sigh.

Sounds filtered up from downstairs. Whatever Gina was watching was accompanied by canned laughter and applause. Since Leigh preferred documentaries, she didn't see them watching the set together. Perhaps she'd get her new lodger a TV for her room and suggest she watched it there.

When Leigh's eyes filled with hot stinging tears, she wasn't sure why. Her silly decision to invite Gina. Matt. A life that suddenly felt uneasy. She brushed a hand across her eyes, annoyed with her weakness, the undeserved self-pity for one who had so much. She reached for the lamp, switched it off and slipped under the duvet.

Usually, the house would be silent. Now, the murmur of voices, squeaks and clunks as doors opened and closed, footsteps in the hallway and on the stairs disturbed the quiet. If she'd given it any thought, she'd have expected the sounds of someone else in the house to be comforting. A pleasant companionable background sound to replace the empty silence she was used to during the week. If she'd given it any thought... she'd have offered sympathy that morning and nothing else.

'Stupid, stupid woman.' She pulled the duvet over her head to dull the sounds, trying to force her tired brain to shut down, to give her some peace. But the same thought ricocheted painfully. *How did Gina know she'd inherited the house, and did it really matter?*

* * *

The question kept her awake long after the house grew quiet. Then the light from the hallway shone under her bedroom door, irritating her. She swung her feet to the floor, listened at the door for a few seconds before opening it and hurrying naked across the landing to turn it off.

The night was a series of periods of wakefulness during which she agonised over Gina, Matt and the job she wasn't sure she enjoyed any more, and periods of sleep with unusually graphic dreams where the common theme seemed to be violent death.

When a drill bit pierced her head with a loud hum, the pain and terror was so real she cried out, the sound waking her from the nightmare. Her hand went to her head, relieved to find no drill bit, no blood. No bogeyman attacking her. The hum, though, was real and coming from the electric shower in the main bathroom. She'd forgotten how loud it was. A glance at her bedside clock made her groan. Six thirty. An hour earlier than she needed to be awake.

It wasn't Gina's fault. It was Leigh's... for having invited her to move in, for not having asked her to shower at night rather than the morning.

She tried and failed to get back to sleep, waiting until she heard the front door opening and shutting before throwing the duvet back and struggling to her feet. A long shower helped to restore a little equilibrium, and slightly heavier make-up hid the pallor resulting from yet another disturbed night. But as she sipped her takeaway coffee – from a different café, unable that morning to face Gina's smiling cheerfulness – she knew she was in for a tough day.

A tough day made worse by Leigh's manager's more intrusive hovering as if sensing vulnerable prey.

'You've missed a connection there.' Bernard Ledbetter leaned over her shoulder to point to something on one of the three computer monitors on her desk. Suddenly she felt a long stream of his breath blow down her cleavage and waft the material of her

hirt. She was tired; perhaps she'd imagined it. But when she
ooked up to reply, and saw the lecherous expression on his face,
he knew she hadn't. It was the final insult to a day that had started
off pretty crap. She jumped to her feet and without thinking, swung
her fist at his smug face.

5

Ledbetter ducked as Leigh's fist flew through the air. He laughed. A sneering condescending sound that floated around the words *you've had it this time* as he scorched the linoleum on his way down the corridor to the human resources department.

She spun around, looking for witnesses to what had occurred. But if there had been any, it wasn't obvious. All her colleagues either had their heads down, their attention fixed on their monitors, or they were staring into space as they listened and spoke on their headsets. Truth was, even if anyone had seen, the floor was often fraught with emotions spilling over and one more wouldn't have made an eyebrow as much as flicker.

Through the open doorway, she could see Ledbetter was almost at the door to the HR department. She could run after him, apologise profusely, maybe invite him for a drink... or dinner... to make up for her flash of temper. It would have been the sensible thing to do. But she couldn't do it because she knew what she'd see on his face if she did. Smug satisfaction that would tell her as clearly as if he'd shouted it, he had her exactly where he wanted her... at a disadvantage.

Instead, she sat at her desk, got back to work, and tried to put Ledbetter and everything else out of her mind. Impossible when she half-expected to hear heavy footsteps stopping at her desk. Ledbetter's round self-important face, the human resources manager standing like an avenging angel at his back, both determined to make her pay for one moment's weakness.

To her surprise, neither appeared. After a couple of hours, she felt her hunched shoulders relax. She hadn't hit the stupid man; perhaps he'd decided against making a complaint.

But when a notification for an email popped into the corner of her screen at six, she realised she'd been too optimistic. Without opening it, she knew it was bad news. It was so tempting to go home; pretend she'd not seen it. Tempting but foolish.

The email was succinct.

Ms Simon,

Following your altercation with Mr Ledbetter today, please attend a meeting at 2 p.m. tomorrow where I will listen to both of you in order to get a better idea of what occurred before deciding how to proceed in the best interests of the company.

Janet Collins, Human Resources Manager

Leigh read it through several times. *In the best interests of the company.* That sounded ominous. But she'd done nothing wrong... she hadn't actually hit the sleazy obnoxious bastard, had she?

They couldn't fire her.

Could they?

* * *

This new worry put everything else out of her head so when she reached home and opened her front door to hear blaring music, she took a step back, startled. Reality came bowling in and she groaned as the kitchen door opened. Gina shimmied down the hallway to the sounds of some rock group Leigh didn't recognise and grabbed her in a hug she neither expected nor wanted.

'Hello,' she said, gently extricating herself.

'Hello.' Gina's smile was huge as she continued to gyrate.

Leigh dropped her bag on the bottom step of the stairway. 'You settling in okay?'

Another shimmy was accompanied by waving arms and twirling hands, Gina's long wildly colourful dress floating around her body as she moved. 'More than okay,' she sang in a surprisingly tuneful voice.

'Good.' Leigh rustled up a smile. She wasn't being fair; it wasn't Gina's fault she was in a lousy mood.

'To thank you, I've cooked dinner.'

Only then did the aroma of something spicy hit Leigh. It made her nose twitch and her mouth water. 'You shouldn't have.' She really shouldn't; Leigh didn't want to get into a cooking for one another routine. Certainly didn't want to sit making small talk over dinner that night with her brain doing somersaults inside her skull.

'It's on a plate; you just need to pop it in the microwave for a few minutes when you're ready to eat, okay?' Gina did a little sidestep into the living room as she spoke, switched off the music, and grabbed a coat from the sofa. 'I'm off to meet friends, hope you enjoy it.'

And she was gone, leaving Leigh standing in the hallway feeling bemused. From not wanting company, she felt suddenly bereft. Shaking her head at her foolishness, she picked up her bag and trudged up the stairs.

Changing her clothes was the perfect way to separate work and relaxation. It should have made it easier to put Ledbetter and the horrendous day out of her head, but it didn't even take the sharp edge off it. She belted her cotton robe tightly and went down to the kitchen for whatever it was Gina had cooked.

A covered plate sat on the counter. Leigh lifted it and sniffed. Couscous, and lamb in a tomato-based sauce. It smelled divine.

As she waited for the microwave to ping, she opened the fridge and took out a bottle of white wine. Two nights in a row. Bad habits were creeping up on her. She dismissed the self-criticism. That night she needed the temporary crutch that alcohol could give. She poured a glass and when the food was ready, she took it all through to the living room.

Rather than the TV, she switched on the CD player and popped in one of her favourite discs. *Cavalleria Rusticana* was the perfect choice to soothe her rattled brain.

She picked up her fork and speared a piece of lamb. It smelled so good. Tasted good too. It was very kind of Gina really. Very kind. *But how did she know Leigh had inherited the house? And was it important?* Suddenly, she didn't feel hungry. In fact, did the lamb taste a little strange? She spat the piece she'd been chewing onto the plate, took it to the kitchen and pressed the pedal of the bin to dump the lot, pulling away at the last minute and allowing the yawning mouth to shut with a snap. If she put it in there, Gina would see and wonder why.

Instead, Leigh scraped the food into a plastic bag and shoved it into the freezer. She could dump it in the bin another day.

Back in the living room, she picked up her wine and continued to obsess over how her new lodger could have known something so private about her. There was no point asking Gina again, she'd simply say the same thing. That Leigh had told her.

But she was sure she hadn't...

6

The waiting room of the human resources department was too small to hold both Leigh and Bernard Ledbetter in any comfort. They took seats on opposite sides, each of them staring directly ahead. Leigh was determined to ignore the man. It was his fault she was there, his fault she was wasting precious time.

Her eyes flicked to her watch. One minute to the appointed hour. She watched the second hand tick its way around the olive-green dial, one diamond after the other. The Rolex had been a birthday present to herself. Crazy money for a watch but when things were tough, she'd look at it and know things weren't so bad.

Like that morning, it didn't always work.

Exactly as the second hand reached twelve, the human resources secretary stuck his head around the edge of the door and glared at them as if they were an inconvenience. 'Ms Collins will see you now.' He said his lines and disappeared before either of the two had got to their feet.

Leigh moved quickly, determined to reach the HR office before him. As if it was a race. As if winning got her the prize. She bit back a nervous giggle when she succeeded and raised her hand to knock.

'Come in.'

Leigh would have preferred not to go in, she'd have preferred to run away. But she was trapped. The manager's door in front, creepy Ledbetter behind. She gripped the handle and pressed, pushing the door open.

Janet Collins was behind an over-large desk in a too-small office. She was a woman renowned for her appalling dress sense as much as her expertise in her role. That day, wearing a mustard-coloured dress with a funnel collar, she bore an unfortunate resemblance to a jar of the condiment.

Leigh hated mustard. It wasn't an auspicious start.

Collins waited until they sat, one hand tapping the file that lay on the desk in front of her. 'We're here today to discuss a very serious allegation.' She continued to tap the file, her eyes pinning Leigh to her seat.

Feeling as if she was back in school during one of her frequent visits to the head's office, Leigh shuffled before shooting a quick glance to the man in the other chair.

'Mr Ledbetter's statement says you attempted to punch him, Ms Simon. Perhaps you can explain what happened.'

'I didn't plan to punch him.' Leigh ignored the loud huff from her right. 'Mr Ledbetter has a habit of invading my personal space. I—'

'And you've spoken to him about this?'

'No, I—'

'Did you mention it to anyone else? One of your colleagues, anyone here in HR?'

Leigh shook her head. She should have. The first time he'd leered at her, she should have called him out on it, should have reported it. Of course, she should have. But she'd a good relationship with the other traders. Banter was an antidote to the high stress environment, and she was reluctant to be seen as someone who couldn't take a joke – worse, as someone who was quick to report any slight infringement.

Far easier to pretend it wasn't happening.

She'd sucked it up until the previous day. She hadn't imagined the warm breath he'd blown down her cleavage. And she'd been too tired to let it pass. Or maybe she'd simply had enough.

Ledbetter looked from her to Collins with a jerk of his head that dislodged a strand of his careful comb-over. He took a shuddering breath and wiped a hand over his mouth. 'This is nonsense. Ms Simon is trying to excuse her unacceptable behaviour by laying the blame on me. I was simply pointing out that she'd neglected an important step in closing a deal.' He shrugged his shoulders. 'Some managers point out errors by email. I've always found the personal touch to be more beneficial to the continued good relationship between traders and me. I think' – his voice caught – 'that most of the traders appreciate this. I thought Ms Simon did.' His loud sigh penetrated the silence that followed.

Leigh watched the oiled lock of his hair bounce as it sought purchase. She might have been amused by it and his amateur dramatics if his following words weren't so damning.

'I know I'm a big man but there was a look in her eyes. It sounds dramatic, but you had to have been there. Seriously, I was afraid.'

There was no point in Leigh arguing, no point in challenging him on the crocodile tears shining in his beady eyes. That stupid bouncing lock of hair was working in his favour too. Not making him look ridiculous but making him look pathetically vulnerable. Leigh knew his account of what happened wasn't true... not exactly. She had tried to punch him, missing only because he had faster reflexes than she'd given him credit for... but he had invaded her personal space and looked down her shirt. She knew he had.

He was still talking, adding a hitch to his voice for effect. Leigh shot him a disbelieving glance and opened her mouth to argue shutting it with a snap when Collins raised a hand to stop her. 'Let Mr Ledbetter finish please.'

And finish he did. He mentioned the impact her attack had had on him, how he'd been so shocked he'd had to go home early the previous day, how he'd not been able to sleep for thinking of it, the negative impact on his work that morning. On and on it went, with the sympathy on the HR manager's face growing with every sneaky word.

'Thank you for putting it all so eloquently, Mr Ledbetter,' Collins said when he finally ground to a halt.

Eloquently? Leigh opened her mouth to argue but this time she didn't need the manager's raised hand for her to stop and snap it shut. Ledbetter had painted such a perfect picture of himself as the put-upon victim, the manager's sympathy was obvious. She'd swallowed every word out of his lying mouth.

Except it wasn't a lie, was it? She had tried to punch the stupid, snivelling creep.

'We can't have staff resorting to fisticuffs in the office, Ms Simon.'

Fisticuffs? Leigh glared. 'I wasn't engaged in any such thing. I—'

'You *did* try to punch me.' He was basking in the sympathy, shaking his head sadly for effect.

The sallow-faced HR manager in her ghastly dress leaned her arms on the desk, her hands pressed together, fingertips gently tapping as she droned on about the level of behaviour the company expected from its employees. A level, it seemed, Leigh had fallen far below.

'Mr Ledbetter has been very gracious; he insists he doesn't want you to be fired...'

Leigh's chin had slumped, her eyes fixed on her feet, but at this she jerked upright. 'Fired?'

'It was attempted assault, Ms Simon. We are obliged to take it seriously.' Collins stopped tapping her fingers and reached for the slim file. 'I've spoken to a number of your colleagues,' she said, opening it and flicking through the contents. 'You're regarded by most as being a hard worker... but rather short-tempered according to some, and decidedly bad-tempered by others.'

'This is a fast-paced, noisy environment. We all speak in loud voices; it possibly comes across as my being short-tempered, but I assure you I'm not.' Leigh was, and increasingly so the last couple of months. Even Matt had commented, calling her grouchy on more than one occasion. Worryingly, she remembered she'd wanted to punch him, too. She hadn't, but the thought had been there.

The HR manager was waffling on about anger issues. A wave of smugness wafted from Ledbetter. It floated over Leigh's head before settling on her, smothering her. She clasped the arms of the chair, panic sizzling as anger bubbled to the surface. There was a long-bladed letter opener on the desk. Her hand itched to grab it and plunge it up to its hilt into the eye of the obnoxious man sitting to her right.

The jar of mustard on the other side of the desk was still babbling... something about an anger management course... Leigh wanted to reach over the desk, twist her head off, and run onto the trader's floor, tossing it to the first person she met.

Her grip on the arms of the chair tightened as the anger threatened to overwhelm her, destroy everything she'd worked so hard for.

'Yes.'

The word silenced the HR manager mid-flow, her mouth hanging open on a vowel. She clamped her lips together and stared at Leigh. 'Yes, what?'

'I'll go on whatever course you recommend.' She ignored Ledbetter's snicker. They were right about her: she'd do the course, learn how to deal with the pressures of her job without snapping at people. And when that was done, when she was back, and this was behind her, she'd record every instance of Ledbetter's sleazy behaviour and she'd hang him out to dry.

7

Acting on impulse was Leigh's biggest character flaw. She should have found out more about the anger management course the HR manager was proposing before she agreed to do it. Because it wasn't, as she'd assumed it would be, a few hours once or twice. No, the course was a week-long residential course in a private clinic in Reading over fifty miles from home.

And to make it a hundred times worse, the only week available for months – who'd have thought anger management courses were so popular – was the following week. Clashing with the half-term holiday and Matt's extended stay in London.

The email from the HR manager, informing her of the details of the course, didn't insist she do one so soon. However, the final line of her email, *attending the course this early will allow all parties to move on*, wasn't subtle.

And the sooner Leigh did the course, the sooner she could make Ledbetter pay for being a treacherous bastard. Anyway, it wasn't as if she and Matt had planned anything exciting. The museums and galleries he wanted to visit would be there the next

ime he was off. Or even better, he could visit the blasted places
himself.

She put it rather more diplomatically when she rang him that
evening. It was a wasted effort; he was less than impressed. 'We had
the week planned. How can they simply insist you do this course
with no notice?'

She'd never mentioned Ledbetter's inappropriate behaviour.
Matt would have insisted she report it. He'd have been right. Now
she was stuck... she could tell him the truth and listen to his
reproaches or tell a white lie.

Past weary, a white lie was easier. 'It's a management training
course. I've been trying to get on it for months so when someone
had to drop out for personal reasons, I jumped at the opportunity.'
Really only half a lie; she *had* been trying to get on a management
course; she *would* have jumped at the chance had one been offered.

'I'd really been looking forward to spending some quality time
together.'

Leigh swallowed the words she wanted to say, the ones she'd
been saying for several months. They'd have longer, they'd have
every day, every night, if he moved to London. She pressed the phone
to her ear. 'It can't be helped. It doesn't start till the Monday morning,
so we'll have the whole weekend together. You can stay here when
I've gone, if you like, and go to those exhibitions you wanted to see.'

'It doesn't look as though I've much choice, does it?'

It wasn't very gracious, but it was probably as good as she was
going to get. Matt didn't like his plans being overturned. She gave
one more try at being conciliatory. 'We could go to some galleries
on Sunday, then go somewhere nice to eat since you won't be
rushing away.'

'Better than nothing, I suppose. Right, I'll see you tomorrow.' He
hung up without waiting for her reply.

'Love you,' Leigh said to the dead phone before dropping it onto the sofa beside her. She heard Gina pottering about in the kitchen. There hadn't been the opportunity yet to ask her about her work schedule. It might be a good idea to get that sorted, try and rescue something of the weekend. It was several minutes before she dragged herself to her feet.

Gina was cooking something that smelled good. Leigh hadn't bothered with lunch, keeping her head down, concentrating on her work. She'd even avoided going for coffee, sipping instead from the water bottle she'd filled at home. Anything to avoid interacting with Bernard Ledbetter.

No lunch and an apple for breakfast. She should have been hungry but, despite the appealing aroma, the thought of eating made her feel queasy. Maybe it was the guilt when she remembered the meal Gina had left for her, still sitting in the freezer waiting to be tossed.

Leigh had been stupid, paranoid. Gina had simply been kind.

'Smells good,' Leigh said as a conversation opener, moving across to shake the kettle, add water and flick the switch.

'Chicken biryani.' Gina gave it another stir before turning. 'I've made loads to put in the freezer; would you like some?'

Leigh opened the cupboard for a mug. 'No, thank you, I'd a huge lunch so I'm not hungry. I'll just take a coffee to watch TV for a while. Tired, actually, so I'll be heading to bed early.'

'You're not going out?'

'No, not tonight.' Leigh couldn't remember the last time she'd gone out during the week. When had she become so dull? Perhaps she should give one of her old girlfriends a shout, meet up for a drink, dinner even. But even as she thought it, she knew it wouldn't happen. Her old girlfriends were either consumed with busy jobs which left little energy for socialising during the week, or else married with children and husbands pulling on their time.

'You should come out with me.' Gina pulled a drawer open with such enthusiasm, every implement inside rattled. She searched for a few seconds, then pulled out a ladle with a grin and a loudly sung, 'Ta dah!' It was a few minutes before she finished putting the food into containers. She dropped the ladle into the sink. 'That's me fed for a few days.'

It was the ideal opportunity for Leigh to ask, 'Are you working all weekend?'

'Off tomorrow, on Saturday and Sunday.' Gina shrugged and picked up the food she'd plated up for herself. 'I don't mind working weekends; the money is better.'

Leigh sipped her coffee. 'Nice to have a day off; have you any plans?' *Like going out of the city all day, going to visit far-flung friends, maybe staying overnight, anything.*

'Not really.'

Great, just great. Leigh couldn't bring herself to ask the woman to absent herself for the evening. What a stupid idea this had been. Matt would simply have to put up with it. 'You'll get to meet my partner, Matt. He usually gets here around seven.'

Gina stopped with the fork midway to her mouth. 'Seven? Sorry, I won't be here at seven. It's a Friday night; there'll be a party somewhere, there always is.'

Of course there would be. Suddenly Leigh felt old. Gina was what, maybe twenty-four or five? Friday night had always been party night when Leigh had been that age. Only six years ago, so why did she feel like Methuselah?

At least Matt wouldn't be complaining. They'd have the place to themselves for a nice, relaxing, dull, boring evening watching TV. Not the documentaries she liked; no, it would be sports of some sort.

And she'd smile, organise dinner, open him beer after beer, drink wine, and wonder what happened to her and her life.

8

The weekend wasn't a disaster... That was the most Leigh could say about it. Matt complained incessantly about having their plans discounted so easily by the demands of her job. Luckily, he didn't ask Leigh what the 'management' course entailed because she wasn't sure she could maintain the lie. If he knew the truth, if he found out she was having to attend an anger management course because of one stupid moment's loss of control, she'd never be allowed to forget it.

Guilt pushed her to keep Matt sweet and it was she who suggested they spend Saturday in the Victoria and Albert Museum, and who asked him to see which exhibitions were open on the Sunday. Unfortunately, there were three, all populated with the kind of people Leigh disliked, the pretentious arty-farty types who spoke in riddles and looked at the frankly hideous art hanging on the walls with far-away looks in their eyes. By the end of the day she was bored and the stress of keeping a smile on her face was giving her a headache.

Matt was happy to eat dinner early and *have an early night* as he put it, with a wink that made Leigh widen her smile as if the thought of sex was exactly what she had in mind, when really she was wishing that, as usual, he was rushing back to Salisbury and leaving her in peace.

As they reached the house, the door opened and Gina came rushing out, dressed in a short, low-cut dress, wearing even heavier, more elaborate make-up than she did during the day. Obviously off to another party.

'Hi,' she said with her usual exuberant smile, her eyes sweeping over Matt. 'You must be the lover. Good to meet you.'

Matt laughed uncertainly and shot Leigh a look.

Did he really think she'd have referred to him as her lover? Ignoring him, she admired Gina's dress. The shimmering coppery shade emphasised her auburn hair and highlighted her green eyes. 'You look lovely. That's a great colour on you.'

'Thank you.' Gina accepted the compliment without demur. 'I'd best be going. Nice to meet you, Matt.'

She was gone in a flash of colour, fluttering down the street like some exotic oversized butterfly.

'Bloody hell. She looks a bit of a tart, doesn't she?'

Leigh, who was searching in her bag for her keys, stopped and looked at him in surprise. 'I think she looks lovely.'

Matt was still staring down the street. 'Tarty. I bet she brings home a different man every night.'

'Don't be silly.' Finding her keys, Leigh opened the door and hoped Matt would let the subject drop. She'd never been a landlady before; hadn't thought to lay out any rules, wasn't sure whether she could stipulate *no men* like some kind of Victorian killjoy. She hadn't thought full stop.

Determined to finish the evening on a good note, she brought beer and wine to the lounge where Matt had already made himself at home, kicking off his shoes, slouching down on the sofa.

'I was thinking,' she said, feeling her way. 'The conference is in a hotel on the outskirts of Reading. Maybe rather than you travelling back up to London next weekend—' She stopped abruptly. He was off the whole week; perhaps he'd planned to stay in the house until she returned. 'Unless of course you're planning on staying?'

He didn't move his eyes from the screen, the screech of a Formula One race piercing the silence as she waited for a reply. 'Matt?'

'What?' With obvious reluctance he turned to her. 'Sorry, you know what I'm like with cars.'

'Like a child in a toy shop.' She had to smile. For a man who didn't own a car, he was obsessed. 'I was asking about your plans for the week. Are you going to stay in London?'

'Not without you.' He moved the beer bottle to his other hand and reached an arm out to pull her close. 'I was really looking forward to this week, Leigh, sorry that I've been such a grump about it. I know you didn't have any choice about the blasted course.' He swigged his beer and wiped his mouth with the back of his hand. 'There's an exhibition I want to see tomorrow afternoon, so I'll probably head back on Tuesday.'

Guilt at misleading him made her squirm. 'Right, as I was saying, maybe rather than you travelling back here next weekend I could go from the hotel to Salisbury. The course doesn't finish till Friday evening, but I could leave early Saturday morning and be with you in time for a late breakfast somewhere. We'd have most of the weekend together.'

He gave her a squeeze. 'That sounds like a good plan. There's a new restaurant opened that I've been wanting to try; I'll book a table for Saturday night.'

It was a good finish to a difficult weekend. Leigh relaxed in his arms and shut her eyes as the cars whined around the track. Within minutes, she was asleep.

9

Leigh had a vague memory of Matt shaking her from a deep sleep some hours later. Barely awake, she leaned on him as they went upstairs where she pulled off her clothes, dropping them where they fell, before climbing under the duvet.

When she felt Matt's hand sliding over her thigh, she pushed it away. 'I'm tired, Matt.'

His hand returned, more insistent. 'Come on, it's our last chance thanks to you deserting me for this damn course.'

It wasn't the first time Leigh had given in to his demands. Usually, it was simply easier. This time, guilt nudged her to be compliant. She tried to show willing; maybe it was obvious or maybe he was making a point by being more, what he referred to as *enthusiastic*, than usual. She was relieved when it was over and he rolled away.

Nervous anticipation of the day ahead woke her early. Matt was snoring softly by her side. Turning, she raised herself on one elbow to look down at him. She regretted not telling him the truth about what had happened. Too late now. He'd be angry at the lie, angrier at what he'd perceive to be her lack of trust in him.

In the en suite, she looked in dismay at the love bite on her neck. Less visible, but worse, was the mark of his teeth on the curve of her breast. She'd yelled in shock when he'd bit down. He'd apologise, of course, he always did.

'It's because you turn me on so much. I can't get enough of you,' he'd said when she'd reluctantly, almost apologetically, mentioned he'd hurt her during one energetic night early in their relationship. He'd kissed her bruises, promised it wouldn't happen again and bought her the biggest bouquet of flowers she'd ever seen.

There'd been several bouquets since.

After a quick shower, she applied her make-up, smoothing concealer over the bruise on her neck. She had her case packed for the week; she'd add a selection of scarves to make sure the damage stayed hidden.

Fifteen minutes later, she perched on Matt's side of the bed. 'Hi,' she said when he stirred. 'I'm going to have a coffee and head off, okay? You go back to sleep; I'll ring you later and see you on Saturday.'

'I'm sorry about last night,' he muttered sleepily. 'I might have been a bit rough.' He lifted her hand and pressed it to his lips. 'Enjoy the course. Drive carefully.'

It was as much of an apology as she was going to get. With an ease she envied, he was asleep again before she reached the bedroom door.

Downstairs, she heard sounds from the kitchen, indicating Gina was up before her. Leigh hadn't told her she was away for the week; she supposed she'd better, and tell her Matt was staying. She left her suitcase at the hall door and propped her handbag and car keys on top.

'Hi.'

Gina waved a slice of toast, sending crumbs sailing to the table. 'Morning; you're up early.'

Leigh patted the kettle. It felt hot enough. She made a cup of coffee and took it to the table, taking the chair opposite Gina. 'I'm heading to Reading for a course.' It was always best to stick to the same story. 'Then I'll be staying with Matt for a couple of nights, so I'll be away until Sunday.' She took a mouthful of her drink. Her hand had deceived her; it wasn't quite hot enough. 'Matt will be here until Tuesday.'

Gina paused with the piece of toast halfway to her mouth. 'Matt will be here, but you won't?'

Surprised at the tone of voice, Leigh nodded. 'Yes. That's not a problem, is it?' To her dismay, Gina dropped the piece of toast on the plate and got to her feet.

'I don't know him. He's a stranger to me.' She pointed to the ceiling. 'There's no key to my bedroom door, no way to lock it from the inside. It didn't seem necessary. But now...'

A decent mug of coffee seemed suddenly essential. Leigh stood, emptied the slop from her mug into the sink and flicked the switch on the kettle. She waited until she had her fingers wrapped around a hot mug, and the first mouthful of coffee sliding almost painfully down her throat before she turned.

Gina was waiting, arms folded across her chest.

'Now, there is no difference,' Leigh said quietly. 'My partner, my boyfriend if you prefer, is staying for a couple of nights. You possibly won't even see him but believe me, you're as safe with him as you'd be with me.'

If Leigh hoped the reassurance would soothe whatever demons were creasing Gina's face, she was disappointed. If anything, her expression turned darker... almost fearful. Leigh had never seen her lodger anything but cheerful and bubbly. This side to her was an unexpected and unwelcome shock. What was it Matt had said? How did Leigh know Gina wasn't an axe-murderer? How indeed.

'You didn't say this would happen when I moved here.'

Leigh gripped the mug tighter. She'd liked to have hurled it at the stupid woman. 'I don't have to explain to you who does or doesn't stay in my home. You're staying here at what is, realistically, a peppercorn rent.'

'I have no idea what that is.' Gina folded her arms across her chest. 'It sounds like an insult though. I pay you rent; I have rights.'

Another mouthful of the scalding coffee made Leigh's eyes water. She couldn't believe she was having this conversation. What a bloody awful start to the day. Anger... and a smattering of guilt that Gina might have a point – she didn't know Matt after all – put Leigh on the offensive. 'Actually, you haven't paid me any rent at all yet, so if you want to move out, you can simply pack up and go.' It would be for the best; inviting her to move in had been a really, really bad idea.

Gina slapped her hands to her face, her mouth opening in a silent wail.

Leigh sighed. God save her from drama queens. 'It's your choice, Gina. I really can't have you dictating to me who can or can't stay here, okay?'

'This is so unfair.'

'Unfair?' Anger pushed Leigh's voice higher, louder. 'Then move out if you want but seriously, I can't handle this right now. I have a difficult week ahead of me. So' – she emptied the last of the coffee into the sink and put the mug into the dishwasher – 'do what you like. I'm off.'

Without another word, she left the room, grabbed her jacket and suitcase and headed out, slamming the door after her. It would have woken Matt, but she was past caring. She hoped he came down for some coffee, naked. That would give Gina something to moan about.

Anger grew rather than dissipated as she walked the short

distance to her car. *How dare Gina? Who did she think she was? What kind of an idiot was Leigh to have put herself in such a crazy situation?*

She was trembling by the time she threw her case into the boot. Slamming it shut, she got in her car and pulled the door closed with a bang. It wasn't until she saw the white knuckles of the fingers clasping the steering wheel that she let her breath out in a loud whoosh.

It was stupid to allow Gina to upset her this way. Leigh was so easily pushed to anger these days, that perhaps this course was what she needed, after all. She was such an idiot; there had been ample opportunity to tell Gina about the course over the last few days and to explain Matt might be staying on. They'd have had time to discuss her concerns, whatever they were. When Leigh got back, she'd have a word, apologise for the lack of warning, and for losing her temper. Maybe over a glass of wine, she could lay down some ground rules.

She wasn't backing down though. It was her house; she wasn't going to ask permission to invite whomever she wished to stay. On Sunday, freshly armed with anger management techniques, she would explain what was what, and clear the air.

10

The anger management course wasn't being held in a hotel as Leigh had told Matt, but in a private clinic in the countryside miles from the temptations of Reading.

She drove through tall elaborate pillars, pleased to see the gates wide open, not locked tightly to prevent a quick getaway. The thought amused her. It was an expensive private clinic, not a Victorian asylum of old. But when the long meandering tree-lined driveway eventually ended in a large car park, she found herself staring in dismay at the gothic building looming before her. The dark brick turrets and narrow windows were distinctly unwelcoming.

If she held any hope this week wasn't going to be too bad, it died in the face of the grim architecture. It was tempting to reverse from the parking space, speed back down the driveway and check in to the nearest hotel. The choice wasn't hers though and the reality check pushed her from the car. With her suitcase bumping off her thigh, she crossed to the entrance. The huge oak door, old and venerable, was let down by an incongruous row of bells set into the wall on one side. Each had a tag beside it, the tiny print forcing

eigh to peer closely before pressing her thumb against the one
abelled *Reception*.

It was several minutes before it was answered, minutes where
Leigh once again wondered about turning tail and heading for the
ills, the thought making her look around nervously towards
er car.

The creak of the door opening was almost her undoing. Luckily,
the woman who appeared in the slowly increasing gap wore a warm
welcoming smile. 'Hello.' Leigh's *hi* in response came on a nervous
exhalation that made the woman's smile widen. 'The building may
ook ominous and scary but honestly we're not a bit.'

'I was just about to run away,' Leigh admitted, reassured by the
sheer ordinariness of the woman in her grey trousers, white shirt,
er nut-brown hair pinned in a neat bun.

'I hear that a lot.' The woman laughed and reached to take
Leigh's suitcase. 'I'm Marie. Come in, I'll register you and show you
o your room.'

Registration was basic, Leigh signing where she was requested.

'Okay.' Marie reached into a cupboard for a key. 'You're on the
econd floor. There's a lift or' – she waved to the cantilevered
tairway that filled the hallway – 'I can take you up the stairs.'

'Stairs are fine, thanks.' They were broad enough to walk up
ide by side. 'This is an amazing place.' It was also, she was grateful
o see, less scarily intimidating on the inside than the out.

'Thank you. We like to think so.' At the top of the stairs, Marie
waved a hand to the corridor on the left. As they walked, she gave a
rief history of the house. 'It was built as a private home but was
old in the nineteenth century and became a school, then a hotel. It
hut about twenty years ago and the building was left empty for
everal years, falling sadly into disrepair. By the time our company
ought it, it was in a sorry state indeed.'

'It looks like they've poured a considerable amount of money into it.' Leigh didn't know much about these things but from what she'd seen so far, no expense had been spared to make the interior discreetly and sumptuously comfortable.

Marie smiled. 'Self-improvement courses don't need to be austere. We've discovered our clientele respond and relate more efficiently when the surroundings are serene.'

Leigh's bedroom was certainly that. Lavishly so, and for the first time she wondered how much the course was costing her employer. Looking around the beautifully furnished room, she guessed it was considerable. 'This is lovely.'

'We recommend spending time in your room after morning and afternoon sessions to better absorb what you've learned, so it's essential to have comfort.'

Any course Leigh had ever attended was usually followed by drinking sessions in the hotel bar or nearest pub. That obviously wasn't going to happen here.

Marie pointed to a folder on a table near the window. 'You'll find lots of information in that, plus your personal schedule for the week. Mobile phones are not permitted anywhere outside your bedroom. We feel many of the problems people come here to address are exacerbated by social media. We also believe in each participant giving their full concentration to what is going on here rather than it being diluted by what others are doing elsewhere.'

'A partial social media detox.'

'Exactly.' Marie handed her the room key. 'There's an official welcome for your course at six, in the conference room which is off the main reception. It will be followed by dinner at seven. We encourage guests to have an early night. Breakfast is at 7.30 a.m.'

Seven thirty! Being big on comfort and a serene environment obviously wasn't the same as letting the attendees have a lie-in.

'If you've any questions, there's always a member of staff in reception who'll be happy to help.' Marie gave a final smile and left

Leigh spent a few minutes exploring the room and the large en suite, pleased to see both a shower and a bath. She ran a hand over fluffy towels, peered at the upmarket toiletries, wondered briefly about having a shower before deciding not to bother.

Back in the bedroom, she moved to the window to gaze at the view that had attracted her before. Nearby, tall trees swayed gently above rows of neatly clipped hedging. In the distance, low hills and farmland ran towards the horizon. When Leigh saw a figure disappearing between the hedges, she realised the garden was criss-crossed with narrow pathways.

Probably designed to encourage introspection... What Leigh would have liked was a large gin and tonic to prevent the same.

* * *

At five minutes to six, she picked up her handbag and opened the bedroom door, then shut it and fished in her bag for her mobile. She checked for messages. A couple from friends which didn't need immediate replies. One from Matt hoping she'd arrived safely and extolling the exhibition he'd seen. She shook her head at his enthusiasm and sent a quick message to say the hotel was lovely and she'd ring later. It felt strange to leave her phone on the bedside table; she'd not realised how used she was to having it as an accessory.

The door to the conference room was open, several people already seated within. As was standard, everyone avoided the front row.

A pale man with sparse blond hair stood to one side of a small table. 'Welcome,' he said, his face creasing in a smile. He waved slim fingers over the table like a magician about to choose the card she'd guessed. 'And you'd be?'

'Leigh Simon.'

He picked up her name badge. 'Here you go. If you could remember to wear it every day, that would be great.'

'Of course.' She took the badge and pinned it to the collar of her shirt.

'Take a seat anywhere.' His smile widened. 'The front row if you're feeling brave.'

Leigh looked across the room and shook her head. 'Maybe tomorrow.'

At a quick glance, the group already gathered looked to be evenly divided between men and women. Leigh was one of the youngest so far; she guessed this came down to the price of the course rather than any demographic slant towards older people having more anger issues. Four rows of seats. Six seats to a row. Twenty-four attendees if all seats were going to be filled.

The end seat of each row, apart from the front, was taken. Leigh hesitated before excusing herself to the woman in the back. 'I'm not brave enough for the front, I'm afraid,' she said as the woman moved aside to let her past.

'Nor me.' She waited until Leigh sat one chair along. 'I'm Melanie.'

It seemed suddenly silly to leave a gap between them and Leigh shuffled across a seat. 'Leigh, nice to meet you.'

'Even given the circumstances?' Melanie arched an eyebrow.

Leigh took in the heavy make-up and obviously expensive clothes. Older than she was, maybe nearer to sixty. Something sad in her eyes. 'In a pub over a G&T might have been better.'

'Nearest pub is six miles away.' Melanie shrugged. 'It was the first thing I checked when I saw the address of the clinic. At least they give us wine at dinner.'

More arrivals drew their attention. Within minutes, the seats, even those in the scary front row, were almost all taken. Melanie started a conversation with a woman in front of her. The woman seated to Leigh's left was chatting to someone the other side so for a few minutes Leigh simply sat, her eyes flicking around the room, assessing. Across the other side, a man around her age was doing the same. When their eyes met, he smiled, then winked.

Leigh looked away without reacting. She knew the type: hand-some, if a little flashy; he'd be charming if he was getting his own way, possibly mean if he weren't. When she was younger, he was the type she'd gravitate towards. Nowadays, she valued her fingers too much to have them burned again. Anyway, she had Matt; she didn't need anyone else, not even a flirtation to pass the time.

11

The introduction address given by one of the course organisers was the usual mix of greetings, instructions and exhortations for each of them to make the most of the opportunity afforded. By the time he'd got to the nitty gritty of what was happening and when, Leigh had zoned out. All the information was in the folder in her room. Time enough to worry about it all the following day.

The restless rustling in the room implied she wasn't the only one getting bored. Whether the organiser read the room and decided to cut his introduction short, or it was always planned to be brief, suddenly it was over.

'I need a drink after that.' Melanie's loud whisper made all who heard giggle nervously. 'Come on,' she said, linking her arm through Leigh's. 'Let's see what the dining room set up is like.'

It turned out to be very nice. A large room to the back of the house with three sets of floor-to-ceiling windows overlooking the grounds where, in the October twilight, solar lights had flicked on to render it almost magical.

Without asking, Melanie dragged Leigh to a table near the window. 'Perfect,' she said, releasing Leigh's arm and sinking onto a hair. 'I suppose it was too much to hope for that they'd have left a ottle of wine on the table.'

Leigh, who anticipated the wine might be doled out by the glass nd perhaps not too generously, was already weary of the woman's xation on alcohol. She liked a drink, but never considered it an ssential.

By the end of the dinner, where they'd been offered one glass nd no more, Leigh understood why Melanie was on the course. he became increasingly vocal and demanding, her manner to the vaiting staff crossing the fine line that separated dismissive from ownright rude.

Leigh glanced around the dining room, wondering about the ther attendees. How did their anger manifest itself? In vocal utburst or physical assaults? For the first time, she acknowl-dged her need to be there. Okay, Ledbetter was a creep, but there vere better ways to handle things than resorting to physical iolence.

When dinner finally ended, Leigh made her excuses and left he table. There was no lounge to sit in, the attendees being encour-ged to return to their rooms. A few, she saw, were heading out for a valk around the gardens, others for a cigarette, yet others were tanding about chatting. She passed by with a smile and a nod and eaded up the stairs.

In her room, she didn't bother turning on the light. Grabbing er mobile she pressed speed dial to connect to Matt. When it went irectly to voicemail, she frowned and redialled. Third time lucky, he thought, dialling again. Same result. He'd probably gone to inner, maybe the pub afterwards. Typical when she really wanted o speak to him.

She tossed her phone on the bed and walked to the window. olar lights gave enough light to access the pathways and she saw everal of the attendees drifting down them; she was amused to see the man from earlier with his hand resting on the waist of one of the women as they headed towards a different path.

It looked as if some people were making their own entertainment.

And this was only day one.

She was asleep when her mobile rang. Disorientated, her hand flailed for where the light switch normally lay, her knuckles hitting painfully against the table. Swearing loudly, she sat up. She'd left the curtains open and sufficient light came through the window to show where her now-silent mobile sat on the bedside table.

She was surprised at the time. 11.15 p.m. The missed call had been from Matt. She tapped his name to ring him back. 'Hi,' she said when he answered. 'I tried you earlier.'

'I saw, sorry. At the exhibition I bumped into some people I used to know, and they invited me to join them for dinner, and you know how it goes.'

She did and, imagining the art-driven conversation, she was relieved she'd not been with him. 'I'm glad you're having a nice time, even if it is without me.'

'How's it going so far?'

'Great,' she lied easily. 'We haven't done much yet, of course, just an introduction. It was tiring though so I was asleep.'

'Sorry, I thought you'd be up late schmoozing in the hotel bar.'

Regretting again that she'd not told him the truth, stuck in a cycle of lies, she told one more. 'I was till about ten thirty. Must have fallen asleep as soon as my head hit the pillow.' That at least was true. She was surprised to have fallen asleep so quickly, having anticipated tossing and turning for hours.

'I'm heading back to Salisbury tomorrow; it'll give me a few days to tidy up before you arrive.'

'Sounds good.' She yawned. 'Have you seen much of Gina?'

'No, I've not seen her at all. Heard her singing last night, that's all.'

Leigh was relieved. Perhaps Gina would understand she'd been making a fuss about nothing. 'Okay, I'll give you a shout tomorrow. Night, love you.'

'Love you too, Leigh, very much.'

She hung up and lay back with a smile. *Very much.* Unusually emphatic for the normally reticent Matt; the holiday was doing him good.

To Leigh's surprise, she fell asleep almost immediately and woke refreshed when her alarm sounded at six thirty.

12

By the end of the first morning, Leigh was bored rigid, and by the end of the day, she was almost catatonic. If there'd been somewhere to get a drink, she'd have spent the whole week drunk simply to get through it.

Maybe it was boredom, or perhaps that younger woman who fell for the most unsuitable men was still lurking inside somewhere, but she felt a flutter of excitement when she saw the man she'd noticed the previous day slip onto the seat beside her at lunch. Close up, he was even more handsome, his devil-may-care air more obvious.

'I'm Philip,' he said, holding out his hand.

She shook it as briefly as manners would allow. 'Leigh.'

Lunch was served with the same care as dinner in the evening but without the alcohol. It was several minutes before she had the chance to look Philip's way. He was in conversation with the woman to his other side, giving Leigh the opportunity to shamelessly stare. Older than she'd first thought. Perhaps forty. No wedding ring but she knew, to her cost, that didn't mean anything.

He turned, caught her looking and smiled.

She wondered what he saw... A glamorous, successful woman with expensively and subtly tinted blonde hair, a well-toned five foot six, make-up perfectly applied to make the most of her blue eyes? Or did he see a slightly weary woman who was finding life so hard to cope with she had to attend courses like this, a woman with the first signs of age in the fine lines fanning out from the corners of her eyes?

She wasn't inclined to accept the invitation she saw in his. Why would she? She loved Matt. *Didn't she?* Okay, their current situation wasn't ideal, but they weren't the first couple to manage a relationship separated by miles. It wasn't Matt's fault that Leigh seemed to tell lies more frequently to make it all work. Lying was simply an easier option at times and if she felt a twinge of guilt, if she acknowledged how she'd feel if she found Matt had been lying to her, she brushed it aside. They were white lies; they didn't harm anyone.

Infidelity was a different matter. She might have been unsure about her feelings for Matt, but it didn't mean she was tempted to cheat on him. In such a small group though, it was pointless trying to avoid Philip. She couldn't deny his charm... if there was a darker side to him, it was well concealed. There was an unspoken agreement among the attendees that they didn't speak about why they were there, but it didn't stop her wondering about him.

She quickly discovered him to be an entertaining companion and his seemingly endless supply of hilarious anecdotes helped to make the boring hours pass more easily. The mind-numbing lectures, tedious workshops, unintentionally hilarious role-plays, and embarrassing one-to-ones with a counsellor where she was supposed to open up about her feelings.

At her first meeting with the counsellor, Leigh was tempted to spin a tale about abusive parents who starved her of affection and had high expectations of their only child. But she couldn't do it.

Instead, she told the truth about her middle-class comfortable upbringing as the only child of parents who adored her, and wanted only for her to be happy.

The counsellor listened, then reached across and laid a hand on Leigh's arm. 'But you're *not* happy, are you?'

Leigh blinked. 'Of course I am. I've a well-paid job, a beautiful home, a boyfriend I love. Everything I could wish for.' The occasional doubts she had... about Matt, her job, the life she'd chosen... they were normal, weren't they? Nobody's life was perfect... everybody had regrets. She had absolutely no right to claim to be unhappy with her life... None.

'Your boyfriend lives with you?'

'No, he lives in Salisbury. He's a teacher.' The sigh floated in the air before she could prevent it from escaping. 'We spend weekends together.'

'Ah,' the counsellor said as if she understood everything. 'Is that enough for you?'

'It's not ideal, but I make it work.'

'I... not we? Do you feel as if you're the one making all the compromises in your relationship?'

Of course she did. It made life easier. 'No.' She sighed, her shoulders slumping. 'Yes... Matt could easily find a job in London, whereas I would struggle to find one in Salisbury.'

'Yes, you're a commodity trader. A high stress occupation.'

'It can be.'

'Fast paced, a lot of adrenaline flowing.'

'Yes.'

'Do you enjoy it?'

'It pays extremely well.'

'But that isn't what I asked, is it?'

Leigh tried a smile, but it wavered. She used to enjoy her job...

ut when? Months, years before? 'It's been more stressful than
sual recently, I suppose.'

'Because the work has become more difficult, or because you're
ot happy with the job?' When Leigh didn't answer, the counsellor
at back. 'Your relationship isn't fulfilling your needs, you no longer
njoy your job, so I ask you again, are you happy?'

* * *

eigh went straight to her room afterwards. She'd have liked to have
one to a bar and got steaming drunk. But as Melanie had informed her,
ne nearest one was six miles away. According to the clinic, *alcohol with
s disinhibiting effect could exacerbate anger urges.* There was nothing in
ny of the leaflets about one-to-one counselling having a similar effect.

Philip had taken to sitting beside her at every mealtime. That
vening over dinner, when she had the opportunity, she asked how
is counselling session had gone. 'I don't mean the details obvi-
usly, just if you found it of any help.'

'Sure, talking about myself, what's not to like.'

She might have been fooled by his glib response if she hadn't
oticed a change in his expression. Her question had been foolish,
ntrusive. 'I suppose that's one way of looking at it,' she said, letting
 drop.

During the lectures, she shut herself down and let the words
wirl around, bouncing off her, harmless, useless, but simple repeti-
on brainwashed even the most reluctant attendee and when she
ound herself mouthing their mantra, *take control, choose to stay
alm,* she had to smile.

'I've been brainwashed,' she told Philip during afternoon coffee.
'm finding myself spouting their propaganda.'

He laughed. 'You'll forget it as quickly.'

She picked up her coffee and tilted it towards him. 'Probably a soon as I get home.'

'London?'

She nodded. 'Camden Town.'

'Nice. Busy though; bet you find parking a nightmare or have you private parking?'

'No such luck. There's residential parking on Gaisford Street. I can be a nightmare though; too many residents, not enough spaces Sometimes I chew my fingernails to the quick driving around. don't use my car for work so it's not so bad during the week.'

'I'm not too far from you. Hornsey. Same problem there.'

A couple sitting nearby entered the conversation and the rest o the break was spent discussing the mundane everyday problems o parking. Leigh was almost pleased when the break was over, and they could head back to the next scintillating talk.

Her second, and final, one-to-one session, followed what Leigh guessed was standard motivational advice – she was to take control decide what mattered to her, write a list of what was important in her life, what she could change, blah blah blah. All the one-to-one had succeeded in doing, she decided, was to make her more unsettled.

More unsettled. The thought jolted her. When had she decided she was unsettled? Matt and she would work things out eventually.

* * *

Leigh would have left the clinic after lectures on Friday if she'd had her way. A quick glance around the bored frustrated faces of the other attendees in the room told her that most felt the same. But there was no point in railing at the enforced delay; she needed the certificate of completion, and the clever beggars weren't handing them out until after dinner that evening.

It was the course director who had the final word... and he seemed determined to make the most of his captive audience as he summarised the main points of what they were supposed to have learnt over the previous dull, boring and seemingly endless days.

Finally, she had the certificate of completion in her hand.

'Makes it all worthwhile, doesn't it?' Philip grinned as he took the seat beside her. He folded his certificate into quarters and stuffed it into his jacket pocket.

'It's over, that's the main thing.'

'We survived it, *that's* the main thing.' His grin faded as he looked at her. 'I expected to be bored to death, but I wasn't.' He shuffled his chair a little closer. 'How about meeting me for a drink next week? We could think of it as a graduation celebration. A platonic drink. No strings.'

He smiled in a way she guessed he thought was sexy. He was right, it was, and she was tempted until she saw the smugness in his eyes. He thought he had her just where he wanted her. That she'd fallen for his obvious charms. Was he really any better than the odious Bernard Ledbetter? 'Now that we're finished here, Philip, I'll want to forget all about it. I'm afraid to say, and I'm sorry if it sounds rude, but that includes you.'

Her handbag was under her chair; she bent to pick it up and straightened with it in her hand. She'd moved faster than he'd expected. He didn't have time to hide the flash of darkness that hardened his face, glinted in his eyes and twisted his mouth.

Charming but dangerous; she'd made the right decision.

13

Leigh left the clinic without bothering to have breakfast, sat in the car and took out her phone. It was only seven; Matt would be asleep. Rather than ringing, she sent him a message to say she was on her way. If the traffic wasn't too manic, she should be there by nine. Maybe even before he was awake.

She dropped the mobile on the passenger seat and sighed. It would be a nice weekend. They'd have a leisurely breakfast, and a nice dinner. Matt would tell her all about the exhibitions he'd visited. Every detail. And Leigh would do her best to look interested.

Suddenly she regretted she wasn't going straight home, even if it meant facing a difficult conversation with Gina. From thinking she'd made a mistake and wishing the younger woman would move out, Leigh now hoped she'd stay. There was nothing boring about Gina; she had the joie de vivre Leigh seemed to have lost over the years. But it was too late to change her plans now; Matt would never forgive her.

The traffic wasn't too bad and at a little before nine she was pulling into the drive of his three-bedded semi on the outskirts of

Salisbury. She'd ignored her mobile phone ringing on the way and reached for it now to see who had called. A voicemail told her it was the clinic and asked her to return the call when it was convenient.

'Leigh Simon,' she said when the phone was answered. 'I had a call.'

'Oh yes, Ms Simon. You left your Kindle behind.'

Damn, damn. Leigh remembered using it the previous evening. 'What a nuisance. Can you send it to me, please?'

'Actually, you are in luck. Mr Dunstable overheard me leaving the message and said he was happy to drop it off.'

A feeling of dread germinated. 'Mr Dunstable?'

'Philip Dunstable.'

'Right, I didn't know his surname. You gave him my address?'

'I wouldn't have done, of course, but he already knew it. Gaisford Street, Camden Town.'

Leigh remembered the conversation about difficulty parking in London. But she was sure she hadn't given him the house number.

'He thought it was number twenty, so luckily I was able to correct him.'

Of course she had. Leigh imagined Philip leaning across the desk with that charming smile. He'd have said *I'll be able to drop it into 20 Gaisford Street tomorrow* and the receptionist would have basked in his attention, probably laughed, maybe even touched him on the arm as she told him, *that would be great but it's number 172.*

Leigh had made it very clear she didn't want to see him again. There was, however, no point in taking it out on the receptionist. 'That's fine, thank you.' She hung up. It crossed her mind she should ring Gina, tell her someone might be calling with the Kindle… warn her not to invite him in… Leigh could get the apology she owed her out of the way too. But before she could dial the number the front door opened, and Matt came hurrying out, a smile on his homily handsome face, arms already outstretched to envelop her in a hug she desperately needed.

She rested her head on his shoulder. Perhaps she was being silly, making issues where there weren't any... perhaps... but the darkness she'd seen cross Philip's face worried her. And now he had her address.

She and Matt walked to a local café for breakfast. When he asked about the course, she raved about the wonderful lectures, the motivational speeches. 'It was really worth doing.' It was all she wanted to say about it. The only lie she wanted to tell that weekend. Far better to encourage Matt to talk about his week. 'You enjoyed the exhibitions?'

Of course he did, and he was more than happy to talk about them. She thought she was giving a good impression of being interested until he reached a hand across the table to take her hand. 'You seem distracted; are you okay?'

It was the perfect time to confess everything: Ledbetter, the anger management course, Philip... but instead, she returned the pressure on his hand and smiled. 'Just a bit tired; the course was far more intensive than I'd anticipated.'

The lines of worry that tracked his forehead didn't ease. 'You're sure that's all it is?'

Another opportunity, a chance to tell the truth, and another one she turned down. 'Yes, of course.'

She tried harder, her face aching from the effort to smile. At times, when she saw Matt's worried frown, she wondered if she looked and sounded a little manic. But it was either that or sink into the dread she knew was waiting to suck her in.

She tried to tell herself she was being silly... melodramatic... but remembering the ugly twist of Philip's mouth and his clever ruse to get her address, she wondered if he was some sort of predator.

Was that why he'd been doing the anger management course?

14

_____

If Leigh hadn't completely convinced Matt everything was okay, by the time she left on Sunday afternoon, she'd done everything possible, and he was looking less angsty.

Before she left Salisbury she stopped off at a supermarket. She didn't want Gina feeling obliged to feed her when she got home. She bought food, and a bottle of Prosecco she hoped would break any ice that hadn't thawed in the intervening days.

It took almost three hours to do the drive to London, roadworks slowing the traffic to a halt in numerous places. If the emotion surging through her at yet another delay was any indicator, the anger management course had been a total waste of time. Then, adding more irritation, there was no parking space near her house. A nail-bitingly frustrating circuit of the roads nearby was also unsuccessful, forcing her yet further away. Finally, she spotted a woman sauntering along the path, a bunch of car keys jangling carelessly from her fingers. Leigh slowed to follow, coming to a halt several metres later to wait for the car to pull out. Her indicator click clicked, the man in the car behind tooted once, then again, before raising both hands in a universal indicator of frustration.

The woman must have seen Leigh waiting, she couldn't have been deaf to the tooting, but she didn't rush, sitting in the car taking off her jacket, adjusting her hair, the mirrors, her seat. Leigh caught between the oblivious woman in front and the increasingly irate man behind, felt her own ire rising, the red tide that had so often consumed her in the past lapping at her feet.

Deep breaths in, slow breaths out.

Leigh tried the breathing. Tried counting to ten. By nine, her fingers were curled around the handle of the car door. She was squeezing ten through gritted teeth when she saw the flash of an indicator and the car finally pull out. Seconds later Leigh had parked her Volvo. She ignored the raised middle finger as the man behind shot past in a road-rage roar of speed that would force him to brake only metres later at the junction with a busier road.

It was a good ten-minute walk to her house and would have been no problem if the boot of her car hadn't been full. A jam packed suitcase, because she hadn't been sure what the dress code was going to be, the carrier bag of food and the second bag holding the bottle of Prosecco. She'd expected to be able to park nearer home and stood staring into the boot for several minutes, searching for enlightenment. It made sense to leave the carrier bags and return for them later. Instead, with a grunt of frustration, she gathered them in one hand and the suitcase in the other. With her handbag swinging awkwardly from one shoulder, she trudged home.

Her house keys, separate from her car keys, had slipped to the bottom of her over packed handbag. She dropped everything on the doorstep and fumbled inside, wondering if she'd lost them, if she'd left them behind with her damn blasted Kindle. Her finger closed over the cold metal with a grunt of relief.

Then she was inside, relieved to be home.

She left her suitcase in the hallway and took the two carrier bags into the kitchen, humming under her breath.

The house was quiet. Gina was probably working late. Leigh was half-relieved, half-disappointed. She'd have liked to have got the conversation over with, then they could have chilled out over the bottle of Prosecco.

Upstairs, she unpacked, sorted her clothes out, tidied everything away. Restless, she decided a bath would be relaxing. If Gina was working, she'd not be home for a few hours yet.

Leigh hadn't been in the main bathroom since she'd shown Gina around. It was exactly as it had been then, no washing accoutrements left sitting on the shelves, no shower gel or shampoo on the side of the shower tray. Leigh had noticed Gina was tidy, now she seemed obsessive.

The scent of her favourite bath oil filled the room as Leigh rested her head against the bath cushion and shut her eyes. Usually, the combined fragrance of lavender and bergamot was enough to settle her thoughts but that evening nothing was working. Her eyes flicked open, glancing around the room, restless. The strange sensation something was wrong wouldn't leave her. It wasn't simply worrying thoughts of Philip, although that didn't help... it was something dodging around the periphery of her mind.

Despite her restlessness, it wasn't till the water cooled around her that Leigh pulled the stopper and climbed out. She dried herself briskly, wrapped the towel around her and opened the door. No sound from downstairs.

Swapping the towel for a cotton robe, Leigh headed downstairs. The ready meal she'd bought wasn't particularly tempting but, hungry, she followed the instructions and popped it into the microwave.

When Gina returned, Leigh would open the Prosecco. Until then, she'd settle for a glass of water with her food. She sat at the small kitchen table, thinking about the week, the weekend, about Matt... and Philip. The last thought took her appetite away. She dropped her fork and pushed away the half-finished meal.

'To hell with this,' she said, getting to her feet. A few seconds later, she smiled at the satisfying pop as she loosened the cork from the Prosecco and poured a glass. Gina was sure to be home soon, she could catch up. Leigh hoped the bubbles would lighten what might be a difficult conversation. She'd had time to reflect on Gina's reaction to staying alone with Matt. Leigh had been at fault. For not laying out the ground rules, for not giving Gina advance warning, for reacting as she had done. Her attitude had been high-handed, unforgivable. She had known Gina's desperate situation, had known the woman had nowhere else to go. Leigh groaned and took a mouthful of her drink. She'd been an absolute cow. But she'd make it up to Gina, somehow.

Leigh took her glass through to the living room. A week's worth of flyers and post sat on the hall table. There were a couple of packets too. Books she'd ordered, she supposed, recognising the Amazon logo on one. Despite having a Kindle, she was still tempted by *real* books, seeing them advertised on Twitter or Instagram, clicking to buy without giving it much thought. They'd join the pile on her bedside locker, waiting to be read some day. She picked up the post as she passed and dropped it untidily onto the sofa.

With the TV on and switched to YouTube, music filled the room. She sipped the Prosecco and reached for the post without looking, picking up one item at a time. Most was rubbish: a couple of letters offering her discounted insurance, one from the council giving advance notice of yet another hike in council tax, a flyer for a local takeaway pizzeria. She assumed the next she picked up... a folded sheet of paper... was yet another flyer until she noticed it had her name scrawled in block capitals across one side.

Puzzled, she opened it. More block capitals. A short succinct note. Two words.

SORRY, GINA.

Sorry? Leigh frowned. Was Gina apologising for her reaction to Matt staying? That would make the conversation Leigh needed to have with her so much easier. Matt had mentioned he'd not seen Gina at all while he'd stayed there so that also helped.

Tossing the note onto the pile of rubbish, Leigh sat back. The uneasy sensation she'd felt earlier returned and she reached for the note again. Rereading the two words, the absence of clutter in the bathroom took on a different meaning. Maybe Gina wasn't being obsessively tidy, maybe she'd left, taking all her belongings with her.

Surely not... Leigh looked up as if she could see through the ceiling to the room upstairs where Gina's belongings would be neatly tidied away in the double wardrobe and chest of drawers.

Slow reluctant steps pushed Leigh up the stairs, her hand hesitating as it rested on the handle of the bedroom door, until with a grunt of irritation she pressed down and threw the door open with such force it bounced against the wall inside. She stood in the doorway, staring. It wasn't necessary to open the doors of the wardrobe or pull out the drawers to know they were all empty. There was an air of abandonment in the room despite the neatly made bed. The bedside lamp stood alone on the bedside table, missing the knick-knacks Gina had positioned carefully behind. The small bookshelf in the corner no longer held her sparse eclectic collection of books. To be certain she was right, Leigh opened the wardrobe. Nothing. Not even the wooden coat hangers she had bought. Gina, in her haste to leave, had simply taken her clothes, hangers and all.

Leigh was glad, relieved, happy. *Bloody delighted!* She slammed the bedroom door and went downstairs. The Prosecco was all hers. She didn't need to share it. Didn't need to apologise for being such a cow. Tears prickled. She'd been so horrible she'd chased the poor woman away.

Bringing the bottle through to the living room, she sat and poured another glass. 'Gina's gone,' she said to Matt when she rang, two glasses later, her voice slightly slurred. 'Left me a note saying she was sorry.'

'Sorry for what?'

Leigh had never mentioned the disagreement she'd had with Gina; she didn't see the need now and have to face his criticism for not telling him. *Yet another thing she hadn't told him.* 'Leaving without notice, I assume.'

'It was a bit abrupt.' He sounded bored. 'Better off though; it was a crazy idea.'

'She must have had a better offer.'

He laughed. 'Right, maybe she's moved into Buckingham Palace.' When she didn't laugh, he added, 'You'll have to refund her rent, won't you?'

No, Leigh wouldn't have to refund anything. No rent had ever been paid. What kind of useless landlady was she? No wonder Gina could just walk off... and with the coat hangers too! But there was no point in telling Matt they'd never got around to sorting out the financial part of it all. 'I'll call into the café tomorrow and have a word about it. I can't believe she left like that.'

'For goodness' sake, you barely knew the woman, maybe she does this all the time. You're sure you're not missing anything?'

Leigh didn't think he meant something as mundane as hangers. 'No, of course not.' Actually, she hadn't looked. As soon as she got off the phone to Matt she went and checked her few valuables, the jewellery gifted to her over the years by the same aunt who'd left her the house. But it was all there.

Leigh sat and finished the Prosecco. She'd let the hangers go, get er usual coffee in the morning, be her normal friendly self and orget she'd ever had Gina live with her.

Forget about her, deal with Philip if he dared show up, and get er life back to normal.

15

On Monday, after a night when sleep had come in fits and starts, Leigh would have liked to have bypassed the café and the confrontation with her erstwhile lodger. Wasn't it enough she'd be facing Bernard Ledbetter again that morning? She was already imagining the smug expression on his face, the wink wink, nudge nudge she knew he'd slip in sometime during the day.

If she had to face him, she needed coffee, and why should she deprive herself of the best? Gina would have to be faced someday. If she'd stayed, Leigh would have apologised; she'd planned to, hadn't she? She'd accepted she'd been wrong. She'd tell her... Maybe they could go somewhere for coffee, lunch even, Leigh's treat.

Her shoulders slumped and her chin dropped as she realised her meeting with Gina wasn't going to happen that morning. She wasn't there. The staff who were, were unfamiliar to Leigh, so she didn't ask where Gina was or if she was working later. On her way home, Leigh would drop in again, see if she was there and if not find out when she would be.

* * *

Although she was, as usual, early, many of Leigh's co-workers were even earlier and the usual air of noisy chaos already enveloped the trader's floor. Relieved to see no sign of her manager, she settled at her desk to check her emails, unsurprised to see they'd piled up. Putting Ledbetter, Gina, and everything else from her head, she settled down to work through them. Most could be quickly dealt with and dismissed, others required more work.

The ring of her desk phone blended in with the surrounding din and it took a while for its persistent brrr brrr to pierce her concentration. Distracted, she looked towards where it sat on the corner of her desk. Reaching for it, she held it in place with her shoulder and continued to respond to the email as she said, 'Leigh Simon.'

'Ms Simon, it's Janet Collins, when you have a minute, could you call in to see me please.'

Leigh swallowed a groan. It wasn't a request, and she knew damn well that the *when you have a minute* meant *get off your ass and get in here now*. Had Ledbetter made a further complaint? Worse, had someone else?

'I'll be right there,' she said. Putting the phone down, she got to her feet.

Perhaps the HR manager simply wanted feedback on the anger management course. As she walked, Leigh searched her brain for a clever quotation from the course she could use and came up empty until she remembered her quip to Philip about having been brain-washed and it came to her. *Take control, choose to stay calm.*

Philip. He had her address; was she going to arrive home some day and find him waiting on her doorstep? Her footsteps slowed. A sensible part of her worried about that dark expression she'd seen, the crafty way he'd acquired her address... but there was a different part wondering if her wariness was partly fear of his undeniable attractiveness. How comfortable she'd felt with him, the way he'd made her laugh. It was easy to feel strongly about fidelity when she'd never been tempted to cheat.

It wasn't the time or the place to be analysing her thoughts. *Take control, choose to stay calm.* She repeated it to herself as she knocked on Janet Collins's office door moments later.

Collins, a vision in a purple long-sleeved dress that looked to be a size too large, nodded to the single chair opposite. 'Take a seat, please, Ms Simon.'

Leigh forced herself to sit back in the chair rather than perch on the edge like a nervous schoolgirl. *Choose to stay calm.* She wasn't sure the anger management course was designed to help her cope with the very intimidating human resources manager.

Collins rested her elbows on the desk in front of her and steepled her hands. A woman who never rushed anything, she looked at Leigh and raised one eyebrow.

Take control. Leigh met her gaze unflinchingly and, taking her lead from Collins, slowly crossed one leg over the other.

'I hope you found the course of benefit, Ms Simon.'

'Yes, I did, thank you.' Leigh had brought the certificate of completion with her. She looked at it before putting it on the desk and sliding it forward. 'For my personnel file.'

Collins took it, and without reading it, slipped it into the file that sat on one side of the desk. 'Thank you.'

Leigh wondered if that was it, if she should get to her feet and leave, but before she could move Collins looked down at her hands. When she spoke, there was a different tone to her voice. 'You may have noticed Mr Ledbetter's absence.'

'With a certain amount of relief, if I'm honest. I wasn't looking forward to meeting him.'

'Indeed.' Collins pursed her lips. 'When you told me about your... issues... with him, you possibly thought I'd discounted them completely. It isn't my way, Ms Simon.' She sighed and pulled at the cuff of her dress, folding it, and pushing the sleeve back. 'Last week, I spoke to a few of your colleagues.' She met Leigh's eyes. 'Your female colleagues. In a one-to-one conversation with three of them, they all said the same thing.'

Expecting validation, Leigh was surprised at the tone of the manager's voice. Perhaps she hadn't wanted her to be vindicated.

'Each said they found Mr Ledbetter to be a kind, considerate manager who treated them with courtesy and respect.'

Disappointed but not particularly surprised, Leigh raised her chin and met the manager's eyes. 'That I'm his only victim, doesn't make him any less of a predator.'

'It does, however, make it difficult when it's a case of your word against his.' She pushed her sleeves back again and rested her hands on the desk. 'For the moment, my concern is more for Mr Ledbetter's welfare. He didn't turn up for work this morning, nor did he ring to say he wouldn't be in. I know from speaking to him during the week that he was finding your accusations difficult to cope with. He said he felt everyone was thinking' – she held up her hands, curled her index fingers in the air and wagged them – 'there was no smoke without fire.'

Leigh was stupidly fascinated by the fingers as they moved out of sync, looking less like inverted commas, more like flashing indicators to highlight Ledbetter's trite cliché. The manager didn't seem to expect a reply which was as well, as Leigh couldn't think of a single thing to say that wouldn't have convinced the manager the money spent on the anger management course was a waste of money.

'Thank you, Ms Simon.'

Not trusting herself to say anything, Leigh settled for a tight smile and a nod before getting to her feet.

On her way back to her desk, she passed Felicity, one of the women the HR manager would have spoken to about Ledbetter's behaviour. They'd never been friends as such but had a cordial working relationship.

Leigh opened her mouth to say hello, to perhaps make some mundane comment about the weather, but shut it with a snap when Felicity turned her head away and walked briskly past without a word.

Stunned, Leigh sat at her desk, angled the monitors and huddled closer. She'd been so busy that morning she hadn't noticed nobody had spoken to her at all. Now, she was conscious of a ring of silence around her desk.

It seemed Janet Collins wasn't the only person Ledbetter had been speaking to. And since, as the HR manager had clearly said, it was a case of her word against his, it was obvious whose word was being believed.

Leigh wanted to climb onto her desk, shout at the top of her voice until she had everyone's attention and tell them... scream at them... that she was the victim here. She... not Ledbetter.

Instead, she huddled behind her computer screens and battled silently with angry frustration.

16

Leigh, for probably the first time since she'd joined Lancaster International, left as soon as the time on the lower right corner of her three monitors clicked from 16:59 to 17:00. Grabbing her jacket and bag, she kept her eyes down and concentrated on walking... not running... to the exit.

Outside, she joined a shoal of pedestrians, swimming from one to another as she crossed paths and roads, anger at Ledbetter and her co-workers churning, making her feel nauseous and numb. It probably wasn't a good time to talk to Gina but when Leigh found herself outside the café, she hesitated briefly before swerving round a group of camera-wielding tourists to enter.

Dealing with one gnawing worry might give her a bit of desperately needed calm. *Worry.* It was only in that second that Leigh acknowledged there was something decidedly odd about the way Gina had moved out without leaving a forwarding address. The café was busy, a queue at the counter waiting to be served. Leigh joined the end, craning over the broad shoulders of the man in front to see who was behind the counter. No sign of Gina but another server she recognised, Isobel, was there.

'Hi.' Leigh smiled, waiting for a sign of recognition, her smile fading when Isobel looked at her blankly. Maybe it would be better to do business first. 'A skinny cappuccino, please.'

She waited until the brimming cup was placed on the counter before trying again. 'I was looking for Gina.'

Isobel barked a throaty sixty-cigarette-a-day laugh. 'You and everyone else!' She glanced at the next customer, then back to Leigh. 'I have a break in ten minutes if you want to wait.'

Leigh didn't. She wanted to leave her coffee, forget trying to discover why Gina had left, forget about the woman completely and run from the café. She swallowed the lump in her throat and picked up her coffee. By the time she reached one of the few remaining empty tables, coffee had lapped over the edge of the cup. She put it down, sat heavily and rested her forehead on her hand. This had been a ridiculously stupid idea. It was better to forget about it, go home, have a private wail.

Before she could make her escape, Isobel approached. She negotiated the crowded café with ease, put her mug of coffee on the table and sat on the chair opposite Leigh. 'I only have a few minutes.' She slurped her coffee and looked at Leigh with curiosity. 'You come in here a lot?'

'Yes, almost every morning.' Often enough to be recognised, she'd have thought.

Isobel shrugged. 'Everyone's face blends into each other after a while. I just want to do my job, get paid. I'm not interested in customers apart from taking their orders.'

'Not like Gina.'

It was a statement rather than a question, and made Isobel tilt her head and smile. 'I may not be interested in customers; it didn't mean I wasn't fascinated watching people being taken in by her sweet-as-pie act. Gina was only interested in Gina and what people could do for her.'

Leigh was taken aback. *What people could do for her?* Like giving her the run of Leigh's home. Had she been taken for a ride? 'You always seemed to get on okay.'

'We did. I'd have preferred it if she'd laughed and joked less and worked more but she wasn't the worst.'

The past tense wasn't lost on Leigh. 'Wasn't? Has she left?'

'Yes, she has.' Isobel checked her watch. 'I need to go. Have to have a fag.' She shuffled in her seat, preparing to stand.

'Please, another minute.' Leigh reached a hand towards her. 'Do you know where she's gone?'

'No.' Isobel's mouth turned down. 'The bitch dropped me in it, didn't bother to turn up for work on Saturday or Sunday. It was impossible to get anyone to cover her shift. Have you any idea how manic it was? A whole weekend, with just me?'

'I'm so sorry.' What Leigh was apologising for she'd no idea, it just seemed the appropriate thing to say.

It seemed to appease the woman sitting opposite too. She relaxed in her chair and leaned her arms on the table. 'Why're you looking for her, anyway?' Her eyes narrowed. 'She didn't hit on you for money, did she?'

Leigh shook her head, then because she saw something in the older woman's eyes she asked, 'Did she hit on you?'

'Owes me fifty quid. Got an advance on her wages too, so the manager isn't happy.'

'Don't you have a way of contacting her?'

Isobel, who'd been anxious to get away moments before, now seemed in no hurry to leave. 'She was living in a flat with a woman she met on the train when she was coming to London from Glasgow. I gather the woman fell for Gina's sob story about having nowhere to stay, and no friends in the city, and foolishly offered her a spare room till she got on her feet.' Isobel gave another of her throaty laughs. 'That was three months ago. Gina'd have stayed there forever, if she'd not been given her marching orders recently. Typical of the conniving bitch though, she managed to fall on her feet and got lodging with some rich woman she met somewhere.'

Leigh, trying to keep her expression neutral, knew she'd failed dismally when Isobel's eyes widened and she started to chuckle, a nasty wet sound that had Leigh lean as far back in her seat as she could. The cackling came to an abrupt halt and Isobel wiped a hand across her mouth. 'This is why you're looking for her! She's fleeced you, has she?'

Leigh doubted coat hangers counted. 'No, she didn't fleece me and I'm not a rich woman.' Is that how Gina had seen her... a rich woman to be manipulated? 'I had a spare room. It was an impulse thing. She told me she'd been living with a friend who was getting married and needed the room.'

Isobel cackled again. 'With people like Gina, truth is an optional extra.'

'I felt sorry for her.' Was that strictly true? Hadn't she been a little jealous of the enthusiastic, exuberant woman who'd reminded Leigh a little of the woman she'd once been? Now it seemed, she'd been taken for a fool. 'I was away for a week and when I came back, she'd packed up all her stuff and was gone. I suppose I was looking for an explanation.'

Isobel checked her watch, then looked across to the counter where her colleague was standing with arms folded and an expression of long-suffering on her face. She waved a hand in acknowledgement before looking back to Leigh. 'I have to go. Gina would have had her reason for leaving, believe me. Something better turned up.' Her mouth twisted in anger. 'Something that allowed her to leave her lodging and chuck her job.' With a shake of her head, she pushed the chair back with a noisy scrape and left.

Leigh watched as Isobel waved to her colleague, held two fingers to her lips and pointed to the rear exit. When she'd gone from sight, Leigh got to her feet and headed away. She walked slowly towards the station as she mulled over what she'd learned about Gina.

How very stupid she'd been to invite a woman she knew nothing about into her home.

She was gone now; Leigh could forget about her.

Couldn't she?

She remembered Gina's delight when she'd been offered the room, how speedily she'd arrived. Remembered how enthusiastic she was about everything. Even that hideous green bathroom suite.

There had been no reason for her to leave.

Now it seemed she'd left her job too.

Despite what Isobel had said, something didn't feel right.

17

Leigh pushed open her front door at about the same time as usual. But if her home was supposed to be a sanctuary, there was none there. When she managed to push the mystery of Gina from her head, the space was quickly occupied by Ledbetter.

She had to keep reminding herself she was the victim, not him. He'd obviously spent the week she'd been away protesting his innocence, enough to have convinced Collins and others, but surely there were those who would wonder if he protested too much.

Only by clinging to that hope, and to it all being a nine-day wonder, had she any chance of staying sane.

Ledbetter's absence that day had been a cheeky sneaky attempt to garner more sympathy, that was all. Despite what Collins had said, Leigh truly couldn't believe her accusation had affected him in any way.

When her mobile rang, she was tempted to ignore it. It would be Matt. If she'd told him everything at the time... the mess with Ledbetter and that stupid anger management course... she could have talked about what had happened that day and maybe received some much-needed sympathy. Maybe he'd hear her distress and ffer to come to London to be with her. Get a taxi and be with her in few hours. She bit back a scoff at the thought of Matt being so ɔolish.

It didn't matter, she wasn't going to tell him. Yes, he'd be sympanetic, but he'd also be critical, and she simply couldn't face it. She eached for her mobile and said an emphatically cheery, 'Hello!'

Maybe too emphatic as there was a moment's silence before Matt spoke. 'You okay?'

She hoped her laugh didn't have a tinge of mania at the edges. Yes, I was upstairs when I heard the phone ring and nearly broke ny neck rushing down the stairs to answer it. I slipped and landed ɪn the sofa.' She was rambling. A deep breath helped steady her. 'm okay though.'

'Good.'

Good. He sounded distracted. 'How was your day?'

It was the perfect question. Matt loved to talk about his job, his tudents, anecdotes about what they did or said. She used to find nem amusing and encouraged him to talk. It was a while before he realised he didn't need any encouragement to talk about his ʳork or himself. Only recently had she noticed she switched off ɔmpletely as soon as she heard *wait till I tell you what...* so never new what Johnny or Sally got up to.

He wouldn't ask her about her day. Not even if she dropped a ₂ss than subtle hint about having had a tiring one. Was it her fault? hould she have immediately jumped in to tell him about her ₂cidedly shit day? Her fault she couldn't, because of all she'd kept ʳom him. It was scrambling her already messy brain. It was better ɔ let him talk.

He'd barely said a word when she heard his doorbell chiming in ne background. 'There's your doorbell. Go answer it. I've had a ʳring day; I'm going to get something to eat and have an early ɪght.'

'You sure?'

'Yes, go, love you.'

'Love you too. Chat tomorrow.'

She changed out of her work clothes, pulling on a colourful silk kaftan in the hope the bright colours would cheer her up. Unfortunately, they reminded her of Gina and sent her thoughts churning even further. She was almost tempted to take the kaftan off and replace it with her plain drab off-white robe until she realised how ridiculous she was being.

Back downstairs, it was habit rather than hunger that sent her to the fridge. When Gina had moved in, Leigh had cleared a shelf for her to use. While her shelves held a sparse amount of food, Gina's one shelf was packed with several neatly wrapped packages from the local delicatessen. Expensive. Untouched.

Leigh took one out. A smoked salmon quiche. Still in date. Why had Gina bought all this food and left it behind? Frowning, she opened the freezer underneath. All the individual portions of food Gina had cooked were still there too.

Strange. Weird even.

Odd enough to wipe any desire for food away. Instead, she made a cup of coffee and took it back to the sitting room, trying to work out the puzzle of it all. A useless task; only speaking to Gina would sort it out.

Leigh drank her coffee and tried to relax. The packages she hadn't opened the day before caught her eye. Gina's note had completely distracted her. Maybe a good book to read was what she needed. She picked up the first. Wrapped with Amazon's usual over the top vigour, it took persistence to open.

The cover of the book with its bloody handprint and blood smeared knife was sufficiently dramatic to have attracted her attention and tempted her in a weak moment to add to her endless pile of unread books. Now she needed something more calming

Hoping the other was a romance, she reached for the second package. So convinced it was from Amazon, it took a few seconds to get through to her addled brain that it wasn't.

This was a plain brown envelope, *Miss Leigh Simon* written in felt pen across the front. No address. No stamp. Hand delivered.

She knew what it was, tearing open the envelope in a faint hope she was wrong. No such luck. It was her Kindle. No note.

Philip. Squeezed from her mind by Ledbetter and Gina, he pushed back in. The Kindle fell from Leigh's hands, hitting the floor with a dull thud that seemed to echo in the silence.

The package had been on the hall table. Not on the mat inside the front door. Philip must have called around and rang the doorbell. Met Gina. Handed it to her.

Then Gina had put it on the hall table, and later, packed up and left.

Was Leigh being silly... paranoid even... to link the two events?

Had Philip used his charms on Gina? What was it Isobel had said? That wherever Gina had gone, she'd have landed firmly on her feet. Perhaps Gina and Philip were the perfect match.

Leigh shook her head slowly. She *was* being silly. Gina had appeared genuinely nervous at being left alone in the house with Matt, a man Leigh was vouching for; it was unlikely she would have left with a man she didn't know.

No, Gina's decision to leave had nothing to do with the delivery of the Kindle, nothing to do with Philip.

It was simply a coincidence. Wasn't it?

18

Perhaps coffee hadn't been the best idea. Leigh's thoughts were running round the inside of her skull in a game of chase that seemed to have no end.

Hoping a glass of wine might counteract the effects of the caffeine, she went to the kitchen, pulled a bottle of red from the rack and opened it.

She hadn't bothered to switch the kitchen light on; enough illumination came through the open door from the living room. There was light from the garden too, shining through the gaps in the hedge from her next-door neighbours whose garden was lit up as if it were Christmas every day. She liked it; Matt moaned about light pollution despite being told, more than once, that the lights were switched off at ten.

She stood at the window, sipping her wine, trying to stay in the moment, to be grateful for all she had. It was great in theory, not in practice. Or maybe she simply wasn't trying hard enough. Whatever. She gulped a couple of mouthfuls and leaned forward to rest her forehead on the glass.

The garden wasn't large. When she'd moved in, five years

before, it had been a tangle of overgrown bushes, brambles and bindweed. Now though, the beds and borders were empty, waiting to be planted in.

Empty. She frowned and peered through the window towards the far corner. Something white was lit up by the neighbour's lights. Her frown cleared. Probably a football. A regular occurrence from the football crazy twins living next door. Putting her glass down on the table behind, she eyed her bare feet dubiously then thought, what the hell, unlocked the door and stepped outside.

It was a lovely evening. She should really have taken her wine outside, but she was waiting until the garden was finished before buying furniture. When Matt was there, he'd haul chairs outside from the dining room. When she was on her own, Leigh would sometimes sit in the doorway on a cushion. Maybe when she'd tossed the ball back, she'd do that for an hour and let the fresh air calm her soul.

She was smiling at the thought as she walked carefully down the curved garden path. With her eyes down, watching for errant snails or even worse, slugs, she was at the end of the path before she looked up and noticed what had appeared ball shaped from the kitchen window, was, close up, acquiring a different form.

The light from next door was sporadic, erratic, changing the shape of the object as she approached. Not a football. Not a ball of any kind.

Leigh didn't stop at the end of the path. Bare feet sank into the soft soil as she crossed to the object. Her tightly clenched jaw was beginning to ache. She stared, afraid to blink, as if what she was looking at might change in that microsecond of darkness.

It wasn't until she was close enough to touch it that she finally admitted what she was seeing, then her feet moved backwards with careless speed. One of her heels struck the edge of the stone footpath causing her breath to leave in a gust as she stumbled, almost falling, eyes still fixed on what she'd seen.

Only when she got to the back door did she turn with a cry of terror and rush into the house. Her mobile, where had she left it? Panic wasn't conducive to thought. She took a deep breath. It was in the living room, where she'd dropped it after speaking to Matt. She grabbed it and pressed the emergency services speed dial.

'Emergency what service do you require?'

'Police. There's a dead body.'

'Are you in danger or in need of an ambulance?'

In danger? 'No, I don't think so, and no, no ambulance.' After answering a few more questions she hung up and waited for the good guys to ride to her rescue. Shock had frozen her in place. It was a minute, maybe longer, before the pain in her cut heel made itself felt. She looked down, lifting her foot to access the gash. It was bleeding a little. Not as dramatic as the bloody, muddy footsteps she'd left on the wooden floor as she'd rushed in for the phone.

When she heard the car pull up outside, she moved in jerky slow steps to the front door, opening it as two officers climbed from the squad car. They stood staring at her before approaching.

If she'd pictured them riding to her rescue, their wary, grimly assessing faces told her otherwise. The child in her, the little bit that lurked deep inside most people, had crawled to the surface, looking for someone to take her in their arms, cuddle her, protect her from the bogeyman hiding under the bed. Or in this case, in the garden.

'Ms Simon?'

Leigh gripped the door frame. 'Yes, Leigh Simon.'

'PC Carter.' He indicated the officer a step behind with a jerk of his head. 'PC Sharp.'

Leigh looked from one to the other... the rather weather-worn, not quite handsome face of the male officer, the pale, high cheeked male officer with hard eyes and oddly narrow lips... and stood ack to allow them in.

In the small hallway, the officers, bulked up as they were with heir uniforms and kit, were an intimidating presence, and Leigh, who had never had reason to deal with the police in any capacity, felt unaccustomedly and ridiculously nervous.

'It's this way,' she said, pointing towards the open kitchen door as if informing them of the location of the buffet table at a party. An nsuitable giggle bubbled; she caught her tongue between her teeth and bit down to stop it erupting and making the hard-faced fficers regard her with even more suspicion.

In the kitchen, a cool breeze came through the open back door. was after ten and the garden, previously lit by the neighbours' ghts, now lay in darkness. 'The lights have gone out,' Leigh said, urrying to explain what she meant. 'I don't have any, not as yet; I'm aving the garden redone.' She stopped and took a deep breath when she saw a hint of amusement creep across PC Sharp's face. 'm babbling, sorry; it's shock. Gina was so alive and now...' Nausea it her. She swallowed frantically, slapped a hand over her mouth nd brushed past the officers to get to the kitchen sink in time for he gush of wine to erupt. She heaved again and stood bowed over he sink, trying to steady herself. A shaking hand reached for the ap and turned it on, stale wine and bile swirling before being ashed away.

Leigh scooped a handful of water to wash out her mouth, then nother to swallow before straightening and turning to face the offi- ers whose lack of concern at her predicament told her this wasn't n unusual reaction to their presence.

'I'm sorry.' She seemed to be always apologising for something. eaching for a towel, she wiped her face.

PC Carter looked out the open door. 'You reported you'd found a dead body in your garden. And you think it's this person... thi Gina?'

'She was my lodger. I was away for a week and when I cam back, she'd packed up and gone. There was a note to say she wa sorry but no explanation.' She wanted to tell them about Philip an the Kindle, but it was such a convoluted story it could wait till late 'I was looking out the window and saw something in the garden. thought it was a football.' She pointed to the house next door. 'M neighbours have twin boys, football crazy, it often happens and... Rambling again, she stopped herself.

'I went down to pick it up and throw it back. When I got closer, realised it wasn't a ball.' She gulped painfully and pressed a han over her mouth again. The kitchen clock ticked loudly in th silence as she tried to regain control.

'It's a hand, pushing out of the soil.'

19

Leigh expected the officers to look shocked, even horrified. When their expressions didn't change, she wondered if she hadn't spoken aloud, if in her shock, she'd only imagined putting her thoughts into words.

'It's a hand,' she said, raising her voice a little. Then, as if trying to make sense of it, she elaborated. 'Gina's hand, pushing from the soil.'

There was still no reaction. Perhaps this was something police officers came across every day. Bodies buried in gardens. Leigh shivered.

'We'll go have a look.' PC Carter pulled a torch from his belt.

To Leigh's relief, the officers didn't expect her to go with them as they switched on their powerful torches and stepped outside, beams of light criss-crossing the darkness.

She stayed propped against the counter within reach of the sink and shut her eyes, hurriedly opening them again as she thought of the darkness of Gina's last moments. Had she opened her eyes as the soil covered her face? Opened her mouth to scream, only to find it filling with the earthy taste of the rich topsoil? Had she tried to claw her way out of her grave, one hand finally breaking the surface? Too late to save her as she gurgled, gasped and sputtered.

Buried alive. It was the stuff of nightmares. Many years before, Leigh had watched a movie adaptation of Edgar Allan Poe's *The Fall of the House of Usher*. A creepily macabre Vincent Price had played the haunted Roderick Usher who'd entombed his twin sister while she was still alive. The claw marks on the inside of the coffin as she'd tried to escape had left an indelible mark on Leigh. For weeks afterwards, she'd woken up in a sweat.

To think of poor Gina going through such horror. The terror of it. Leigh would never be able to get it out of her head.

When the officers returned, she'd tell them about Philip. It had to have been him. The Kindle was proof he was one of the last people to see Gina alive. Maybe *the* last person. Had he expected to see Leigh when he'd called with the package, and taken his frustration out on the poor unsuspecting Gina?

It might have been an accident. He possibly took fright, thought she was dead and attempted to hide the body. The soft soil in the garden was the perfect place. Gina was tiny, slight; it would have been easy for the well-built Philip to have dug a hole and carried her down to drop her body inside. Intent on getting it done, he'd possibly never noticed signs of life and Gina... poor poor butterfly... regained consciousness too late to do anything but die in agonising terror. A wave of nausea hit Leigh again and she hung over the sink, retching. Saliva and bile dripped from her mouth, tears from her eyes, mixing in the stainless-steel basin until washed away by a jet of water.

She rinsed out her mouth and spat. Her arms were braced against the sink, her head hanging low, vomit-clumped strands of her hair falling forward. She pushed them back with a grimace and listened as static from the police radios drifted from the garden. One of the officer's voices was raised. Staccato words Leigh couldn't make out. Unlike some of her friends, she didn't avidly watch crime series; she had, however, seen enough to know her home would soon be swarming with crime scene investigators.

Reporters too.

Leigh lifted her head as a terrifying thought hit her. Would she be a suspect in this macabre murder? Despite her having called it in, it was her house. Her garden. A suspect... Reporters would poke into her life. The anger management course would be highlighted. They'd ask questions. Get all the wrong answers. Ledbetter and his supporters would point fingers her direction. And if it was in the papers, on the news, as it was sure to be, Matt would hear about it. And he'd know she'd lied. About so many things.

There would also be those who'd question why Leigh had invited the tiny, butterfly-like woman to move in with her. Assigning insidious motives to her spontaneous *bloody stupid* generosity.

Perhaps it would be better to take more time off work. Get away. To Salisbury if Matt forgave her for her lies... or maybe it would be better to go home to her parents in Yorkshire. If she was allowed... if the police didn't say she wasn't to leave town. Or did that only happen in bad movies?

Tears of self-pity stung; she brushed them away in disgust, horrified to be so self-centred while Gina lay buried in her garden. What kind of a woman had she become?

Heavy footsteps on the garden path alerted her to the officers' return.

She straightened as they came into view, her eyes widening to see what PC Carter was carrying in a gloved hand. Her knees failed her when he held it forward, and she staggered to a chair, her eyes never leaving the hideous sight of Gina's hand, the wrist hacked and bloody.

20

PC Carter held the hand closer.

Leigh saw his mouth moving, but all she could hear was the swoosh that deafened her as she tried to blink away the blackness filling in the edges of her vision.

It was PC Sharp who saw her dilemma, grabbing Leigh's shoulders and pushing them forward so her head was between her knees. 'Breathe, you're going to be okay.'

Leigh didn't think she'd ever be okay again. A hand on her back kept her splayed out, facing the floor. Only when she held hers up in surrender, was the pressure removed, allowing her to straighten.

PC Carter still stood in front of her. Gina's hideous hand, however, was thankfully nowhere in sight.

'How could you?' Leigh muttered, taking the glass of water PC Sharp handed her. She took a mouthful, put it down, and wiped the sleeve of her kaftan over her face. 'I don't understand.' Why had they removed Gina's hand? What was the point in scaring her? Was it some sort of trick to make her confess to her part in her lodger's death?

'It's a joke-shop hand.'

'What?'

Carter reached behind him and brought the hideous hand into iew again despite remonstrations from his partner. He held it orward as if proximity to it would make what he'd said clearer.

It didn't. Leigh looked from Gina's dreadful bloody muddy hand ɔ Carter and back, unable to make sense of anything.

'It's not real.' PC Sharp's voice was surprisingly gentle. She eached across and squeezed the hand's thumb. 'Latex rubber, I'd uess.'

Latex rubber. The swooshing noise returned. It grew louder, lling Leigh's head. A dazzling bright light filled the room. Blinding er. Fireworks exploded. Light, noise and pain.

When she came to, she was on the floor, on her side, one of her ands tucked under her cheek. A hand pressed to her side revented her jerking upright. 'Easy does it.' PC Sharp's voice was rm. 'You fainted and gave yourself a nasty bang when you hit the oor.'

The silk of Leigh's kaftan gave little protection from the cold ard tiles. 'I'm okay.' The hand was immediately removed. She sat p and got unsteadily to her feet. 'I've never fainted before. I don't nderstand what's going on.' She felt as pathetic as she sounded.

'It looks like someone played a nasty trick on you.' PC Carter sat n the chair opposite. 'The hand wasn't real. Probably bought in a ɔke shop or more likely online.'

Leigh looked around but there was no sign of the offending em. 'It looked so real.'

'Often we see what we want, or what we fear the most.' Carter aned forward. 'You mentioned a woman called Gina. Is she ɔmeone you're worried about?'

Leigh nodded. 'Yes.' Immediately she shook her head. 'No.'

'Which?'

'I don't know. She was my lodger. I went away for a week and when I got back, she'd moved out. No notice or explanation. Just a note saying she was sorry.'

'Sorry? For what?'

'I assume for moving out without notice.' Nothing to do with the row they'd had before Leigh had left for that blasted course.

'How long had she been living here?'

'Only a short while.' Leigh wasn't surprised to see him raise an eyebrow. 'Almost two weeks.'

He nodded, almost as if to say that explained everything. 'Had you known her long?'

Leigh had reached the conclusion she hadn't known Gina at all. 'She was the barista in the café I go to on my way to work. A couple of weeks ago, I noticed she wasn't her usual bubbly self and asked what was wrong. When she said she had to move out of her accommodation and didn't think she'd be able to find anything affordable, I felt sorry for her and offered her a room.'

PC Sharp was leaning against the wall behind Carter. She stared at Leigh as if she was an unidentified specimen. 'Were there strings attached?'

It had been a hellish day. Leigh's head was thumping, and the question made no sense. 'I don't know what you mean.'

'Maybe it's why she left. You were coming on to her, wanting payback for your' – she crooked her fingers in the air – 'kindness.'

Leigh pushed her chair back and got to her feet. Swaying a little, she reached a hand for the table to steady herself. 'If there's one thing I hate more than people doing this' – she waved her index fingers in the air – 'it's people who think everyone has an ulterior motive for being kind.'

The back door still hung open; she went to it, shut it with a bang, and turned the key in the lock. She rested a hand on the door for a moment before turning back to the two officers. 'I had no ulterior motive in offering Gina a room, I can assure you.' No point in trying to explain to them that she'd hoped some of Gina's joie de vivre might rub off on her. That the younger vivacious woman might fill a hole in her life. No point at all, especially since Leigh was only just facing the truth herself.

Carter lifted an appeasing hand. 'How old is she?'

Leigh stopped glaring at Sharp and turned to him. 'Mid to late twenties.'

'Old enough to look after herself. If there was no sign of foul play, she probably had a better offer. I wouldn't worry about her.'

Since it was much like what Isobel had said, Leigh nodded. 'Right, thank you. I won't.' She waved a hand towards the garden. 'I'm sorry for dragging you out for what looks like a horrible trick.'

'Probably kids having their bit of fun.' Carter got to his feet. 'Your garden is quite accessible from the rear. It might be worth having motion sensor security lights installed to deter unwanted visitors.'

'Yes, good idea. Thank you.' *Now please go away so I can sit and cry in peace.*

She didn't show them out. Instead, she stayed leaning against the counter until she heard the front door shutting. Then the house echoed with her howling.

21

Despite knowing Gina wasn't buried in the garden, hadn't died a horrible death trying to dig her way out of a grave, Leigh woke several times during the night, clawing her way from under the duvet. The last straw was when she swore she felt latex rubber fingers crawling up her leg. She squealed and threw the duvet back, expecting to find that hideous hand dripping blood onto her white cotton sheets.

There was nothing, but the feeling that something was moving up her leg didn't fade. She twisted each limb desperately searching for a cause. Finally, unable to rid herself of the sensation, she clambered awkwardly from the bed and hurried into the en suite shower. It took twenty minutes under a stream of hot water with a soapy loofah before she was satisfied. Legs red and fingers wrinkled, she stepped out.

She'd done such a good job the night before of convincing herself Philip was to blame for Gina's disappearance, the thought had become embedded. Needling her. All so silly. She'd made the man into a monster.

If she was going to survive the day ahead being ignored by her colleagues, she needed to put him and Gina out of her head. If Ledbetter was back, the day would be worse; she'd have to cope with his smug lecherous glances.

No point in hiding in her en suite. Time to face the day. Her work clothes were organised to require little thought. Jackets and trousers in navy or grey were designed to match randomly. M&S shirts in various colours and patterns were chosen to go with any of the jackets. It made dressing easy, if a little dull and boring.

A long way from the exotically flamboyant Gina.

Perhaps it was that thought that made Leigh reach for a bright red lipstick she'd bought but never used. Channelling her inner Gina... The thought almost made her smile. Her chin-length bob simply required a brush through, and she was ready to go.

Physically perhaps; mentally she was anything but.

* * *

It was almost nine before she reached her office, officially on time, but unusually late for her. Slipping behind her desk, she glanced around, half-hoping to see Ledbetter's hulking presence, catching instead sideways furtive glances from her co-workers. She dropped her eyes to her desk and, once again, angled her screens and shuffled her chair closer to give herself more privacy.

Too close. It made working difficult and slow and she quickly fell behind. Worse, she made errors. Easily corrected, but she was good at what she did; she didn't usually make mistakes and her confidence was shattered. She started double checking everything, slowing her work down further, stressing her, causing her to stumble over decisions, miss things, and make more errors. Her eyes filled with tears of frustration.

When she heard the human resources manager's voice raised to get attention, Leigh pushed back from her desk and looked up in surprise. It was unusual for Collins to make a personal appearance.

'This will only take a second, but I wanted to inform you all in person.' She looked around the room until silence fell. 'We were understandably worried regarding Mr Ledbetter's unexplained absence yesterday. It was completely out of character, plus we're all aware he's been finding things a little difficult recently.'

Leigh saw Collins' eyes flick to her and cringed.

'In view of what I considered to be his fragile state, I told the police of our concerns.' Collins spoke slowly, her expression more than usually grim. 'They have informed me they called to Mr Ledbetter's home yesterday evening and found no sign of him. Neighbours told the police he hasn't been seen recently. One of them was a keyholder, so the police checked inside the house and found no sign of foul play. For the moment, they're keeping an open mind.' She clasped her hands together. 'I know you'll all keep him in your thoughts. I'll let you know if I hear anything new.'

She didn't look in Leigh's direction again. Others did. Leigh could feel their eyes on her. Condemning, criticising. *Blaming.*

A wave of muttering broke the silence following Collins' departure.

Leigh didn't need to hear the words to know they were all discussing her part in whatever had happened to Ledbetter. She didn't hear the words; the tone, however, was clearly judgemental.

She wanted to stand up. Meet their eyes. Reclaim the status of victim.

Instead, with tears stinging, she shuffled as close as she could to her desk again, shoulders pressed down by the words of blame floating in the air. Guilt Ledbetter was probably sunning himself on some beach in Spain. He'd arrive back in a few days, be feted as a survivor, have Collins and others fawning over him. His life would be easier, and Leigh's would be hell.

For the remainder of the day, she was unable to trust herself to work without making a serious error. Instead, she pretended. Better to do nothing. Huddle down behind her monitors. Avoid attracting anyone's attention and wipe her tears from the keyboard.

That day, she didn't wait for the clock to tick to 17:00. At 16:30, she made the mistake of peering over her monitor and was immediately pierced by a poisonous dart from Felicity's hard eyes. How long the woman had been standing there waiting for the opportunity, Leigh had no idea, but it was the final push she needed.

It would have been nice to have stormed off dramatically but for one, she hadn't that type of personality, and for another there was no point in handing the human resources department further ammunition. She typed up a concise email to explain she was leaving early due to feeling unwell and sent it off.

Two minutes later, she exited the office building.

She was feeling weary and stressed. And weak. The latter she decided was possibly due to having had so little to eat over the last couple of days. At least that was something easily sorted. In King's Cross station she found a Starbucks and had a coffee and a sandwich. She lingered over both, reluctant to leave, to go home to the empty house, to an evening filled with hours of angst. It was tempting to get a second coffee, maybe a pastry. She did neither. No point in putting off the inevitable.

It was silly to be reluctant suddenly to go home. Over the years, the house had been a place of comfort, almost a sanctuary from the hustle and bustle of London. When her aunt had been alive, Leigh had frequently spent nights with her, revelling in being spoilt and cared for.

She refused to let something as stupid as a fake hand ruin everything for her. It had simply been a cruel joke. Probably done by kids living in the houses behind. She'd talk to a gardener about re-enforcing the back boundary, make sure it never happened again.

She'd forget about it.

And about Gina.

But the incessant annoying voice that kept nudging a painful shard of guilt into Leigh's thin hide wouldn't allow her to forget her old lodger. If, instead of shouting, she'd listened to Gina's concerns perhaps she wouldn't have left.

22

Perhaps she wouldn't have left. The thought made Leigh sigh as she trudged along Kentish Town Road. She was almost home when it struck her; she'd been thinking of Gina as having left of her own accord... not as being *missing*.

The difference between gone and missing was a chasm Leigh hadn't thought to cross till now. It brought her to an abrupt halt. She'd been so wrapped up in her own problems that she'd accepted a young woman leaving her home and job without notice as being normal. Maybe Leigh had been too quick to accept Isobel's scathing summation that Gina was only interested in herself and what people could do for her.

Maybe it had suited Leigh to believe Isobel. It had made it easier to throw off the guilt she'd been feeling.

Those police officers hadn't seemed concerned Gina had left without notice. They'd even been dismissive. That didn't mean they were right. Leigh had never been to the local police station but she knew where it was. A short walk from where she was standing. Maybe this was fate lending a hand, or even giving her a shove in the right direction. She waited for a break in the traffic and dashed to the other side of the road, then walked back to the corner of Holmes Road. Opposite, a gang of teenagers were laughing and shouting, filled with an exuberance that reminded Leigh instantly of Gina dancing across the café the day Leigh had offered her the room.

If she had any doubts, they disappeared in that second. Something was wrong. Leigh was suddenly sure she was right.

She turned down Holmes Road in search of Kentish Town Police Station. She needn't have worried; it was impossible to miss. Her eyes widened at the Victorian police lamp suspended on a wrought-iron stand in the stone archway of the front door. Should there be any doubt, *Police* was carved into the arch, a metal sign on one side announced it was the *Metropolitan Police* and on the other, *Kentish Town Police Station*. No room for misunderstanding.

If Leigh hadn't been so nervous, she'd have been amused.

On the outside, the old building may have been a Victorian gem, but inside it was determinedly twenty-first century, all glass and yellow metal. There was only one other person. Sat on a fixed yellow-metal seat, eyes shut, arms folded, legs crossed, he looked as if he'd been there a long time.

Leigh approached the reception area.

A solid glass barrier separated her from a middle-aged officer. He regarded her with interest, almost as if he was waiting to be entertained. 'Yes, can I help you?'

Here goes. 'I want to report a missing person.' In her determination, it came out louder and with more emphasis than she'd planned.

The officer took it in his stride. 'Okay,' he said, looking down at his keyboard.

Leigh waited while he tapped some keys.

'Name?'

'Leigh Simon.'

'And when did he go missing?'

Leigh gripped the edge of the counter. 'No, sorry, Leigh Simon is my name. The missing woman is Gina Henderson. She was my lodger. I was away for a week and when I came home on Sunday, she'd packed up all her stuff and left, leaving a note to say she was sorry.'

The officer frowned.

He was taking it seriously. Leigh felt a release of tension.

'How old is Ms Henderson?'

How old? Leigh had initially thought she was six or seven years older than Gina but had revised that gap after she'd moved in. 'Maybe late twenties.'

'You don't know for sure?'

'No, I don't. She was my lodger, not a friend. It wasn't something I needed to know.'

'A lodger?'

'Yes.' Hadn't she already said that? Why wasn't he taking notes?

As if he'd read her mind, the officer tapped a few keys before asking, 'How long had she lived with you?'

'Two weeks.' She waited for a sarcastic comment and when none came, relaxed a little.

Too much, and too soon. When the officer looked up from his keyboard his expression was less friendly. 'You're Leigh Simon, Gaisford Street?'

'That's right.' A feeling of dread hit her. What had those officers who'd answered her emergency call last night written about her?

The officer behind the desk sat back on his seat and folded his arms. 'You mentioned to PC Carter yesterday that you thought this woman was buried in your garden, and here you are today reporting her missing.'

'I thought she was buried because there was a hand sticking out of the soil.'

'A fake hand.'

'Yes, but I didn't know that, did I? It looked so real.' Ringing the police for that had been a mistake; was it going to be held against her? 'Gina *is* missing. I'm anxious to know what's happened to her. Isn't that a good thing?'

He wagged his head, unconvinced. 'How long did you know her?'

Hardly at all. No point in telling the man it had been a crazy, spontaneous, stupid, stupid impulsive decision. 'Only a few months.'

'A few months, but she wasn't a friend, she was just a lodger?'

'Yes.' She hoped he wasn't going to suggest as the other officers had, that she'd an ulterior motive for asking Gina to move in.

'Looks like she changed her mind.' He scratched his nose with his thumb. 'Before you went away for the week, did you have some sort of disagreement with her?'

'Not a disagreement as such.'

'A difference of opinion maybe?'

'Something like that.' Leigh loosened her grip on the counter and shoved her hands into her jacket pockets. 'Does it matter? She's still missing.'

The officer shook his head. 'Sounds to me as if she left of her own accord. She'd be classified as a *lost contact*, not a *missing person*.' He unfolded his arms and laid his large hands on the counter his side of the glass partition. 'We don't have the resources to deal with lost contacts, Ms Simon. There are tracing agencies who do though. If you do an internet search, you'll find them.'

And that was it. Leigh was dismissed. The officer turned back to his computer and didn't give her a further glance. She stood for a moment, shuffling uncertainly from foot to foot, caught between a desire to insist something was done, and the feeling she was wasting her time on a woman she barely knew.

She turned in time to see the occupant of the seat, arms still
folded, legs still crossed, one eye now open, regarding her with
amusement... or was it pity? She glared at him before hurrying
from the station.

With her handbag pressed to her chest and her shoulders
hunched, she didn't stop until she was outside her house. That was
it. She'd done all she could. Gina wasn't missing... she was a *lost
contact*.

But the idea she hadn't left of her own accord, once established
in Leigh's head, wasn't in a hurry to leave.

23

Leigh dropped her bag on the hallway floor and went into the kitchen. Usually, unless she was away, she'd wait for Matt to ring. He was often delayed in the school with extra-curricular activities and didn't like to be disturbed unless it was something urgent. This was. She needed the sound of a friendly voice.

She was in luck. He answered on the first ring. 'Leigh, hello.'

'Hi.' It was almost tempting to pour out her problems in one hurried gush of words. He'd rant at how stupid she'd been, complain he was disappointed she hadn't confided in him sooner and when he'd run out of words, he'd offer the support she so desperately needed.

Support... and the comfort of his arms around her. She needed both. Perhaps it would be better... easier... to wait until he was with her. She'd be able to gauge how annoyed or disappointed he was if she was able to see his expression. It wasn't chickening out, nor was it the sudden doubt that Matt may not play the part demanded of him, that of loyal supportive loving partner. It was simply better to wait till the weekend when they were together. She'd tell him everything then. About her prob lems at work, the anger management course, Philip, Gina. Everything.

With the decision made to put off the inevitable, she sat, rested her elbow on the table, and pressed the phone to her ear. 'Did you have a good day?' It would unleash more of his anecdotes but at least she wouldn't have to talk.

'It was okay.'

To her surprise, that was it, no stories about his students. No wisecracks about his fellow teachers. Nothing. 'Are you all right, Matt?'

'Sure. A bit tired perhaps. Listen, I've dished up dinner so d'you mind if I go? We can chat more tomorrow.'

Leigh was taken aback. It wasn't the first time either one of them needed to end a conversation abruptly. Things happened, after all. When they did, when their chat was interrupted with something boiling over on the cooker, the doorbell ringing, an urgent call needing to be returned by a certain time... any number of reasons... the abrupt halt to their talk was generally tempered by a promise to ring later the same evening. Never tomorrow. It was so unlike Matt she was lost for words and merely agreed. 'Of course.'

When he rang off without his usual declaration of love, Leigh was stunned. She stayed staring at the phone. Matt was a fast eater, ten minutes or so and he'd be finished his meal. He'd ring back then, wouldn't he? After fifteen minutes, she was less sure, and after twenty, she knew it wasn't going to happen. She could ring him again, ask if there was a problem.

No, because if she did, and he admitted there was, could she handle more trouble? Worse, if he said there wasn't, she'd have the problem of what was wrong with him to pile on top of everything else she was worried about.

It was probably nothing anyway. Matt was allowed a bad day.

Trying to put him out of her mind, she got to her feet.

She headed to the fridge for some well-deserved comfort eating. The food on the shelf she'd given to Gina was still in date. She pulled out a wrapped quiche and put it in the oven to heat. When it was ready, she slipped it onto a plate and took it to the table. It looked good, smelled delicious but when she sliced through it with her fork and lifted a mouthful to her lips, she couldn't bring herself to eat it. She simply couldn't get over the idea there was something very wrong with Gina's sudden disappearance.

Nor could she forget her paranoid belief Gina had poisoned her food. The quiche was from the delicatessen on Kentish Town Road. But she could have put something in it, couldn't she? Might have known Leigh would be tempted to eat it. Was that why she'd left it all behind?

There was absolutely no logic to Leigh's suspicions but it didn't stop her getting up and emptying the food into the bin.

Weariness and the stress of the day were making themselves felt: heaviness in her limbs, slowness in her thoughts, a stinging in her eyes. Early as it was, she decided to go to bed and leaned heavily on the banisters as she climbed the stairway one step at a time.

The bedroom curtains were heavy and once pulled they created a dark haven for sleep. Leigh slipped naked between the sheets, snuggled her head into the pillow, and shut her eyes in expectation that exhaustion would help her to drift away despite her worries.

But her troubles easily outweighed her weariness and, in the darkness, they marched heavy-footed behind her eyelids. Two hours later, she was wide awake. She wondered if hunger was the problem. The thought nagged her until she threw the duvet back and went downstairs.

Unwilling to try any of Gina's abandoned food again, and there being nothing on her shelves that appealed, she heated some milk, poured it into a mug and took it back to bed with her. She switched on the bedside lamp and reached for a book from the pile that had built up over the last year. Opening it wide, she balanced it on her bent knees and read as she sipped the warm drink.

Whether it was the milk or the book, she wasn't sure, but her eyelids were drooping by the time she finished the first chapter. She switched off the light and snuggled down again.

It was still dark when she woke. When she saw the time on her bedside clock, she groaned. 3 a.m. She lay for a moment, frowning. Something had woken her.

It had taken her a long time to get used to the various noises the old house made: the creaking floorboards, gurgling pipes and when the heating was on, the hissing radiators. But in the middle of the night, hours after the house had settled down, it should be silent. There certainly shouldn't be creaking floorboards.

Leigh held her breath. When the creak came again, she didn't hesitate. Jumping from the bed, she grabbed her phone and fled into the en suite bathroom, locking the door. Her fingers shook as she dialled emergency services, her voice a barely audible squeak when the call handler asked which service she required. 'Police.'

Another voice asked, 'What's the nature of your emergency?'

'There's someone downstairs in my house. A burglar. I've locked myself into the en suite. Please hurry.' She whispered her name and address and hung up. It was chilly, and she was naked. She pulled the bath towel from the rail and wrapped it around her.

How long would it take the police to get there? Not as fast as it would take the burglars to arrive in her bedroom. They'd see the rumpled sheets and know there was someone there and it wouldn't take them long to discover the locked door. An internal one. A few heavy kicks and it would cave in.

A knock on the en suite door made her squeal in shock. She looked around for something to use as a weapon. The toilet brush didn't look too sturdy. The only other option, and the one she went for, was to pull dried grasses from a tall narrow glass bottle that stood in the corner of the room. She dumped the grasses and grabbed the bottle by the neck, swinging it to and fro, ready to defend herself.

'Ms Simon?'

A polite burglar who knew her name?

Another knock. 'Ms Simon, it's the police.'

The police? It had only been minutes since she'd rung. 'I don't believe you.' She looked around her, wondering how much protection the shower enclosure would offer her if they broke down the door. Not a lot. No, her best bet was the bottle she held. She dried her fear-sweaty hand on the towel wrapped around her and gripped it tighter.

'Ms Simon. It's PC Carter; I was here Monday night. The hand in the garden, remember?'

PC Carter. Of course she bloody well remembered. She wasn't going crazy.

'Ms Simon, can you open the door?'

Leigh slapped the glass bottle into the palm of her hand. It didn't make any sense. But a burglar wouldn't have known about the hand, or PC Carter. Unless, of course, Carter was the burglar. That had to be it.

'Police,' she said when she redialled emergency services. 'Are they on their way? I think the burglar is PC Carter who was here on Monday night. He's here now, banging on the door, trying to get me to come out.'

'Ms Simon.' The call handler's voice was calm and firm. 'PC Carter is on duty and answering your emergency call. I assure you; you can safely open your door.'

It was unlikely the whole of emergency services was in cahoots with the officer outside. With a sigh, Leigh hung up. She set the mobile on the edge of the sink, gripped the bottle in one hand, undid the lock with the other, and slowly opened the door.

Carter had moved back and he eyed her warily as she stepped out. He pointed to the bottle. 'Best if you put that down, Ms Simon.'

Leigh looked at it. She wanted to weep. Everything was confusing, disorientating. She tried to claw her way towards something solid. 'How did you get here so quickly?'

'We were already here.'

His reply was so unexpected, she staggered to the bed and sat, her eyes never leaving him, the bottle now grasped in both hands. 'What?'

'I said we were already here. Downstairs.' He took a step closer, then slowly and carefully, he reached for the bottle and took it away. 'We were on patrol, driving down Gaisford Street. We slowed as we passed your house. PC Sharp was commenting on the puzzle of that latex hand when she noticed your front door was wide open.' He shook his head. 'Not a normal occurrence at 3 a.m.'

Leigh stared. Her door was open. How? She'd shut it when she came home. And even, if by some weird moment of forgetfulness, she'd left it open, she'd have noticed it when she passed on her way upstairs. Wouldn't she?

'I'm sorry.' For what she wasn't sure. 'I thought someone had broken in.'

Carter put the bottle on the dresser. 'There's no damage to the lock or door; it looks as if you simply left it open. We were checking to make sure we weren't interrupting a burglary in progress, when we got a call to say you were holed up in there.' He jerked his thumb towards the en suite.

'I thought maybe you were the burglar.' Leigh laughed as if she thought the whole thing was hilariously funny, her laughter turning quickly to tears.

It was PC Sharp, arriving in time to see Leigh's meltdown, who grabbed a robe from where it was hanging on the back of the bedroom door and draped it around her shoulders, holding it there as Leigh struggled to regain control.

'Would you like us to call someone for you?' Carter asked.

Leigh took a shuddering breath and let it out slowly. She grabbed the corner of the bedsheet and wiped the tears away. 'No thank you, I'll be fine.'

Sharp tucked the robe in place and stood back. 'Perhaps tomorrow, you could speak to someone.'

Someone? Leigh looked at her, then at PC Carter who stood a little behind. Both of their faces were saying the same thing. *They thought she needed help.*

Carter was determined to make their point clear. 'You called the emergency services to report a dead body in your garden, called to the station earlier to report a missing person, and here you are reporting a burglary in progress.'

She could hear his unspoken diagnosis – she was a pathetic sad lonely woman looking for attention. 'You think I put that hideous hand in the garden? Left my front door open on purpose?'

Sharp's handset crackled with static, drawing Carter's attention. 'We need to go,' he said, looking back to Leigh. 'I'm not saying anything, Ms Simon, but perhaps you should see someone, you do seem to be a bit...'

Leigh rolled her hands into fists. If he said *hysterical*, she was going to show him just how wrong he was.

Luckily for both the officer and Leigh, it wasn't the word he chose. 'Distraught, if you don't mind me saying.'

She did mind. Her world appeared to have imploded and when she desperately needed some support, first Matt had cut her off and now these two officers were telling her she was a time-waster. Worse, an attention-seeker.

'Fine.' That wonderful catch-all word that said so much, an

nothing. She couldn't think of anything else to say and it beat saying *I'm sorry* when yet again she'd nothing to apologise for.

Carter and Sharp left together, clumping noisily down the stairs. The front door slammed after them, as if to make a point.

Leigh flopped back on the bed and reached for the bedsheet to dab uselessly at the tears running from the corners of her eyes into her hair. Were they right, these pillars of law and order? Had her life become so desperate she was seeking attention from anyone who'd give it? It happened; she'd read about cases but had never pictured herself in the role.

The hand in the garden... could she have done that? And then forgotten about it? She rubbed the sheet over her face again and sat up. No, she couldn't have, but Matt might have done. It was the kind of thing he'd have found amusing. He'd have done it as a joke, not to scare her.

He'd no reason to want to scare her, had he?

24

It was impossible to get back to sleep with her head churning. Hadn't she suggested Matt give her a hand with the garden to cut down on the expense? Planting the latex hand might have been his idea of a pun on that.

Staring at the ceiling, she considered whether she would have seen the hand in the garden for exactly what perhaps it was supposed to be... a practical joke... if her thoughts weren't so occupied with Ledbetter and Gina. Matt had probably been expecting her to mention it, laughingly, amused at his sense of fun. Either it wasn't the slightest bit funny, or she'd lost her sense of humour somewhere in the last few months of working too hard over too many hours.

There was an easy way to find out. She'd ask him. Hopefully he'd be chattier that evening than he'd been the previous night. This was another puzzle to add to the mix. It was so unlike the normally garrulous Matt to be so quiet.

It struck her then, with a blow that took her breath away, that there might be a good reason. Perhaps he'd grown tired of her hints that he should move to London... perhaps he'd decided his future lay with someone else.

If she were being honest, hadn't she thought the same now and then? And hadn't she wondered if their inability to move past where they should base themselves as a couple was a reflection of their basic lack of commitment. Because if they'd really wanted to be together, wouldn't they be? It had come down to pig-headed stubbornness in the end, each of them wanting to be the winner.

Why too, had it come down to a toss-up between Salisbury and London? There were other cities where both could have found work. They'd never bothered having that discussion, never got past the either-or argument.

Perhaps he'd finally realised the end was nigh when she'd accepted the position with Lancaster International three months before. Had that been the final straw? The point when he knew it was all over bar the shouting.

She tried to think back... Had they been happier before the stresses and pressures of her new job had made her tired and irritable? Hadn't Matt called her grumpy, more than once?

Grumpy, quick to anger, coming to blows with her manager.

It was her night for facing the truth. She hated that damn job. And she wasn't sure she loved Matt any more.

It seemed a good idea for Leigh to get to work early. She'd get into the safe place behind her desk and keep her head down. Not too low though because, despite the noise and bright lights of the trader's floor, she was so incredibly tired, she might fall asleep.

Sitting close to her monitors, she avoided the sharp, cutting glances she knew were flying over her head. Some of her co-workers went out of their way to make their displeasure felt, passing close to her desk, muttering audible criticism with the word *bitch* slotted in somewhere.

Leigh wanted to ignore them, to keep working, to prove she couldn't... wouldn't... be intimidated by them. She was the victim, not Bernard Ledbetter. Reminding herself of that fact didn't seem to help; didn't stop her eyes stinging or tears falling.

Mid-morning, she gave in, got to her feet and walked, eyes straight ahead, to the HR department.

She was in luck and caught Janet Collins between meetings. 'Do you have a minute?' Leigh asked, peering around the office door.

'As long as it's quick.' Collins, wearing a vividly patterned dress, pulled at the cuff of the sleeve and sat back. 'Have a seat.'

Leigh wrapped her arms around her chest and sat on the edge of the chair. 'I assume there's no word on Mr Ledbetter.'

'I'm afraid not.'

Under her arms, Leigh could feel her heart thumping. If she had a heart attack from stress, would she get sympathy, or would her co-workers say it was revenge for what she'd done to Ledbetter? I think it's better if I take some time off until we know what's happened to him.'

Collins played with the cuff of her dress again before pushing the sleeve up and clasping her hands together on the desk. 'I'm aware some of your colleagues have been making things unpleasant for you, Ms Simon. If you think it would make things easier, I could have a word with them.'

Leigh hadn't expected sympathy and her eyes filled again. She pulled a tissue from her pocket and wiped them away. 'I don't think it would make any difference.'

'Probably not.' Collins sighed. 'I'd like to make it quite clear there is no blame being laid at your feet by anyone in HR. As I pointed out, your allegation against Mr Ledbetter may have been a contributory factor behind his disappearance, but it was unlikely to have been the only one.' She hesitated before unhooking her hands and opening them out. 'Although none of the other staff corroborated your allegations, I've never ruled out the possibility there was truth behind them and, strictly between me and you, Mr Ledbetter makes my skin crawl.'

Leigh was surprised into a bark of laughter.

Collins sat back. 'I'll deny ever having said that, of course, but I thought it might make it easier for you.'

It did. 'Yes, thank you, it does.'

'Good. As for taking time off, I agree it might be for the best. Hopefully, by the end of the week we should have some information regarding Mr Ledbetter.' She clasped her hands together again, the cuffs falling to envelop them. 'Go home, Ms Simon. Get some sleep. It looks as if you haven't had much recently.'

The kindness in her voice was almost Leigh's undoing. She swallowed and held a hand tightly over her mouth to stop the sobs. Unable to speak, she resorted to nodding before getting to her feet and exiting the office.

She went to the ladies and locked herself into a cubicle until she could get in control of cascading emotions, pulling reams of toilet paper from the roll to dam the flood. It was almost five minutes before she could face returning to the trader's floor.

Ignoring the glances sent her way, she picked up her handbag, slipped on her jacket, turned and walked with her chin in the air towards the exit.

26

Leigh thought about going to Salisbury. A short while before, faced with unexpected free days, she wouldn't have hesitated about going to stay with Matt. Now, facing all she had to explain to him, and what he might tell her in return, she decided against going. By the weekend, she'd have her thoughts lined up.

She could go to Yorkshire. Her parents would be delighted to see her. Her father would drag her to the pub. Her mother, a woman with a keenly astute brain and all-seeing eyes, would take one look at her and ask what was wrong. She wouldn't be fooled by Leigh's protestation that all was well.

No, she loved her parents; she wasn't going to offload her problems on them.

Instead, she'd fill the days with getting herself in shape both physically and mentally. First, she was going to have something decent to eat. She was in London; the choice was vast. With her head set on good food with no fuss, she decided on a restaurant she used to go to frequently but hadn't been to in... She shook her head, unable to remember the last time.

She walked with her head down. Only as she reached King's Boulevard, did her mood lift, and she smiled as the restaurant appeared. Vinoteca, unchanged as if it had been days, not months, maybe years, since she'd visited last. The menu was British and European, so she'd never brought Matt, who preferred Indian or Chinese.

'A table for one, please,' she asked the smiling waiter who greeted her inside the door.

'Certainly.' He picked up menus and led her to a table in the far corner overlooking the square outside. 'This one okay?'

'It's perfect, thank you.' Leigh gave him a smile and sat to peruse the menus. It wasn't difficult; she chose her favourites and gave her order. 'And a large glass of Chenin Blanc, please.'

The wine came almost immediately. She picked it up, curling her fingers around the bowl, the pleasant chill building anticipation of pleasure to come. One sip and she immediately regretted she hadn't ordered a bottle. It was delicious. She wasn't hurrying home; she could have sat there all afternoon, eating, drinking wine and watching the crazy world as it passed by outside.

Perhaps it was the wine, or pleasant memories of having been in the restaurant with friends, colleagues from the last place she worked, a couple of boyfriends, or perhaps it was simply that her brain had reached the limit of its endurance and had locked down.

Whatever the reason, she felt surprisingly mellow and when the food arrived, she tucked in with gusto, washing the main course down with a second glass of wine.

'That was delicious,' she said, when the waiter came to take her cleared plate away.

He stood with it in his hand, smiling down at her. 'Looks like you were hungry. Can I tempt you with dessert?'

Leigh laughed and shook her head. 'I think I've reached my limit. I'd like a coffee though. A double espresso, please.'

'A double espresso coming right up.'

Good food, great wine, pleasant staff. Leigh remembered why she'd enjoyed coming here. It had been a good choice. She'd have liked to rest her arms on the table, drop her head on top and sleep. Perhaps if she did, the pleasant waiter would take pity on her and leave her be.

She smiled at the thought, drank the excellent coffee when it arrived a minute later, then sat with the last drop of wine before reluctantly leaving for home.

The food had helped to settle her, or perhaps it had been the place. The happy memories. She frowned as she walked back to King's Cross station. Memories of laughing and chatting, of getting pleasantly merry with friends. Old memories. She tried to recall the last time she'd laughed with Matt; not a polite laugh at one of his stories but a belly laugh of sheer enjoyment. Her frown deepened when she couldn't remember.

In the beginning, when he'd come to London for the weekend, they'd met up with friends until Matt complained about having to share her when their time together was so limited. She'd been flattered. A willing accomplice. She'd allowed her friendships to slide for the sake of her grand romance.

Her grand romance. She'd worried she didn't love him any more; now, she wondered if she ever had.

She'd met him at an exhibition in an art gallery she'd been reluctantly dragged to by a girlfriend who'd fancied the artist. Leigh had seen Matt across the crowded gallery, admired his physique, his thick curly slightly messy hair, his smile when he caught her looking.

Embarrassed, she'd looked away only to find him at her side seconds later as she was gazing with no interest at a painting so ugly it made her eyes hurt.

'I find it fascinating too,' he'd said.

She'd turned with a laugh bubbling, swallowing it when she realised he was serious. 'It drew me in.'

And that was it. After the exhibition, her friend vanished with the artist and Matt suggested they go for a drink.

He was in London staying with friends for the weekend. They spent all day Saturday together visiting exhibition after exhibition. It wasn't Leigh's thing; in fact, they bored her rigid, but Matt was so enthusiastic, so knowledgeable, so interested. When he realised her knowledge was basic, he was happy to share what he'd learned.

Leigh had been going through a romantic dry spell and before that there had been a couple of short-lived but heartbreaking failures. Matt's obvious interest was flattering and by the end of their second weekend together she'd fallen in love with him.

Hadn't she?

Or had she simply convinced herself she had because Matt seemed to be perfect boyfriend material: good-looking enough, tall, well-built. It had been a relief to have someone reliable and dependable. A relief! How romantic a thought was that? Anyway, it turned out he wasn't so perfect. Leigh rubbed her fingers over where he'd left bite marks on her breast.

She'd thought it was pressures of work in the last few months making her stressed and a little glum, but maybe it wasn't that at all. Maybe she was simply weary of lying to herself.

Lost in her thoughts, she did the journey home on automatic and was soon turning from the busy Kentish Town Road onto the quieter street where she lived. She was almost at her house when she saw a figure approaching... floating clothes in dramatic hues, a halo of curling hair... Leigh slowed to a halt in anticipation as the woman came into focus.

Gina!

elief sent Leigh racing, arms wide in anticipation of greeting her
x-lodger with a welcome-home hug. Only when it was too late,
hen she'd swooped on the woman with a genuine yell of pleasure
: having the mystery of Gina's disappearance sorted, only then did
1e realise the woman was far older, taller and wider than she
1ould be.

The woman didn't hesitate. She'd obviously read the advice on
hat to do if attacked – scream your lungs out and keep screaming
1ntil help arrives. And she did it with gusto. 'Help! Help! I'm being
1ugged! Help!'

Loud enough to make Leigh step back in dismay but not fast
1ough to miss the swinging clenched fist. It caught her on the
1eek and sent her stumbling backwards. Unable to keep her
1alance she fell to the ground and lay stunned.

The woman's effective vocal reaction drew every pedestrian
ithin hearing distance. Soon there was a circle around the
istraught victim and her fallen attacker. Mobile phones were held
1p to capture the scene, all of them hoping their footage would be
orthy of a TV spot. Or maybe it would be a YouTube sensation.

Leigh wanted the ground to open up and swallow her whole. She raised a tentative hand to her already swelling cheek. It was only the woman's shrill demand for someone to call the police that made Leigh forget her aches and pains and hurriedly scramble to her feet. 'No, please, there's been a mistake, I'm so sorry, I thought you were someone else. A friend I haven't seen for a while.'

'Yeah, right,' one of the onlookers muttered, moving to get a better angle with his mobile.

'You were trying to swipe my bag!' The victim held out a patchwork leather satchel. 'I felt you tug on it.'

'No, honestly, I wasn't.' Leigh pointed to her home, three houses further on. 'Look, I live there, I thought you were a friend coming to visit.' She looked around at the staring faces. 'It was a mistake.'

Whether they believed her or not, when there was no further drama, the crowd began to disperse, leaving her alone with her irate victim.

Leigh looked at the colourfully dressed woman. Close up, there was little comparison to the ethereal Gina whose clothes floated fairy-like around a tiny frame. This woman was stouter, and far older. Leigh had simply seen what she'd hoped to see. 'I really am so sorry.' Her cheek was throbbing; she wanted to get indoors and hold an ice pack to it. And cry.

'You scared me silly.' The older woman gathered the edges of her coat together and shoved the straps of her bag over her shoulder. 'I'm feeling a bit weak from the shock, actually.'

Leigh was too relieved there was no more talk of calling the police to argue she had more reason to be shocked. For one horrifying moment when the crowd had gathered around, she'd imagined those two police officers, Carter and Sharp, arriving to see her embroiled in yet another ridiculous scenario. Anything was better than having to suffer that, even extending the woman an invitation to her home. 'Why don't you come in and have a cup of tea. Afterwards I'll ring for a taxi to take you wherever you want to go, okay?'

'Very generous.' A large, worn hand was extended in Leigh's direction. 'Beatrix Austin.'

Leigh wouldn't have considered herself to have a small build, but her hand was swallowed by Beatrix's big blunt fingers. Feeling their strength, she considered she'd been lucky to have a bruised cheek and not a broken one. 'Leigh Simon.' She pointed towards her front door. 'That's mine.'

'I hope you've something stronger than tea,' Beatrix said, striding towards the house.

Leigh, following behind, shook her head. Inside, she showed her unexpected guest into the living room. 'I have wine or whisky. Gin but no mixers.'

Beatrix sank onto the sofa with the air of a woman who was looking forward to a long stay. 'Whisky sounds good to me.'

With her cheek still throbbing, it sounded good to Leigh too. She opened the door of the drinks cupboards in the corner and took out a bottle. 'Would you like water with it?'

'I always think it's a sin to dilute good alcohol.'

Leigh left the bottle on the coffee table and went into the kitchen for two glasses. When she returned, her visitor had removed her multi-coloured coat and draped it over the arm of the sofa. The dress she wore underneath was equally striking, this one a garish mishmash of colour and pattern that made Leigh blink and wonder vaguely if her visitor was colour blind.

She poured two generous measures of whisky, handed one over and sat on the other end of the sofa. Her cheek ached. She hadn't wanted to draw attention to her injury by applying a cold pack. Maybe later; for the moment she'd settle for the analgesic effect of whisky.

'Cheers.' Beatrix took a tentative sip, nodded as if in approval, and took a longer swig. 'Good stuff.'

Leigh sipped hers and put it down. 'I'm really sorry I startled you.'

Beatrix used her free hand to point a finger at Leigh's cheek. 'I'm sorry my aim was so good. You're going to have a fine bruise.'

'I'll put an ice pack on it in a bit.' She wondered if her visitor would take her less than subtle hint to drink up and go.

It seemed not when she leaned forward to pick up the bottle, refilling her glass almost to the brim. 'One more should do the job.'

If the job was to get blotto, she was certainly on the right road. Leigh, conscious of the wine she'd had with lunch, put her glass down after each tiny sip. 'Do you live around here?'

'You're thinking of that taxi you promised to get me.' Beatrix reached a hand out and patted Leigh's arm. 'Don't fret, I'm not going to take you up on that kind offer; it'd be faster to walk. I only live about fifteen minutes away, on Haverstock Hill.'

Leigh watched the level in the glass going down at speed. 'It might be better to get you a taxi.' She picked up her glass. 'This is strong stuff.'

The older woman grinned and knocked the rest of hers back in one. She coughed, banging her chest with the flat of her hand with enough force to send her back against the cushions. She lay there, looking perfectly relaxed. 'This woman you thought I was, did you have a falling out with her or something?'

Leigh's fingers tightened around her glass. 'What makes you ask?'

'Unless I look remarkably like your friend, which I doubt since I'm at least twice your age, you were seeing what you really wanted to see.' She sat up and met Leigh's eyes. 'Strikes me you must have wanted to see her a lot.'

'She was my lodger. Only for a short while. She moved out suddenly. No explanation.' This time Leigh took a healthy gulp of her drink. 'I'm trying to forget about her but when I saw you and thought you were Gina…'

'You realised she wasn't that easily put out of your mind.'

'If I knew why she left, I probably could. I was away and when I came back she was gone.'

'No note?'

'Yes, there was. It said she was sorry, that was it. No forwarding address, nothing.'

'What about the police?'

'They won't do anything about what they call a lost contact rather than a missing person.' Leigh swirled the end of the amber liquid in the glass before taking another mouthful.

'It looks to me as if you're not going to be able to let it rest till you find out what happened to this woman.' Beatrix scrambled to her feet. 'Until you do, you'll have to rein in your tendency to see her in every strange woman with a weird sense of clothes.'

'You do have a rather unusual style about you. Gina was equally colourful but—' She realised what she'd been about to say might offend.

'She was younger so able to carry it off?' Beatrix laughed. She picked up her coat and held it out. 'I was such a boring dresser until I hit seventy, then I stopped worrying about what people thought of me and went for it.' She slipped her arms into the sleeves and pulled the coat on. 'I read the poem "Warning" and took it to heart.' Leigh's bemused expression made her laugh. 'You don't know it? Jenny Joseph's poem about being old and wearing purple?' She took a beret from her bag and pulled it down over her crazy wild hair. 'A red hat, the final touch.' It took a few adjustments before she was happy with it. 'Do you know what my biggest regret is, Leigh?'

'Tell me.'

'Waiting till I was seventy. Take my advice. Don't wait. Not for anything. Do whatever you can to find this Gina woman, then get on with living.'

———————

eatrix refused the offer of a taxi and left on foot, a walking atchwork of colour lighting up the grey London streets. Leigh ood in the doorway and watched until she disappeared into the eflection of neon lights in the distance.

What an odd afternoon it had been. Leigh slammed the door hut, opened it and shut it again, pressing the snib down to dead-ck the Yale.

It was tempting to ring Kentish Town Police Station, tell them he door was definitely shut. But they probably wouldn't believe er, would think she was simply looking for attention again. She inged at the thought of what they'd have said had any of those ystanders earlier rung them.

Back in the living room, she sat with the last trickle of the hisky in her glass and thought about what that surprisingly enter-ining woman had said. Maybe she was right. Maybe only solving e mystery of what had happened to Gina would let her get past it.

Leigh remembered something the officer in the station had said her about using a tracing agency. She picked up her mobile and

did an internet search, surprised at the number of agencies sh
found.

'Who'd have thought,' she muttered, opening a few of th
websites. They didn't make any promises apart from doing thei
best and setting out their fee structure.

She could hire one, give them all the information she had
which wasn't much. Tell them about Philip who was the last perso
to see Gina... Her breath caught when she realised what she wa
thinking, how she'd been about to finish that sentence... the las
person to see Gina alive. There was no reason to believe she wa
dead.

Anyway, Leigh couldn't prove Philip was the last person to hav
seen her ex-lodger. All she could be sure of was that sometime afte
he'd delivered the Kindle, Gina had upped and left.

Perhaps Leigh's suspicions and wariness of him was cloudin
her judgement, making her see intrigue where there was simpl
coincidence.

She needed to forget about him, concentrate on Gina. Thinkin
back, when Leigh had mentioned Matt was staying without he
hadn't Gina's reaction been a little over the top? Maybe there was
reason. As was becoming patently clear, Leigh knew nothing abou
her ex-lodger. Perhaps despite her rather devil-may-care manne
and careless attitude to the truth, she had a history with men tha
made her wary of them. She'd been left alone with Matt, and
perhaps had to deal with an angry Philip. Were the two event
enough to have made leaving the better option?

It was a rather far-fetched idea, but no crazier than Gina fillin
the fridge and freezer with food then simply deciding to pack u
and leave for no reason.

'Oh for goodness' sake!' Leigh got to her feet and moved to th
window. The street outside was quiet now. No shrieking womer
Her hand crept to her cheek. It wasn't too late to apply that icepack

She finished the dribble of whisky, took both glasses to the kitchen and dropped them into the sink.

Upstairs, she switched on the en suite light and checked her face in the mirror, pressing her fingers gently along her cheekbone. It was red and swollen. The next day it would probably be as colourful as Beatrix Austin's dress. The thought made Leigh smile.

It was probably too late to do any good, but back in the kitchen, she opened the freezer. Ignoring Gina's neat pile of frozen dinners, Leigh took out the ice cube tray and knocked some cubes into a tea towel and sat on the living room sofa with the pack held against her cheek.

Forced into immobility, her thoughts settled in sympathy. It seemed sensible to talk to Philip herself before going to the trouble of hiring a tracing agency. Her mobile was on the sofa beside her. She picked it up and scrolled through her contacts for the number of the clinic.

'Mind and Body Clinic, my name is Harriet, how may I help you?'

Harriet, the muppet who'd given Leigh's address to Philip. She had a lot to answer for. But playing nice would get Leigh what she wanted. 'Hi, Harriet.' Sweet and light as if they were besties. 'It's Leigh Simon here; I wanted to thank you so much for getting my Kindle back to me. It was so kind. I was absolutely lost without it.'

'We were pleased to have been able to help, Ms Simon.'

'I wanted to thank Mr Dunstable too. Unfortunately, I don't have contact details for him. Obviously, I realise you can't divulge them' – a subtle dig she guessed would pass straight over the woman's head – 'but I wonder if you could contact him, pass on my phone number and ask him to ring me?'

'Certainly. Is this the number you're calling me from now?'

'Yes, that's it.'

'Not a problem, I'll do that right away. Is there anything else?'

'No, that's it, thanks so much.' Leigh hung up with a grin. *Easy peasy*.

Doing something made her feel good. The earlier wine and whisky helped, and the icepack eased the ache in her cheek. Now, especially since the police hadn't been called, she was able to view the afternoon's incident with amusement. Beatrix Austin was one of a kind. Leigh had liked her and was sorry she hadn't asked for her number to stay in contact.

She shrugged away the regret and reached for her phone again. It was early but Matt might be home. The idea that she was ringing him to get their nightly call over with, succeeded in dampening her good mood. 'Hi,' she said when her call was answered.

'Hello.' There was a clunk before he came back. 'Sorry, just in the middle of something.'

'Oh. Would you prefer if I hung up? We could talk later.'

'No, that's fine, I can talk as I'm working.'

Delightful. There had been a time when she'd have been his priority, when he'd have dropped anything to concentrate on her. It worried Leigh that she couldn't remember when this time had passed. She'd been fooling herself about their relationship for months. 'What are you doing anyway?'

'Fixing one of the kitchen cupboards; it was hanging a little askew.'

Since this comment was followed by more clunks and bangs, Leigh waited before answering. She wanted to point out the cupboard door wasn't exactly an urgent repair. Instead, she asked, 'Did you have a good day?' It would have been nice to have told him about her afternoon, about the eccentric Beatrix, but it would have given rise to questions she didn't want to answer till the weekend.

'Yes, thanks, and you?'

Leigh frowned. Were their conversations always this strained? 'Same old, same old.'

'Good.'

She tried to inject some enthusiasm into her voice. 'About this weekend, I thought I'd take you to a restaurant I used to go to years ago, I—'

'Listen,' he interrupted her. 'I'm afraid I'm not going to be able to make it up this weekend. There's an open event at the school and they've asked me to be available.'

'Really? That's short notice, isn't it?' Instead of an answer, there was a series of bangs and knocks. 'Matt?'

'Sorry, just finished. What did you say?'

'That it was short notice.' Her brain was desperately trying to adjust. She'd wanted to sit down with him, tell him everything that had been happening with her, discuss their relationship. Broach the idea that it had run its course. She didn't want to put it off for another week. It might be even easier in Salisbury. 'It's not a problem, I'll come down instead. I enjoyed the last weekend.' Well, if she was being honest, she hadn't hated it. 'I can do some shopping while you're busy.' When he didn't immediately leap in to greet this suggestion with delighted relief, she added, 'I know you prefer to come to London, but it's nice for me to get away sometimes.'

'Yes, but not this weekend.'

It wasn't only the words, but the tone of voice that made Leigh draw a sharp breath and let it out in a nervous laugh. 'Not this weekend? Why not?'

'I'm going to be up to my tonsils, that's why. The open days are all day Saturday *and* Sunday, so I'll have no time to spare and will be too exhausted in the evening to be good company.'

She was going to argue that he still needed to eat but didn't get the opportunity.

'Listen, there's the doorbell, I have to go. We can talk more tomorrow.'

He hung up before she had the chance to complain it was what he'd said the previous night. No exchange of endearments. No expressions of regret for cutting her call short. Nothing. Leigh threw the phone to the far end of the sofa. When it bounced and slid to the floor, she glared at it, as if the fault lay with it and not the spurt of anger that faded as quickly as it had erupted to leave her feeling completely drained.

She rested her head back and shut her eyes. Tears squeezed through her eyelashes and trembled there a moment before sliding, one after the other, down her cheeks.

Perhaps their relationship was over, but she'd still depended on being able to talk to Matt, discussing her problems, getting his support, his calm advice.

It looked as though she was on her own.

_____

nger could be destructive, but it could also be energising. Leigh llowed the tears to fall before realising how many times she'd ried or worried over men recently. Ledbetter, Philip, Matt. It was nough to have her sit bolt upright and wipe her face with the eeve of her shirt.

Restless, she got to her feet and went to the kitchen for a mug of a, choosing camomile in the vague hope it would soothe her free-lling thoughts and help her sleep. She took it back to the living om and sipped it as she watched TV. A movie she'd saved for ich an evening. The kind of movie Matt hated and dismissed as a hick-flick. It was perfect light entertainment, requiring nothing iore than she suspend belief for ninety minutes. Plus, if her atten-on wandered, when she dragged it unwillingly back minutes later was easy to pick up the simple storyline.

It was enjoyable enough to keep her watching till the redictable happily ever after ending. Whether it was from the iindless fluff she'd watched or the camomile tea, she was feeling almer. Switching off the TV, she shuffled down on the sofa, snuggling her head into a cushion. She should go to bed, not sleep there and wake up with a crick in her neck.

Exhaustion pressed her down. It seemed far too much trouble to move.

Her thoughts were swirling and dipping into dreamland when the chime of the doorbell brought her back to reality with a start. She'd pulled the curtains earlier and the room was in semi-darkness, the only light coming under the door from the hallway where a table lamp was on a timer.

The house was quiet. She'd imagined the sound. Or dreamt it. Rubbing her eyes, she got to her feet. Time to go to bed and try to get a decent night's sleep.

She took her empty mug back to the kitchen and had returned to the hallway when the doorbell sounded again. More insistent, someone holding their finger on it. Her immediate reaction was to freeze, eyes wide. Nobody she knew would call without ringing first. She took a step backwards, planning to make a run for it to the back door. She could push through the shrubbery at the end, escape into the neighbour's garden, call for help. Do Beatrix's trick: scream till her lungs hurt.

The back door was locked. She used to leave the key in the lock but the last few days, for security, she'd removed it and put it in a nearby drawer. Too secure. It would take precious minutes to find it and unlock the door.

She should ring the police. Oddly, the thought succeeded in calming her fear a little – she'd been wrong the previous two times she'd called them; perhaps she was wrong this time too. It might be as simple as someone calling to the wrong house. It was unlikely there was a herd of monsters on her doorstep filled with evil intent. Perhaps she could talk to whoever it was through the door. Find out what they wanted. First, to be on the safe side, she'd get her phone. As she hurried forward to grab it from where she'd left it on the living room floor, her foot caught in the trailing straps of the handbag she'd carelessly dropped earlier. She dragged it with her as she stumbled, the bag itself catching her other foot. She was unable to save herself, and it was only the proximity of the front door that prevented her from falling to the floor. Her shoulder hit it, her painful *ooof* loud in the following silence.

'Leigh?'

Monsters wouldn't know her name, would they? Nor would they sound vaguely familiar.

'Leigh, it's Philip.'

Stunned from the blow, she pushed away from the door, and held her arm. If tomorrow ever came, she was going to be multi-coloured.

'Are you all right?'

Her face and her shoulder ached, and she knew she was close to tears. What was he doing on her doorstep? Had that stupid Harriet given him the wrong message and told him to call around rather than ring? Or had Leigh been right about his being a predator, and this was proof. She'd ignore him. He'd go away. *Like she'd ignored Ledbetter, and where had that got her?*

'Leigh? Are you hurt?'

She rubbed her bruised shoulder, wondering how long it would be before he gave up and went away.

'I'm going to call the police.'

Leigh shut her eyes in dismay. She imagined those two police officers arriving and looking at her bruised face with snide looks of disbelief. She took a step closer to the door. 'No, please don't. I'm okay.'

'Okay.' He sounded perplexed. 'Are you going to open the door?' He waited a beat before adding, 'There's obviously something wrong so I'm not going away until you do.'

He sounded caring, or was that how predators operated, lulling unsuspecting women into their lair? But it was her lair. And she wasn't unsuspecting. Being wary was a good thing; it would keep her on her guard.

'Hang on, I need to get the keys.' Seconds later, she undid both locks and pulled the door open. Philip stood with one hand in his trouser pocket, looking James Bond debonair and dangerous in a dark suit and white shirt with the top button opened. Leigh had forgotten how handsome he was. 'I wasn't expecting you.'

'Really? Yet you rang the clinic looking for me.' His eyes narrowed and he took a step forward.

It took great strength for Leigh not to step backwards. But that would have been an invitation for him to enter, and she didn't want him inside her home.

'You've been in a fight,' he said, pointing to her face.

She lifted a hand to her cheek. 'I fell.'

'Earlier today obviously, it's already starting to turn a lovely colour.' He frowned. 'And again, just now I heard you slam against the door.'

She waved at the handbag on the floor. 'I'm having a bad day, I tripped over the straps.'

'Are you sure you're okay? Do you need to go to the hospital?'

She simply needed him to go away and to sleep for twenty-four hours. Maybe take a few painkillers for her aches and pains. 'No, I'm fine.'

Neither spoke, the silence lingering until broken by a couple walking past whose voices were raised in inebriated amusement.

'Aren't you going to ask me in?'

It was late; she needed to sleep. She'd wanted a quick conversation on the phone, not this intrusion. But if she sent him away, she might never get the answers she needed. 'Yes, okay, for a few minutes.'

She led the way into the kitchen, deciding it was less cosy and intimate than the living room. It was too late for social niceties too. She waved to a seat at the table, waited till he'd sat before taking one on the far side. Conscious of his assessing eyes, she dropped hers to her clasped hands. 'I wanted to thank you for having dropped off my Kindle. I asked the clinic to pass my number to you so you could phone me, not call around.'

She looked up in time to catch the smirk that twisted his lips.

'The lady doth protest too much, methinks.'

'Oh please,' she groaned. 'If you're going to use quotations, try for something a little less done to death.'

To her surprise, he laughed, a deep belly laugh of genuine amusement. 'You are something else, you know that?'

'I know I'm impervious to your rather obvious charms.' She sat back and folded her arms. Being rude possibly wouldn't get her the answers she needed but right then she didn't care. She'd had her fill of troublesome men.

'I'm supposed to believe you went to all that trouble, ringing the clinic, asking them to pass on your number, simply to say thanks?'

Better to admit the truth than have him think she was interested in pursuing a relationship with him. 'No, I didn't, there was something I wanted to ask you.' She got to her feet so abruptly she startled him.

He jerked backwards, raising his hands defensively. 'Hey!'

'What?' She was surprised at his overreaction. Maybe he wasn't as self-assured as she'd assumed. 'Did you seriously think I was going to hit you?'

His sallow skin flushed an unattractive crimson. 'To be honest, I've no idea what you're capable of. You aren't the kind of woman I'm used to dealing with.'

'You mean ones who fall for your—'

'Rather obvious charms, yes, I heard you the first time. Thanks very much but that wasn't what I meant.' He shoved his hands into his pockets and tilted the chair back to look up at her. 'The women I'm used to meeting wouldn't think twice about having a fling despite being in a relationship. They're women who know what they want and take it regardless of consequences.'

Leigh was surprised at the bitterness of his words. Strangely, they made her less nervous of him. 'Sounds like you've been meeting the wrong kind of women.' She pointed towards the kitchen. 'I was simply going to put the kettle on for a cuppa.'

'Okay.' He frowned. 'You said you wanted to ask me something.'

'That's right.'

'I'd answer more eloquently if I had something stronger than tea.'

Her eyes flicked to the ceiling. 'God forbid I should hamper your eloquence.' She went to the fridge and took out the open bottle of wine. 'White wine or nothing.' She still didn't trust him; he wasn't getting anything stronger.

'Wine sounds good.'

She poured two glasses, put the bottle back in the fridge and took the glasses to the table. Sitting, she shoved one across to him.

He raised an eyebrow. 'Your social skills need a bit of polishing.'

'This isn't a social event. I didn't invite you here.' She sucked a breath in and let it out in a long hiss. 'I'm sorry, my life is a bit complicated these days.'

'Complicated?' He picked up the wine and sipped. Putting the glass down, he looked at her with a more serious expression than she was used to seeing from him. 'Did the boyfriend hit you?' He waved a finger at her cheek.

'No, Matt isn't violent.' Not in the way Philip meant; Matt had never hit her.

'But someone did, I'm guessing.'

There was no point in continuing to claim she'd fallen. 'Yes, but it was an accident. It's long and boring story and not what I wanted

talk about.' She cradled her glass without drinking. 'I wanted to
ask about when you called here with my Kindle.'

'Okay...' He dragged the word out, his brow furrowing.

'What day did you come?'

Philip wasn't a man who answered questions without thinking.
The furrow on his brow deepened before he finally spoke.

'Saturday. Late morning.'

'And you handed it to my lodger, Gina?' She watched as he
picked up his glass and made a big deal about swirling the wine
before taking a sip. He swished it around his mouth as if he was at a
very expensive wine-tasting and not drinking cheap supermarket
plonk. Obvious delaying tactics. Why did he need to use them?

'Yes, I did. The clinic had put the Kindle into a plain brown
envelope; I wasn't happy about dropping it through the letter box in
case it was damaged when it hit the floor.'

'I appreciate that,' Leigh said when silence lingered. 'It was
lucky Gina was in to take it from you.'

'I was about to leave a note saying I'd called and would call
another day when the door finally opened.' He took another drink
before continuing. 'I was expecting you, so when a stranger opened
the door, I thought I'd gone to the wrong house. I asked if she knew
you...'

Leigh felt her gut tense when he stopped. What wasn't he telling
her?

30

This time it was Leigh who was startled when Philip stood abruptly. He went to the fridge and took out the bottle of wine. 'I'm making myself at home.' He sat, filled his glass and waved the bottle at Leigh who shook her head.

'I've had enough to drink for one day.' She waited till he'd taken a drink before saying, 'You'd better tell me the rest.'

'Before I do,' he said, looking at her curiously. 'Why are you asking me about this?'

'After the clinic, I went to Salisbury to stay with Matt. I didn't get home till late Sunday afternoon. Gina had packed up and gone. All she left was a note saying she was sorry. No explanation, nothing more than those two words. She didn't turn up for work that weekend. In fact' – Leigh kept her eyes fixed on his face for the slightest hint of guilt – 'you're the last person I know to have seen her.'

The one unsaid word *alive* floated in the air between them.

Philip stared. 'She's dead?'

'I've no idea, I hope not. All I know is, sometime after you saw her on Saturday, she packed all her belongings and disappeared.'

He gulped a mouthful of wine, then lifted the glass to his mouth again and drained it. 'I owe you a bottle of wine.' He picked up the bottle and poured the remainder. He said nothing for a few minutes. With frown lines criss-crossing his forehead, and his voice tight, he said, 'You're not implying I had something to do with her disappearance, are you?' He pushed his drink to one side and leaned forward towards her, arms sliding across the table. 'Shit, have you told the police this?'

'No!' Leigh shook her head too emphatically and saw disbelief flicker across his face. 'I went to the police to report her missing, but they're not following it up since there was no sign of any foul play. They said she was a lost contact, not a missing person.' If they had decided to investigate, she'd have given them his name without compunction. He didn't need to know that.

'But surely they thought it was suspicious that she moved out without warning after—' He stopped, tilting his head in question. 'How long had she lived here?'

'Not very long,' Leigh hedged.

'Not long? Years, months?' He laughed when she didn't reply. 'Don't tell me it was only weeks?'

'Does it matter? She's still missing—'

He stopped her with a raised hand. 'That's not what the police are saying though, is it?' He seemed to take pity on her because when he spoke next his voice was kinder. 'Did you have a falling out? Was that it?' When she didn't reply, he asked a final question. 'How long were you friends?'

Refusing to answer, Leigh made an obvious point of looking at her watch. 'Look, it's late, I'm shattered, so if you could simply tell me what happened when you met Gina, you can go home, and I can try and get some much-needed sleep.'

Philip downed the remainder of the wine. 'I asked Gina if she knew you, right?'

'Yes, okay, so what did she say?'

'That she did... in the biblical sense.'

Leigh was tired, her brain on a go-slow. It took several seconds to make sense of what he'd said. Comprehension made her eyes widen in surprise. 'She told you we were lovers?'

He nodded. 'She said you were away for a few days, trying to gather enough courage to finish your relationship with your boyfriend, then you and she would be together.'

'Me and Gina!' It was almost a shriek as disbelief and anger collided. 'That's the most outrageous thing I've ever heard. Why would she say such a thing?'

'She didn't mention the anger management course.'

'Because she didn't know about it.' Leigh's voice still bristled with annoyance. 'We weren't friends at all; she was simply a lodger. A woman I'd felt sorry for.'

'It's not true then?'

Leigh glared at him. 'No, it's not bloody well true. I don't understand why she would have lied about that.'

'Has there ever been anything...' He coloured. 'You know.'

'No!' Leigh was horrified. 'What? You'd think I'd have Matt in Salisbury, and another lover here in London? There was never anything like that between us. I thought she was stunning, like a butterfly, sometimes as ethereal as a fairy, but my desires don't run that way. And I've never given her any reason to believe otherwise. I don't understand why she would tell a stranger such a lie.'

'How long have you known her?'

Leigh, who'd already reached the conclusion she hadn't known the woman at all, sighed heavily as she admitted, 'Not long, only a few months.'

'Seems like maybe you didn't know her very well,' Philip said, unwittingly echoing Leigh's thoughts. 'Perhaps it's as well she's gone.' He got to his feet. 'I should be going too. I'm sorry my answers weren't what you were expecting.'

Leigh shrugged and stood. 'Well, put it this way, if I was puzzled before, I'm twice as puzzled now.'

31

Leigh walked with Philip to the door. Lost in her jumbled thoughts, she wasn't aware of his intent regard and was taken aback when he leaned in and planted a kiss on her cheek.

'Don't,' she said, wiping it away with the back of her hand, wincing as she brushed her damaged cheek.

'I'm sorry. You looked so sad.'

And he thought taking advantage of that was acceptable. Leigh pulled open the door. 'Goodbye, Philip.' In case he hadn't got the message, she slammed the door hard enough to send the sound echoing down the street in his wake.

If she wasn't so weary, she'd be steaming mad at everything... Gina and her lies, Matt and whatever the hell was going on with him, Philip and his ego, even the missing Ledbetter for casting her as the bad guy.

She left the glasses on the table, hers still half full of wine, and trudged up the stairs. The bed looked so inviting, she didn't bother with anything apart from taking her clothes off, dropping them on the chair and crawling between the sheets. Exhausted as she was, despite whirling thoughts, sleep came almost instantly.

* * *

o her surprise, Leigh slept solidly till seven. A recuperating sleep;
ᴇ felt better, less confused and anxious. She had no regrets about
ᴐntacting Philip. With his input, a clearer picture of her late lodger
ᴀd emerged. Gina may have looked ethereal and butterfly-like, but
ᴇigh was discovering hidden and unattractive depths behind the
ᴌossy exterior. Isobel had been right with her summation – a
ᴐugh, manipulative woman, Gina was always going to land on her
ᴇet.

It was time to forget about her.

It didn't mean her head was empty of problems, though. With
ina gone, Matt came front and centre. Leigh laced her fingers
ᴇhind her head and stared at the ceiling for a long time going over
ᴇcent conversations. There was nothing suspicious, nothing out of
ᴌe ordinary till this week.

Having to wait until the following weekend to have a face-to-
ᴄe conversation with him was going to be murder. How many
ᴌore stilted conversations on the phone could she endure without
ᴄreaming?

He said he'd be busy all weekend. But it was only Thursday.
ᴎhy couldn't she drive to Salisbury that day, surprise him, take
ᴌm out to dinner, have a long talk and clear the air? If he was
ᴐing to break the news that he'd met someone else, she could
ᴐunter with her belief that their relationship had wound down
ᴌyway.

It would be good to get the conversation done. Hopefully too,
ᴌce they'd got everything out in the open, she'd be able to spill all
ᴇr secrets. She might have no romantic feelings for Matt any more,
ᴌt she knew he wouldn't let her down. He'd give her problems the
ᴇnefit of his clear, objective thinking; set her straight.

Energised from the good night's sleep, she swung her feet to the

floor. Her shoulder ached a little and bruises stretched from it t
her elbow. Leigh ran a hand down it. She'd been lucky.

Or maybe not. The sight of her bruised face in the bathroor
mirror made her groan. Overnight the colours had come up. Shin
purple edged with green over her cheekbone, a paler shade of puc
creeping up to her eye. She did her best with make-up, but it wasn
going to fool anyone. She looked like someone who'd bee
punched.

'Thanks a million, Beatrix!' A final dab of powder to dampe
the glowing purple achieved nothing and she gave up.

There was no point in heading to Salisbury until late mornin
at the earliest. Matt was generally home from the school late afte
noon, unless there were after-school classes. It didn't matter; sh
could sit in the car and read till he arrived.

With her day mapped out, she ran down the stairs, feelin
lighter than she had in days. She filled the kettle, searched in th
freezer for bread, took out a couple of slices and popped them int
the toaster. Humming a song, she waited till the toast popped the
slipped it into the toast rack and put it on the table. That's when he
good mood vanished with an almost audible *poof*.

Her hand was trembling as she reached for the glass she'd le
on the table the previous night. It had been at least half full. Th
memory was clear. Distinct. But now... the glass was empty. A dro
might have dried overnight, but half a glass, that wasn't possible.

And if it wasn't... Leigh looked around, her mouth suddenly dr
It meant someone had been here. With a groan, she remembere
her lapse. After Philip had left, she hadn't double-locked the doo
or pushed the snib down on the Yale.

Those police officers had convinced her she'd stupidly left th
front door open. This was proof she hadn't. Someone had come int
her house while she was asleep both nights. She sank onto a chai
a hand over her mouth, feeling nausea curl. Had they crept up th

stairs and into her bedroom? She slept naked, frequently throwing the sheet back if she was too warm... Had they stood there, staring lecherously? Who would do such a thing?

She went to the front door and opened it, peering at both locks. The police had said there was no sign of forced entry when they'd found the door open. There wasn't any visible damage to either lock now either.

Someone with a key.

Gina!

Leigh slammed the door shut, feeling stupid. She'd been so taken aback by Gina's short, unexpected note, by her abrupt departure, that she'd never given any thought to what she'd not left... the damn front door keys.

32

Leigh was trembling as she sat at the kitchen table. After what Philip had told her, it seemed Gina was capable of anything, but what reason could she have for sneaking into the house? She could have come back at any time and asked Leigh for a second chance.

And because she was a stupid gullible fool, she would probably have agreed. Self-pity made her lower lip quiver and tears gather but anger at being taken for a fool drove her to action. She could make sure Gina wouldn't get inside her home again.

It took a quick internet search to find a local locksmith and the payment of an emergency call-out fee to have them attend immediately to change both locks. 'How soon is *immediately*?' she asked. It was a relative term; she'd been caught out before.

'They'll be with you within the next thirty minutes.'

'Good, that's good, thank you.' She hung up, went back to the door, pressed the snib on the Yale and put the key into the lower lock, making it impossible to open from the outside. That would do for the moment; only changing the locks would make it safe again.

The company was true to its promise, the doorbell ringing

twenty minutes later. She answered the door to a short rotund man with a thick shock of curling hair.

'Larry, the locksmith,' he said, introducing himself, in case she might have missed the less than subtle hint in the bright red over-alls with its pattern of silver keys. He chatted cheerfully as he worked, oblivious to her monosyllabic replies. 'There you go,' he said less than an hour later. 'All done.' He held out two bunches of shiny new keys.

Her fingers closed over them. 'That's great, thank you.'

'All in a day's work.' He packed up his tools, gave her a quick wink and headed away.

Leigh shut the door again, pressed the snib down on the Yale, slipped the new key into the lower lock and turned it. She stepped back with a sigh. It might be more secure, but she didn't feel any safer.

Back in the kitchen, she threw the cold toast into the bin and made a mug of coffee. If she didn't have such poor history with her local police station, she could have gone in and told them again about Gina. Not that it would have made any difference. Leigh needed proof, not airy-fairy speculation. Perhaps she should look into getting a CCTV camera for over the door... if she could capture footage of Gina trying to get in, wouldn't that work? It was worth a try.

She also needed a working alarm. She'd been relying on the deterrent of the alarm box over the front door. The system, installed by her aunt years before, had worked for the first few weeks after Leigh had moved in, stopping one day never to work again. The service company had come to assess it and shaken their head. Beyond saving. They'd quoted a breathtaking amount of money to replace it. Money she hadn't had.

She'd didn't have it now either, but she could borrow it. Until a new alarm was installed, the new locks would have to do.

It was time to get on with the rest of her planned day. Preparing for her trip to Salisbury, she packed an overnight bag with enough for one night's stay. If the conversation went as she expected, there really was no point in her staying longer.

It was the usual chaos getting out of London and it wasn't until she joined the A303 that she could relax and enjoy the drive, turning the radio up, rolling tense shoulders.

Matt's semi-detached house was in Bishopdown, a little over two miles from the centre of Salisbury. Planning to spend a few hours in the city, Leigh left her car in the nearby London Road park and ride. A bus, ready to move out, waited for her to climb aboard and this touch of good luck served to lift her mood further.

The bus dropped her in the centre; she stepped off and looked around, anticipating a pleasant few hours. She wandered lazily around the streets, stopping now and then, window shopping. A Costa reminded her she'd skipped breakfast and she went inside to have a sandwich and a coffee. More wandering, another coffee at a small independent café, and finally she dropped into M&S where, being a fan of their underwear, she made her only purchase.

A glance at her watch told her it was an hour, maybe more, before there was any hope Matt would be home. Not for the first time, she was irritated he'd never given her keys for his house.

'You won't need them,' he'd argued. 'I'm always here when you arrive, aren't I?'

He was, but it wasn't the point. She'd given him keys to her home; she'd expected it to be a reciprocal arrangement. 'I'd still like to have a set.'

'Right!' He huffed in exasperation. 'I'll get some cut. My spare set are with my parents so they can check on the house when I'm away.'

But despite reminding him, more than once, Leigh still didn't have keys.

She could drop into the school where Matt worked. Classes couldn't be over, but she could ask the administrator to give him a message. If he had after-school commitments, he could give her the keys. It beat sitting in her car for hours.

Bishopdown Senior School, where Matt taught, was near the park and ride. Leigh caught the bus back and walked the five minutes to the school. An old building, it had been added to over the years. Some of the extensions blended in with the original, others, especially recent ones, had been designed with an eye on the purse strings rather than aesthetics. Altogether it was an ugly mishmash of styles. But the grounds it occupied were lavish. Leigh walked up the tree-lined driveway, admiring the well-maintained playing fields to each side.

The glass entrance door was locked. Leigh pressed up against it and peered into the large reception area, then stood back to look for a bell.

Before she had a chance to press her finger to it, a buzzer told her she'd been seen, and she hurried to push the door open. Inside, immediately to her right, a door was designated reception. Next to it was a window with sliding glass panels. An elderly woman with dyed black hair, matching dramatically arched eyebrows giving the appearance she was eternally surprised, smiled through the glass as Leigh approached. 'May I help you?'

'Hello, I'm Leigh Simon, a friend of Matt Gibbs. I wonder if it would be possible to get a message to him.' Her smile faltered at the woman's instant reaction, lips forming a tight line, eyes flitting from side to side as if looking for escape.

'Is there something wrong?'

'Not as such.' The woman licked her lips so energetically Leigh wondered if the pink lipstick she wore was flavoured.

Leigh wanted to push the glass panels apart, reach through the gap and shake the woman until the information spilled from her in

jigsaw pieces that would fall onto the counter and form a clea
picture. 'What's going on?'

'It's not really my place to say.' She looked behind her as i
hoping someone was going to rush out and rescue her. When it wa
obvious she was on her own, she sighed. 'He's not here. Hasn't bee
since Monday.'

'What?' Leigh leaned forward, her nose almost touching th
glass. It didn't make anything any clearer. 'Is he sick?' If the woma
answered with *not as such*, Leigh was going to scream.

But after being reticent up till then, suddenly the informatio
came in a barely audible gush. 'No, he was suspended.' She leane
closer to the glass, bringing her almost to kissing distance, he
words a whisper. 'It's being kept hush hush, but since you're
friend, I'll tell you. He's been accused of sexual assault.'

Leigh reared back. 'What?'

'You heard me.'

'Matt?' Leigh shook her head. 'You sure you're talking abou
Matt Gibbs?'

'It's not something that happens in Bishopdown Senior School
Her sniff was disdainful. 'Certainly not something I'm likely t
make a mistake about.'

Leigh was staggered. Matt was a lot of things. Irritating, sel
opinionated, often contrary, but he wasn't capable of this. *Sexu*
assault? She looked at the receptionist in horror. 'Oh no, was it
student? You hear about teachers being wrongly accused, I'm—'

'No!' There was equal horror in the receptionist's voice. 'No, w
haven't had to suffer that calamity. Now, really, I can't say any more
Her face creased in worry as if she suddenly realised she shouldn
have said anything at all.

'Thank you for telling me.' Leigh waved towards the exit. 'I'll g
to his house and find out what's going on.' She lifted her chin. 'He'
be cleared and back before you know it.'

For the first time, the receptionist looked pointedly at Leigh's bruised cheek, her arched eyebrows rising to her hairline. 'Whatever you say.'

Leigh's hand instantly went to her face. There wasn't any point in explaining; she could see by the condemning eyes that it was too late for that. Outside, she took a deep breath. *Sexual assault.* Poor Matt. Now she could understand why he'd been odd the last couple of days; what she couldn't understand was why he hadn't told her. Why lie about having to attend the school open event to avoid coming to London? What a dreadful reflection on their relationship... he lied to her... she lied to him. Her eyes blurred with tears. She hurried back to the park and ride to get her car and a few minutes later pulled into the driveway of Matt's house.

The curtains were shut. He was probably inside, glued to the TV to keep his mind occupied. She left her overnight bag in the car and stepped up to the front door to ring the doorbell. The sound echoed but when there was no sign of him coming to answer it, she pushed her finger against the bell again, twice, longer each time.

Still no answer. Frustrated, she moved to the window and rapped on it. 'Matt, are you there? It's Leigh.' There was a slight gap between the curtains; she peered through. There wasn't much light. Enough to tell her the room was empty.

The side gate wasn't kept locked. She went through it to the back of the house but here too, curtains and blinds were pulled shut. *Sexual assault.* Leigh wasn't a fool; even unfounded allegations could ruin a teacher's career. So many times, she'd listened to Matt telling her how much he loved what he did, how he could never do anything else. This would destroy him.

She returned to the front of the house and looked at the upstairs windows. Then, desperate, she bent to look through the letter box. There was no sign of him.

A call to his mobile went straight to voicemail. 'Matt, it's Leigh.

I'm outside your house. Where are you?' If he'd heard it, he wasn't replying. She stood, staring, wondering whether to ring the police or not.

A woman came out of the house next door, a gurgling toddler balanced easily on her hip. Seeing Leigh, she raised a hand to wave.

Leigh had met her once before. She remembered her name as she crossed to speak to her. 'Hi, Poppy, I wanted to surprise Matt with a visit but he's not answering the doorbell. Have you seen him recently?'

'No, not since Monday evening.' The child on her hip wriggled. She jangled a bunch of keys for his benefit and smiled at Leigh. 'If I put him down, he'll be gone like a bullet.'

Leigh reached out for one pudgy leg and shook it gently. 'He's growing quickly.' She tried to keep her expression and her tone of voice unconcerned. 'You saw Matt on Monday?'

'Yes, getting into a taxi.' Poppy's eyes softened in understanding. 'Have you two fallen out? Relationships! They're a nightmare. I told my husband if he left me and made me go through all that dating crap again, I'd kill him.'

Leigh managed to force a smile. 'It's certainly not easy.' She sighed. 'I don't suppose, by any wild chance, you know where he went?'

'Oh, I'm sorry, I don't. If it's any help, he wasn't carrying any luggage.'

'Actually, that does help. He's probably gone to his parents. He still has stuff there despite having moved out years ago.'

'Mothers and their sons.' The neighbour's smile faded. 'You sure you're okay? A nasty bruise you have there.'

For the second time that afternoon, Leigh raised a hand to her cheek. 'It's not what you think, honestly, Matt isn't the violent type. This was a genuine accident.'

Whether the neighbour believed her or not, Leigh wasn't sure.

'I'd better go.' Poppy cuddled her son closer and with a *good luck*, strapped the child into the back of her car and was gone while Leigh stood wondering what her next step should be.

She still hadn't decided when she got into her car. Going to his parents was an option... but what if she was wrong and he wasn't there? They were a kind, loving elderly couple. It wouldn't be fair to worry them.

No, she'd ring him again, this time tell him she knew everything. She fished in her bag for her mobile and dialled his number. When it went to voicemail she hung up and rested her head back. What was the best way to put it? *I know about the accusation against you...* it sounded too bald, almost accusatory. She dialled again. This time, when she heard his voice inviting her to leave a message, she said, 'I know about the accusation, Matt. I'm here for you. In Salisbury. Outside your house. Ring me. I'll come to wherever you are.'

She sat with the phone in her hand, begging it to ring. An hour later, she sent a message repeating what she'd said, adding an *I love you* to the end of it. After another hour's frustrating wait, she threw the phone on the passenger seat and started the engine. It didn't look as if she had a choice; she'd go home.

33

An accident somewhere slowed traffic to a crawl and it took over three hours to reach Gaisford Street and another ten minutes to find parking. Weary, Leigh pulled her overnight bag from the boot and walked back to her house.

The new keys worked smoothly. She opened the door and stepped into the quiet house. Dropping her bags on the floor, she turned to lock the door behind her. She wished it made her feel safer. True, Gina could no longer enter freely, but it didn't mean she'd leave Leigh alone or wouldn't find some other way to unsettle her. Tomorrow, she'd investigate both the alarm and the CCTV camera.

The big question of course, was why Gina was doing this? There was no logic to her behaviour, no logic to the lie she'd told Philip. It was certainly a cruel repayment for the spontaneous act of kindness in offering her lodging.

Leigh needed to forget about her and concentrate on Matt. He was her priority now. She tried phoning him again, left another message to tell him she was back at home. Perhaps he'd be happier

nging her if she was at a distance and unable to descend upon
im with words of comfort he wouldn't appreciate.

She threw her jacket across the newel post and went into the
tchen. It was a night for camomile tea. She made a mug and stood
pping it, staring out the window. This late, with the garden in
arkness, it was her reflection she saw, bruised and worried.

Every time she tried to make sense of her life it became more
visted. It devastated her that Matt hadn't felt able to share what
ad happened but then neither had she shared what had happened
 her. It proved more than anything their relationship was shallow
nd meaningless. *Over.*

Tomorrow, she'd ring his parents, make up some reason to need
 call them, see if he was there. If not, what would she do, go to the
olice? The idea made her cringe.

The allegations against Matt were ridiculous. *Weren't they?*
adn't she had cause to remonstrate with him numerous times over
ie last year when he'd been a little too enthusiastic during sex?
nthusiastic... was the word he used; she'd have said rough, in fact,
ie'd have said bloody painful at times, but she'd said nothing.
he'd taken the easier option and made herself into a doormat.

The idea made her squirm. Is that what she'd become? And just
ecause Matt was a bit rough, did she really believe he was capable
 sexual assault?

Suddenly another thought squeezed through all the others with
ich a sharp intensity it made her gasp. She'd blamed Gina for
iose two nightly incursions, but she wasn't the only one who had
eys to the house, Matt did.

Leigh remembered giving him the two keys attached to a key
ng she'd bought. A small silver heart. 'A bit mushy,' she'd laughed
hen she'd handed it to him.

Later, weeks, months, she couldn't quite recall, she'd noticed the

heart was missing. 'It must have fallen off,' he'd said with a shru
when she'd asked.

She'd seen the lie in his eyes but hadn't called him on it. Wha
did it matter? It was only a silly charm. Looking back, was that th
point where taking the easy way out in their relationship ha
started? Had that been his first lie?

With tear-filled eyes, she picked up her mobile, blinking whe
she saw there was a message. Matt?

But it wasn't; it was from an unknown number. She opened it.

I wondered if you'd come out for a drink with me. Philip

Yes, because what she needed in her life was more trouble. Sh
didn't reply. There was nothing from Matt.

She dropped the mobile on the counter. He had no reason t
enter her home clandestinely, but then neither did Gina. Ye
someone had. Leigh had to cling on to the few solid truths in he
life. That there were far fewer than she'd have assumed only day
before scared her.

Since she couldn't think of anything better, she pushed he
chair back and got to her feet. A night's sleep might give her som
clarity. She'd switched out the light when the phone rang. For
second, she stood staring at it, wanting it to be Matt... afraid
would be Philip.

It was another number she didn't recognise, making her hes
tate longer. When it stopped, she relaxed. Then it rang again. Thi
time she picked it up, her faint *hello* barely recognisable even to he
Who was this scared woman she'd become?

'Leigh, it's me.'

'Matt, thank God!' Her voice was high-pitched with relief. 'I'v
been trying to get hold of you all day. Where are you?' When ther

was no reply, she added, 'I called to the school; I know about the allegations.'

'You don't know anything.' His voice was defeated.

'Talk to me. I don't understand why you were keeping it a secret, why you lied about being involved with the school this weekend. Unnecessary lies, Matt. Why couldn't you tell me the truth? Where are you? With your parents?'

'No, I can't go there. They'd guess there was trouble and would be horrified. I'm staying with an old school friend, Doug Bedford; you've heard me mention him.'

Leigh vaguely remembered the name. 'Is he the guy who lives in Southampton?'

'Yes. He has a spare room, says I can stay as long as I want, didn't ask me for an explanation.'

As she was doing... but didn't she deserve one? 'I'm your partner, Matt; we're supposed to be there for one another.' The irony of it didn't escape her. 'Why don't you tell me?'

'You're not going to like it.'

Leigh had wanted to hear him say there was nothing to the allegation made against him, to hear him say he'd been devastated by the unfounded lies this nameless person or persons had spread. What she hadn't expected him to say was she wasn't *going to like it*. 'You'd better tell me and let me be the judge of that.'

'Right, okay.' A loud sigh came down the line. 'It was Monday before last, the night I stayed without you.'

A wave of weakness hit Leigh. She sank onto the chair, holding the phone in one hand, resting her forehead on the other. 'Go on.'

'I was watching TV. Gina came home and joined me. She had a bottle of wine, had brought through two glasses, poured me one without asking. We finished the bottle between us. I'd been in the pub in the afternoon after the exhibition, and already had had a bit to drink. Quite a bit, Leigh. Enough to be flattered, when she started flirting with me, moving a little closer on the sofa, resting a hand on my leg... I didn't mean for it to happen, but one thing led to another.'

This couldn't be true; Leigh had fallen asleep at the table. It was a nightmare. It had to be. Any moment, she'd wake up, shake her head and laugh at the impossibility of such a thing happening.

'I'm so sorry, Leigh.'

34

Leigh couldn't find the words. Gina and Matt? Impossible. A joke. Like that stupid hand. For some reason, it seemed important to know if he was responsible for that. More important than facing up to her boyfriend sleeping with her ex-lodger. 'Did you plant a latex hand in the garden?'

'What?'

'I found a hand sticking out of the new bed at the end of the garden. It scared me; for a few minutes I thought there was a body buried there.' No point in telling him she'd believed it so strongly she'd called the police. Absolutely no point in telling him she didn't know which way was up any longer.

'And you think I'd do something so stupid? Jesus, Leigh, do you know me at all?'

It seemed she didn't. 'Someone put the damn thing there, and it had your rather weird sense of humour written all over it. To be honest, I'd have preferred to believe you did that, and not have to try to get my head around you cheating on me with the damn lodger. Do I know you at all? How about you're a ridiculous fucking piece of shit? Is that close enough to the true you?'

'I knew you'd be angry.'

Angry! Was he being serious? 'I trusted you. It never entered my head you'd cheat on me.' Not until recently anyway. 'And with Gina!' Leigh got to her feet and paced the floor of the dark room, pushing aside furniture in frustration. 'I can't believe this is happening.'

'It was nothing, I swear. It didn't mean anything to either of us. We were just scratching an itch.'

'What?' Her shin hit against the edge of a chair. She grimaced in pain. 'You were willing to ruin our relationship for something as basic as scratching an itch? What kind of a man are you?'

'Oh, get off your bloody high-horse, Leigh, I'm a normal healthy male. We were supposed to be spending the week together, remember? I'd been looking forward to more time together, days, nights. But no, you put your blasted job before me, yet again, and went off on that management training week to that fancy hotel and left me to fend for myself. I'd have *fended* for myself just fine, but when a beautiful woman showed more than a bit of interest, it seemed like I was going to get some holiday fun after all.'

Holiday fun! Leigh wanted to reach into the phone, drag him through it and punch him till he bled and begged for mercy. She felt for the back of a chair, pulled it out and sat. There didn't seem to be anything for her to say. If he was waiting for her to say she understood and accepted his apology, he'd be waiting a long time.

She didn't know if she could forgive him; worse, she didn't know if she even wanted to. What was the point? Hadn't she already reached the conclusion their relationship had come to an end? An unedifying one as it turned out. She supposed she should be grateful he'd told her. Why had he? She frowned. They'd been talking about the allegation against him, hadn't they? 'Why did you tell me? Gina has vanished; I'd never have known.'

Was it why Gina had left so suddenly? Had she been struck with

ilt for sleeping with the boyfriend of the woman who'd kindly
fered her a room when she'd been desperate?

She was waiting for Matt to answer. When he didn't, she felt a
uiver of nausea. 'Why did you tell me?'

'You were never supposed to know about it. On Tuesday morn-
g, I got up early, spoke to her before she went off to work,
xplained it was a mistake, that I loved you and didn't want to
urt—'

'Didn't want to hurt me? It was a bit late for that, Matt!'

'I know.' He sounded genuinely contrite. 'She seemed okay with
, agreed it had been a bit of fun. It was only later, I realised she
adn't precisely said she wouldn't tell you, but I assumed she
ouldn't.'

'She didn't. I never saw her again. Is this why she left, Matt? Do
u know where she's gone?'

'No!'

His shout was loud enough to have Leigh move the phone from
er ear.

'I'm sorry,' he said. 'I don't know where she's gone, but I know
hat she did. Because it's her. Gina.'

Leigh wasn't stupid, but her thoughts were a maelstrom so she
uld be forgiven for taking longer than usual to make sense of
hat he'd said. When she did, she let out a nervous disbelieving
uffaw. 'Do I understand you correctly? Are you saying it was Gina
ho made the allegation of sexual assault against you?'

'She wrote to the school principal and told him I'd forced her to
ave sex.'

Forced? 'You raped her?'

'No! No, I swear to you, she came on to me, it was absolutely one
undred per cent consensual. I don't know why she's doing this, she
emed okay that morning when I was talking to her.'

'I don't understand any of this mess,' Leigh said slowly. 'What have the police said?'

Matt sighed heavily. 'That's the weird thing. She said in her letter she wasn't going to involve the police in deference to the school. The principal thought it was noble of her.'

'Of course he did! He wouldn't want his precious school embroiled in a scandal by being linked to a sexually predatory teacher.'

'That's so unfair; you know I'm not a sexual predator.'

Did she?

Matt didn't appear to notice her lack of response. 'I explained to the principal that I'd made a mistake, you were away, and I was stupidly tempted. He's going to talk to the board and see how they're going to proceed.'

Leigh was only half listening to him. 'Why did Gina move out so abruptly?'

'I don't know, do I? She seemed quite happy there, was behaving as if she owned the bloody place. I heard her on the phone to someone telling them how great her new rental was, going on about all the space, the stylish furniture. She called it a rental, Leigh, as she was renting the whole damn house, not just one room. I'd have thought she had no intention of leaving.'

'Until you and she—' She wanted to say *fucked*, but angry as she was, she couldn't bring herself to use the word, couldn't bring herself to think of the two of them having sex either. A vague question as to where they'd done it was batted away before it took root. She didn't want to know they'd done it on the sofa, or the floor of the living room, nor in any of the beds.

'She said nothing about moving out. I swear she seemed okay with it all. And the letter didn't arrive until the following Monday. A full week later, Leigh.'

It was odd Gina hadn't reported it to the police. She could have phoned as soon as it had happened, or if she was afraid of Matt, she could have left the house. It wasn't far to the police station; she could have gone that night or the morning after he'd left. 'Perhaps she was so traumatised—'

'Traumatised! It sounds like you believe her. I swear, I did nothing wrong.'

'Nothing wrong?'

He groaned. 'You know what I mean. I'm sorry, I know I shouldn't have cheated on you, but I promise you, me and Gina, it was totally consensual.'

'Right.' Although it was anything but. 'So what's going to happen with the school?'

'She didn't ring the police which is good and bad. Good, because if I can prove I'm innocent, it should be easier for the school to forget it. Bad, because if the police aren't investigating, how can I prove I did nothing wrong? It then comes down to my word against hers, but you know how that'll go. It'll always be a case of there's no smoke without fire and any hope I had of being the next principal would be shot to hell.'

He was fooling himself. Regardless of whether he proved his innocence or not, there would always be a whiff about him now. It wasn't a matter of being pure as the driven snow, it was more a case of being perceived as such. Matt, admitting to cheating on Leigh, had tainted his image even if he could prove Gina's allegation was a lie. He'd be kept as a teacher, probably, but that's as far as they would go.

'The letter is printed. No signature. I'm hoping the principal will be able to convince the board it's merely someone trying to cause trouble. I've been with the school ten years without the slightest hint of controversy. That should count for something.'

It should, but it probably wouldn't. 'Hopefully.' It was the best she could manage.

35

Leigh allowed Matt to talk for a few more minutes. Listened to him apologise again. As if saying sorry multiple times might work. It didn't.

Pleading tiredness, she finally hung up. She checked the locks on the door before going upstairs, then a minute later, to be sure, went down and checked them again. Paranoia was creeping over her, but the wave of exhaustion was the winner when she got into bed, sweeping her into a deep sleep for a few blissful hours of escape.

Friday dawned like it always did, the last day of the working week. It was usually brimful of promise and cock-eyed optimism for the weekend ahead. Leigh's weekend, already a disaster, was off to a poor start. As soon as she woke, rather than lying there staring at the ceiling and going over and over every word of the conversation with Matt, examining each and every utterance for tone, believability, credibility, she got up, slipped on a robe and went downstairs for breakfast.

Nibbling a slice of toast and sipping on a mug of strong coffee, she thought about her ex-boyfriend and his dilemma. *Ex-boyfriend.*

It sounded good to have that straight in her head. She wondered if Matt realised it was over between them, that it had been over before he'd cheated, that his liaison with Gina had simply confirmed Leigh was right.

It was odd, but she found herself separating Matt the ex-boyfriend, from Matt the superb, enthusiastic, totally committed teacher. Perhaps if she could find Gina, she could ask her to withdraw her allegation and save the latter. Leigh and Matt might be over, but it didn't mean she didn't care about his future.

Back to her original plan. Hire a tracing agent to locate Gina. She did an internet search and brought up the long list available. There didn't seem to be much difference between them. Finally, she chose the one with the 'no find, no fee' tagline. If they wanted money, they'd perhaps work harder.

There didn't seem any point in waiting. She dialled the number. Unfortunately, she quickly found she would indeed have to wait. The offices didn't open until nine, and it was still minutes before eight.

More coffee passed the time. Worrying over Matt had condensed Ledbetter into a corner of her head. He oozed out now and wrapped his fingers around every thought, so when she worried about Matt's future, Ledbetter was there screaming *what about me?* It was stress. There had been too much of it over the last couple of weeks. There was time enough to worry about Ledbetter on Monday, when she had to return to work and face the sea of condemnatory faces. Since there had been no word from the HR manager to say Ledbetter had contacted them or had been found, the situation wasn't going to have changed.

Leigh would have liked to have gone in on Monday and handed in her notice, but she wasn't a fool. Moving jobs after three months would indicate to a prospective employer that there'd been trouble of some sort. She'd need to wait at least three more months, assuming that is, they let her.

She mulled over this until nine, then dialled the tracing agency again. This time, she was in luck.

'Grafton Tracing Agency, how can we assist you?'

'Hello, I want to trace someone.'

'Okay, just hold for a moment, please, and I'll check which of our agents is free.'

Leigh hadn't given the agent much thought. Had she been asked what she expected, she'd probably have shrugged and said a badly dressed man with a hoarse, rough gravelly voice and nicotine-stained fingers, not the high-pitched voice of a young... maybe even very young... woman.

'Hi, I'm Spring, I believe you want to trace someone. Great, that's what we do.'

Leigh was tempted to be sarcastic. *Really, I thought you sold cheese.* And what kind of a name was *Spring*? Did she have siblings named Winter, Summer, and Autumn? Perhaps Leigh needed to go back to that clinic, do an extended version of anger management. She sighed.

If the annoyingly named and irritatingly vivacious Spring heard the sad sound, she didn't comment on it. 'Okay, let's get started. If you can tell me as much as you can about the person you're trying to locate.'

It didn't take long to tell her what little she knew about Gina. 'That's all I know.'

'Right, well it's not much to go on, but we've traced people on less.' Spring hummed for a few seconds. 'Okay, so this Philip Dunstable was the last to see her.'

'That I know of.'

'Okay, great. You don't happen to have an address?'

'Only a phone number. He did say he lived in Hornsey but that's
ll I know.'

'No matter, we can find him. And this workmate of Gina's,
obel, no surname?'

'No, but I think there's only one woman of that name working in
e café.'

'Okay. That's great. Right, I just need credit card details and
e're good to go.'

'Credit card details? Isn't it "no find, no fee"?'

'Exactly, but we've had experience where we find missing
eople, then our clients change their minds about wanting to
ontact them and refuse to pay. If we find this Gina Henderson, we
ke a fee regardless of whether you wish to pursue the contact or
ot.'

It seemed logical, and fair, but Leigh handed over her credit
rd details with extreme reluctance. 'Nothing will be taken until
m contacted?'

'That's it exactly. Right, great, we'll get on with this and be in
uch as soon as we know anything.'

Leigh couldn't resist replying, 'Great, that's great.'

Spring did indeed grate, but perhaps the woman was an excep-
onally good tracing agent and would be back with details of where
ina could be found. Leigh would go to her then, and ask her to
consider the allegation against Matt.

First – and Leigh couldn't help the doubt that ran through her
ead – she'd ask her if it was true.

36

Leigh had a whole day to fill. It was unlikely she'd hear back from the irritating Spring until the following week. The thought of sitting around, mulling over her myriad woes didn't appeal. Neither though, did meeting any of the girlfriends she hadn't seen for a while. Not the single ones who'd want to hit the bars and clubs in search of that elusive right man, or the married ones who'd be quizzing her on the progress of her relationship. If she told them it was over, she'd have to listen to their commiserations and a variety of comments all based on *there's plenty more fish in the sea*. There might even be a few who'd say, *I never liked him anyway*.

Nothing anyone said was going to make any difference. She simply didn't want to have to listen or justify her existence to anyone. Nor did she want to have to say, emphatically, every time that it had been a mutual decision. She had absolutely no intention of saying Matt had cheated on her with the damn lodger. The younger prettier lodger that she, Leigh, had brought into the home.

Because, how pathetic was that.

She filled the morning by clearing out every item Gina had

bought from the fridge and freezer. Leigh found herself grimacing as she picked up each, imagining Gina and Matt together. She took some satisfaction in firing each item into the rubbish bag with such unnecessary vigour one of the tinfoil containers perforated the plastic rubbish bag. Swearing loudly, she took another from the roll and squeezed the burst bag inside.

Late afternoon, she stood restlessly at the living room window and watched the occasional passer-by. She wondered about wandering along Haverstock Hill in search of the eccentric Beatrix. Leigh should have taken her phone number. Should have... story of her life.

It was a man passing outside that put the idea into her head. A stranger, but he bore a vague resemblance to Philip. She should have been flattered by his interest. Had it been loyalty to Matt that made her turn him down... misguided loyalty as it turned out... or something else? There'd been that flash of darkness she'd seen at the clinic, his underhanded behaviour in acquiring her address, turning up on her doorstep out of the blue, and that definitely out-of-line kiss.

All very good reasons for having nothing more to do with him.

But he'd been good company, making the interminable hours in the clinic pass quickly. Wasn't that exactly what she needed now? It was a crazy idea but the more she thought of it, the better it appeared. What harm could it do? It would pass a boring evening. She'd never need to see him again... unless she wanted to. That thought troubled her. He was a handsome man with undeniable magnetism, but she wasn't interested in a relationship with him.

Or was she? She sat back on the sofa and reached for her mobile. It was another minute of staring at it before she rang his number.

Half expecting it to go to voicemail, she was startled when it was answered immediately by a gruff, 'Dunstable.'

It struck her then: she had no idea what he did for a living. He'd been chatty at the clinic, but with a frown she realised he'd asked a lot of questions but had given little away. This was a crazy idea; she would hang up, forget it.

'Dunstable, can I help you?'

His voice sounded part irritated, part impatient. Strangely, it made him more human than his usual slightly oily approach. 'It's Leigh... Leigh Simon.'

'This is a surprise.'

She laughed. 'To me, too.' When there was no quick rejoinder, no flattering insistence he was delighted to hear from her, she hesitated, then decided to be honest... as much as she was willing to be. 'I find myself with a free evening and wondered if you'd like to meet up for a drink.'

'I, on the other hand, find myself puzzled.'

Leigh, who'd expected him to jump at the invitation, was taken aback. She was tempted to ask what happened to the brash Philip Dunstable she'd met but before she opened her mouth to say anything sarcastic, he spoke again.

'Okay. What time were you thinking?'

It was possibly too late to play it cool, but she tried. 'I'm busy till eight—'

'I thought you said you had a free evening?'

He was making this surprisingly hard. 'I do, but not till after eight.'

'Right.' He seemed to be giving her every utterance more consideration than necessary. 'As it happens, I've no plans tonight either. Did you have somewhere in mind?'

'The Windsor Castle, on Park Road. Do you know it?'

'Sure. Okay, I'll see you there at eight fifteen.'

He hung up without another word, leaving Leigh staring at her phone in bemusement. Had she completely misread the signals he'd been giving? Her thoughts were in such a turmoil she couldn't decide. It didn't matter; all she was interested in was filling in a few hours in pleasant company. *Nothing more.*

Despite this assertion, she found herself taking more care than usual in choosing what to wear that evening, throwing garment after garment on the bed before deciding on a dress she hadn't worn in a while. Matt had been more into casual nights out. Jeans and T-shirt type places. The pub where she was meeting Philip was one she used to frequent in her single days; it catered to a smarter clientele.

She was early, as she always was. The pub, as expected, was busy, clusters of drinkers standing, mingling, flirting. Leigh skirted the groups, stretching to see over shoulders to the edges of the venue for a free table. Seeing one, she hurried to take possession, sitting with a satisfied sigh.

It was ten minutes to the hour. She'd have liked a drink but going to the bar risked losing her table and there was no sign of any staff taking orders from the seats. Busy looking for staff, she didn't notice Philip until he loomed over her, his face more serious than she remembered.

'You're early.' He sat on the chair opposite, shuffling it closer to the table.

'I always am, it's one of my quirks. Never could do late.'

'Not a bad quirk to have.' He finally smiled, then looked around the pub. 'I've never been inside before.' He tilted his head towards the bar. 'A drink?'

'If I remember correctly, I'm the one who invited you, so I'll get the drinks in.'

'If you were remembering correctly, you'd admit I asked you first.' He got to his feet. 'What'll it be?'

It seemed childish to continue to argue. 'I'll have a white wine, please.' She watched him manoeuvre through the crowded pub to the bar. He moved with easy assurance... not quite a swagger, more a happy-in-his skin confidence. She noticed more than a few women turn to give him the once over. No doubt they would do as she'd have done, and search for the ring finger of his left hand. Seeing no ring, the more experienced among them would peer for the telltale narrowing, indicating one had been worn not too long before.

It was a couple of minutes before Philip returned. To Leigh's surprise, he held a bottle and two glasses. 'Seemed to be a good idea,' he said, placing the glasses on the table and taking his seat as he twisted the cap on the bottle. He poured. 'I hope Chenin Blanc is okay.'

'Yes, thanks.' Leigh picked up the wine, wondering if she should make a toast, feeling unaccountably nervous. She reminded herself this wasn't a date; she didn't have to make a good impression. It didn't matter if she said the wrong thing, if he didn't laugh at her jokes, or ever want to see her again.

'Where's what's his name tonight? I thought he came to London at the weekend.'

Leigh wished she could remember what she had and hadn't told him during the week in that blasted clinic. Far too much, she guessed. 'He does, usually, but he had obligations in the school where he teaches so he's staying in Salisbury this weekend.'

Philip tasted his wine and gave a slight grimace. 'Not the best, is it?' He put the glass down and sat back. Burying his hands in his jacket pockets, he looked at her. 'Seems to me you could have gone to Salisbury, and I'm wondering, since you didn't, if there's trouble in paradise.'

Leigh tried for an amused laugh. She knew she hadn't pulled it off when one of his eyebrows rose. 'You're reading too much into it.' She took a large mouthful of her wine. It was irritating to find he was right about both the wine and her relationship with Matt. 'I have plans for the weekend; it was only tonight I was at a loose end.

here's something about spending a Friday night alone I find a
tle depressing.'

'So you decided to ring me for companionship?'

'You could have said no.' She was surprised when he frowned
d looked away.

He picked up his glass and swallowed half the contents. 'I
ould have. It would have made a lot more sense and been a lot
fer.' He played with the stem of the glass before lifting it to his
s again and emptying it. Reaching for the bottle, he held it
wards her.

She'd barely touched her drink. 'I'm okay.' She waited for him
explain what he'd said and when he didn't, asked, 'What did you
ean, *a lot safer*?'

His smile was the flirtatious, sexy one she'd seen him use at the
inic. It was odd how he suddenly seemed a different man. Unset-
ng. Worrying. Like walking along a beach and finding you'd acci-
ntally wandered into quicksand.

'You're a very attractive woman, Leigh, the kind of woman to
ad a man astray.'

It was her turn to raise an eyebrow. She wasn't vain, nor
aware she was considered attractive, although she'd always
ought herself a little on the bland side. Attractive or bland, one
ing she was certain of: she wasn't the type of woman who drove
en wild.

She saw something in his eyes that she'd not seen before. Wari-
ess. What had changed between them since they'd last met only a
uple of days before? She was so tired of mysteries.

Picking up her glass, she drained it in two mouthfuls, then put it
own and got to her feet. 'This has been interesting, but I think it
as a mistake to meet. Thanks for the drink, Philip.'

She glared when he grabbed her arm. 'I think you'd better let
e go before I scream and make a scene.'

He took his hand away, raising both in surrender. 'I'm sorr
please don't go. Sit, I promise I'll explain.'

She looked towards the door, then shrugged. 'You have
minute, and if I don't like what you say, I'm gone.'

'Fine.' He poured her a glass of wine. 'You might need a drink.'

She ignored it.

He took a mouthful from his glass and cradled the bowl in h
hand. 'Why did you really ring me, Leigh?'

The question surprised her. 'I told you, I was at a loose end an
– she remembered the long day she'd spent trying to fill th
minutes – 'I wanted company. You'd helped pass the time in th
clinic; it seemed a good idea.' She threw him a sharp glance. 'No
I'm not so sure.'

He put his glass down and leaned forward, dropping his voic
so she had to move closer to hear. 'You're certain that's the on
reason?'

Leigh blinked, then shook her head. 'What other reason could
have, for goodness' sake? You're turning a simple meeting into som
kind of mysterious assignation.'

'So you're absolutely positive it had nothing to do with Bernar
Ledbetter?'

37

It was so unexpected that all Leigh could do was stare, her mouth and eyes both wide open. Neither of them had spoken about their reasons for doing an anger management course so she knew she'd never mentioned her manager's name in conversation at the clinic. 'Why would it have anything to do with him? I don't understand; how do you know about Bernard Ledbetter? I know I never mentioned him.'

Philip's expression was shuttered. 'No, you didn't.'

'Then how do you know?' She frowned, trying to understand. 'You don't work for Lancaster International, do you?'

This drew a smile. 'No, I don't.' He shook his head. 'It was a mistake to agree to meet you, I should never have come.' His eyes swept the crowded premises. 'I could get into serious trouble if I'm seen with you.'

At this, she laughed, genuinely amused. 'We're straying into James Bond territory here. Next, you'll be telling me you work for MI5.'

'No, not MI5. I work for the MPB.'

He had to be joking; her laugh however was a little less amused. 'What's that then, a branch of *Men in Black*?'

He glanced around again before he spoke, leaning a little closer so there was only a short stretch of table between them. She could feel his breath brushing her face when he spoke. 'It's the Missing Persons Bureau, Leigh. I'm a detective inspector.'

Stunned, she sat as far back as she could and glared at him. 'You're a police officer!'

It was his turn to laugh in amusement. 'You sound shocked. It's a perfectly acceptable job, you know.'

Of course it was, and it wasn't his fault her recent dealings with the police had been so disastrous. 'You don't strike me as typical.' She lifted her hand and waved a finger up and down. 'Designer suits, expensive shirts; I didn't think police were so well paid.'

'They aren't, but I have a sister who works in retail who is happy to pass on her discounts to me.'

Leigh wanted to ask where his sister worked, she would have liked to have had a long conversation about clothes. Anything rather than asking him what he knew about Bernard Ledbetter. She was afraid to ask, afraid of the answer; there wasn't enough room in her head for more angst. 'I should go,' she said, looking towards the exit and wondering if she'd manage to manoeuvre her way through the mass of customers who were drinking and laughing without a care in the world.

'The case landed on my desk this morning. Perhaps you can understand then why I was suspicious when you rang me to ask to meet. You'd emphatically rejected my invitation when I asked you to go for a drink at the clinic. You ignored my last message. Then suddenly you contact me. What was I supposed to think?'

'I promise you; I had no idea you were a police officer or that you'd be in any way involved with the search for Bernard Ledbetter. How could I? You never mentioned what you did.' She reached for her glass and took a mouthful. 'I enjoyed your company in the clinic and tonight, as I said, I was at a loose end and needed some pleasant company.'

'Pleasant company?' He looked unsure of what to make of this.

'Yes.' She smiled at him. 'But since it seems you know more about me than I'd expected, tell me what you meant about *the case*.'

Philip sat back, picked up his glass and swirled the wine around without drinking. 'Local police are required to submit missing person details to the bureau after seventy-two hours.' He stared into his glass. 'I know all about your dealings with him, your allegation against him, the reason you were at the anger management course.'

Leigh reached for her glass and gulped a large mouthful. 'My colleagues in Lancaster International think he left because of my allegation. Nobody believes me, but I'm not making it up. My crime was not to act the first time he leered at me. I was the new kid on the block, trying to fit in, so I ignored it until I couldn't any more.'

'You assaulted him.'

She looked up at that. 'No, I didn't! Or at least' – her shoulders slumped in defeat – 'I tried to hit him when I caught him peering down my shirt, but I missed.'

Philip looked at her pityingly. 'Most people aren't aware you don't need to make contact; a raised fist is enough to be classified as common assault. According to the report, Mr Ledbetter refused to press charges.'

'Yes, he took great pleasure in that,' she sneered. 'He was the noble forgiving victim and I the aggressive offender.' A burst of laughter from a nearby group of people grabbed their attention for a few seconds. Leigh envied them. It had been a long time since she'd experienced such careless enjoyment. 'Some of my colleagues were making my life hell which is why I took this week off.' She sighed heavily. 'I've decided the job isn't for me anyway but I need to stay a few more months, if I can. It's not going to be easy; meanwhile, I bet the sleazy bastard is sunning himself somewhere in Spain. Probably laughing himself silly at my predicament.'

'I shouldn't be talking to you about this. Hell, I shouldn't even be here.' Philip was still holding the glass; he put it down and leaned forward once more. 'Your theory is unlikely. The police did some preliminary investigations before passing the case to the bureau. The HR manager, Collins, said Ledbetter's absence was totally out of character so despite no sign of foul play the police took it seriously from the off. There's been no activity on his credit card, or his phone. And disputing your idea he's sunning himself somewhere in Spain, his passport was found in his apartment.'

Leigh's image of Ledbetter lying by a pool with his pasty skin turning an unpleasant shade of red, dissolved in the face of Philip's words. 'Okay, so he's still in this country somewhere, waiting it out to make me suffer.'

'Leaving aside the fact this would make him out to be some sort of psycho, the police have checked with his bank. There have been no withdrawals from his account.'

Leigh felt tears prickle. Had her allegation forced Ledbetter to do something desperate? For the first time, she wished she'd let his behaviour pass, shut it away with all his other lecherous moments. Those she could eventually have put behind her... but this, to be held responsible for a man's death, would be impossible to forget. She was mulling over her dilemma when something Philip said struck her as odd. 'What did you mean when you said you shouldn't be seen with me, shouldn't be talking to me?'

Another shout of laughter, more raucous, drew his attention. Or he was using it as an excuse to delay answering. When he turned back to look at her, his expression was shuttered. Now she could see the policeman and wondered why she hadn't before.

'You're not a stupid woman, Leigh. Think of it. You accused Ledbetter of inappropriate behaviour. Nobody was able to corrobo-

te your claims. You attempted to punch him. There's no doubt
.is would all have gone into your personnel file. You're still in your
-obationary period, you must have been concerned your actions
ould impact the company's decision to keep you on the staff
·not.

'The human resources manager recorded some reports of anger
sues; combined with the attempt to hit Ledbetter, it was sufficient
·r her to demand you attend that anger management course.' He
oked at her intently. 'Then Ledbetter disappears.'

Leigh held his gaze as she felt the colour leech from her face.
·ell me you're joking!' When he said nothing, she clenched a fist
id banged it on the table with enough force to make their glasses
ttle. 'This is unbelievable. You're telling me I'm under suspicion.
hat they think I might have killed him. Seriously?'

'You're a person of interest in the investigation. As such, I
iouldn't be getting involved—'

She huffed an unamused laugh. 'Rest assured, you're not getting
volved.' She picked up her bag and jacket. 'It seems this was a bad
·ea all around. But it's easy to fix; I'll take myself off and you won't
·ar from me again.'

The pub was more crowded than it had been when she'd
itered. She pushed through, forcing space where there wasn't any,
·noring the slightly inebriated comments that followed her as she
ruggled to reach the door. Outside, she stood trembling before
king off down the street as fast as jerky steps could take her, afraid
iilip would attempt to follow.

It would have been faster to take a tube home, but when she
·w a taxi, its vacant light seemed to call to her and she waved fran-
·ally, reaching for the door almost before it had pulled to a stop.

'Gaisford Street,' she said and sat back. She shut her eyes,
·eling the tears burn. *Damn him and every other blasted man who
is determined to make her life a misery.*

She was mentally kicking herself for having contacted him i
the first place. If she hadn't, she'd never have known about his *cas*
She'd never have known they were looking at her with suspiciou
eyes.

He'd mentioned reading reports. Did he know about her dea
ings with the local police? Colour bloomed in her cheeks. He'
have had a good laugh at them no doubt.

When the taxi pulled up outside her house, she stared at it fc
so long the driver turned with an impatient grunt. 'You want to pa
and get out, miss?'

'Sorry.' There she was again, apologising. She paid the far
adding a tip she didn't want to give. A slam of the taxi door was th
only indication of her annoyance... with the driver, with herse
with everything.

Inside, she double checked the locks on the door befor
heading straight for the stairs and trudging upward. It seeme
better to leave the lights out so she couldn't see the reflection of th
stupid, stupid woman in any of the mirrors. She checked h
mobile for any messages from Matt, unsurprised to see nothin
What was there left to say?

She didn't bother to clean her make-up off, merely dropping h
clothes on the floor where she stood and crawling under the duve
pulling it over her head, looking for comfort in the darkness. The
wasn't any of course. No comfort anywhere. Ledbetter – she wa
struggling now to remember him as a lecherous creep, his featur
changing, becoming sadder, softer, his eyes looking upon her wit
fondness, his voice now sounding supportive, encouraging.

Had she got it wrong? Matt had said she'd been more stresse
since she'd started with Lancaster International. Was that it? Ha
stress twisted her vision to make her see things that weren't ther
Was that why nobody else had complained about his inappropria
behaviour... because there hadn't been any?

It would explain why he'd taken time off... he'd been devastated by her allegations. She didn't know anything about him. Had never tried to get to know him. Perhaps, contrary to the view she had of him, he was emotionally fragile, and her allegations the last straw.

How could she cope if they found his body, and she was to blame? She didn't think she could.

38

Leigh didn't sleep. She stayed hidden under the duvet, waiting for daylight to brighten the room, if not her thoughts. Then she threw the covers back and crawled wearily from the bed. The weekend stretched ahead of her, but this time she'd keep to herself. A safer, if uncomfortable, place to be with her churning thoughts.

Saturday was spent in front of the TV, drinking tea and eating whatever she had in the fridge with little desire for anything except for something to do to pass the time.

She ignored a message from Matt asking if she'd managed to get in touch with Gina, ignored messages from friends asking if she was free for a chat, and deleted a message from Philip without reading it, blocking him in case he tried to contact her again.

When her mobile rang late afternoon, she looked at it listlessly. The number wasn't one she knew. She ignored it. A beep a few seconds later told her whoever it was had left a message and she picked it up to see who it was, more to pass the time than from any real interest. But when she saw who it was, she jerked upright. *Spring!*

Leigh hadn't expected to hear from the tracing agent until

Monday at the earliest. Could she really have found the missing Gina already?

When she pressed to return the call, she got a message asking her to leave her name and number and Spring would get back to her as soon as possible. *Damn!* She left a message, then sat staring at the phone, willing it to ring. And preferably with good news. She was due some, wasn't she? For goodness' sake, could her life get any worse?

When ten minutes passed without a call, she rang again, left another, slightly more desperate message. 'It's Leigh Simon again, I'm really keen to hear what you've found out so please get back to me. It doesn't matter how late; I'll be waiting.'

She sat with the phone in her hand, the TV on mute, feeling numb, weariness soaking through to her bones, making them heavy. The next hour passed in a daze only broken by the need to check the phone every few minutes in case she might have missed the call, in case she'd lost the ability to hear as well as think.

It was nearly ten before she dropped the phone on the seat beside her and got to her feet. The room was warm, but she felt chilled. A hot drink would probably have helped. Whisky seemed a better option. She sat again, a tumbler half full of amber liquid in one hand, the phone once more in the other. Another hour passed. The glass was empty, the chill replaced by a pleasant warmth. When the phone rang, Leigh stared at it, unwilling to dispel the hard-acquired fragile calm by hearing whatever it was the tracing agent had to tell her. Remembering the lie Gina had told Philip, she knew it was going to be bad news.

'Hello.'

'Hi, it's Spring, sorry to be so late getting back to you, it's been one of those days.'

Leigh didn't have sympathy to spare. Nor was she in the mood for chit-chat. 'You found Gina?'

'Not precisely.' Spring proceeded to relate all she had done since speaking to Leigh the previous day... the series of computer checks, phone calls to various government departments, and what sounded like hundreds of internet searches. If Leigh had been under any illusion that being a tracing agent was an exciting job, by the end of Spring's account she was enlightened. She'd have liked to have asked the woman to cut to the end but hadn't the heart to stop the enthusiastic monologue. Spring's voice was lilting, hypnotic. Leigh's eyelids drooped.

'There's no mistake. I double checked.'

What? Leigh shook off the sleep creeping over her, getting to her feet to speed up the process. 'Sorry, there was a connection issue, I missed that last bit. Can you repeat what you said?'

'I said there was no mistake, I—'

Leigh clenched her free hand. 'Not that, before that, what is there no mistake about?'

'Right.' Spring sounded puzzled and there was less enthusiasm when she spoke again. 'I told you we traced Gina Henderson to an address in Glasgow.'

Had she? Leigh wiped a hand over her face, pressing fingers into her eyes and rubbing hard. 'Sorry, okay, and after that?'

'I told you, she's dead. The police are investigating.'

Leigh staggered backwards and collapsed onto the sofa. 'Dead!' Leigh remembered the bubbly butterfly-like woman. Whatever her faults, and Leigh probably didn't know half, Gina didn't deserve her life to end so terribly. 'Poor Gina, that's so awful. I remember Isobel telling me she'd come from Glasgow before starting work in the café. Maybe she was homesick and decided to return.'

'No,' Spring said sharply. 'You've missed some of what I said.'

'Gina is dead. What else?'

'Gina Henderson *is* dead. The problem is, she died over three months ago.'

eigh wondered if she'd fallen asleep again. 'What did you say?'

Spring huffed an exasperated sigh. 'I said Gina Henderson died
over three months ago.'

This couldn't be happening. 'It has to be a coincidence surely;
it's not an uncommon name.'

'No, I agree, it's not, but I didn't simply go with the name.' The
underlying *I'm not an idiot, I know how to do my job* remained unsaid.
'I got her National Insurance number from the café who were only
too happy to help after she'd let them down so badly. It didn't take
me long to track down her previous employer. The real Gina
worked in a nightclub for several years. A quick phone call to the
premises in question got me the rest of the facts. They're still in
shock over her death.

'My contact in the Strathclyde police is very interested in
hearing more about your Gina. They're treating Henderson's death
as suspicious and have been looking for a woman who was lodging
with her for a few months before she died. This is the first lead
they've had.'

'Right.' For the life of her, Leigh couldn't think of anything els
to say.

'They'll be looking for her now, but I can go places they can't, s
I'll keep looking, assuming that's what you want me to do.'

Was it? Leigh was feeling overwhelmed. She would have like
to have forgotten all about Gina... or whatever her name was... bu
that would mean casting Matt adrift. And it was Leigh's fault. If sh
hadn't invited Gina into their lives, he'd never have becom
ensnared in her web of intrigue.

Whatever had made her ex-lodger decide to leave, she'd no
done so without leaving chaos in her wake – the lie she'd tol
Philip, the lie she'd told the principal of Matt's school, the mone
she owed the staff in the café. Leigh was almost embarrassed t
have been swayed by Gina's exotically colourful exterior. It was
difficult step to acknowledge that behind that pretty facade la
something vile. Leigh remembered the intruder and gave thanks fc
her new door locks. She should probably be grateful she'd escape
a similar end to the real Gina. 'Yes, keep looking please, but don
take risks. It seems the woman is capable of anything.'

Spring laughed. 'Don't be fooled by my fluffy voice. I'm ex-arm
a professional boxer in my spare time, with a black belt in judo.
can take care of myself.' She hung up, leaving Leigh to stare at th
phone in bemusement.

Sometimes, a brain can overload, decide it's not going to proces
anything else. So it was with Leigh. This last twist was the end c
her capability. In a daze, she headed upstairs and got ready for be
a routine done without thought. Then she was under the duve
burying herself in its warmth.

* * *

The brain fog allowed Leigh to sleep most of the night. Once, a noise pushed its way through... a distant rattle. It might have been someone at the front door, trying to enter, but in her half-asleep state, she thought of the new lock. She was safe.

When the morning light woke her, she cursed her stupidity in not shutting the curtains the previous night. She rolled onto her side, pulling the duvet over her head. But sleep had ebbed and after a few minutes of desperately trying to coax it to return she gave up. She lay for a while, thinking about what the tracing agent had told her. Gina... Leigh had got her completely wrong.

Throwing a robe on, she went downstairs. At the front door, she stopped and stared, a faint memory of a dream about someone trying to get in, flitting through her head. It had been a dream, hadn't it? Unlocking the door, she opened it and examined the two locks. They still looked shiny new. If someone had tried with the old keys, there'd be scratch marks, wouldn't there?

She was being silly. It *had* been a dream.

Normally on a Sunday, she and Matt would have gone to their local pub for breakfast and afterwards they'd sit for hours with the papers, swapping sections back and forth, she folding each neatly, laughing at his inability to do the same. Her smile at the memory quickly faded.

There was no reason she couldn't go on her own. The breakfast would be as tasty, the newspapers as filled with news and gossip as usual, the pub as busy. With couples and families, and the odd sad lonely person... the ones she used to feel smugly sorry for. She refused to join their ranks that morning.

Instead, she sat with a coffee and wondered where it had all gone wrong, examining the what ifs and if onlys. It would have been nice to have been able to blame everything on Gina but that would have been foolish. She wasn't to blame for Leigh's work woes, nor could Gina be held responsible for Matt's cheating behaviour.

Leigh looked at her mobile. Matt needed to be told the news about Gina; it would help his case to prove she wasn't who she said she was, that she might be responsible for the death of the real Gina. It wouldn't change everything; he couldn't recant telling the principal he'd cheated on Leigh. Couldn't paint a picture of himself as being an upright, honest man, one who'd be a credit to the school as the next principal. Poor Matt; that wasn't ever going to happen now.

She wondered how long it would take him to blame her for inviting the evil woman into her home.

40

Despite Leigh's worries about returning to work the next day, it would be a relief to get back, be busy, not spend another day frantically trying to occupy herself. Thanks to Philip, she knew Bernard hadn't returned. No doubt, as a result, she'd have to suffer harsh comments and sharp glances. She could put up with it for three months... just three and then she'd leave. Put it all behind her. Even Matt.

Maybe it was time to see more of the world. She could rent out the house. London rental prices were crazy; she'd have enough to live on somewhere abroad. Somewhere sunny perhaps.

It was something to think about, rather than any of her troubles. *All of her troubles.*

Late afternoon, when the doorbell rang, she wouldn't have cared if the devil himself was at the door so tired she was of her restless company. But when she opened the door and saw two stern-faced strangers, one of whom held out police identification, she wasn't so sure.

'DI McLeod,' he said. He waved his identification towards the other man. 'DI Riley.' He slid the card into the inside pocket of his jacket. 'We're with Strathclyde police; we believe you might be able to help us with a case we're investigating.'

When the tracing agent had mentioned a contact with the Scottish police, Leigh had stupidly assumed any information passing between them was confidential. It appeared not.

'You'd better come in.' She stood back and waved them into the living room. 'Would you like coffee or something?' She didn't want to give them anything, she wanted them to say whatever it was, ask any questions they needed to ask, and leave. Her recent dealings with the police had left a sour taste in her mouth.

'Coffee would be good,' McLeod said, looking around the room as he spoke. He turned back to her. 'Black for both of us, thanks.'

'Have a seat, I won't be long.' What she'd liked to have done, was opened the front door and legged it. She wondered what would happen if she did. The Kentish Road police would be involved. She held a hand over her mouth to stifle the laugh as she imagined their faces. Seriously, she was losing it.

With a shake of her head to get her brain back in the right groove, she made the required coffee. The whisky bottle was on the counter; it was tempting to lash a drop into her mug, but she resisted.

'Here you go,' she said, putting the mugs on the coffee table within reach of the two men.

Deciding to take the lead, she sipped her coffee and put it down. 'I assume you're here about Gina Henderson... or should I say the woman who was calling herself that when she lived here.'

McLeod picked up his mug and blew noisily into it before taking an even noisier slurp. 'That's it,' he said, replacing the mug on the table and straightening to look at her. 'You seem unusually keen to find your ex-lodger.'

It wasn't a question, so Leigh sipped her coffee and waited.

'Keen enough to pay a tracing agent to find her.'

It still wasn't a question.

McLeod smiled as if acknowledging her win. 'Can you tell us why?'

It was so tempting to say she could, and nothing more, but it was probably a bad idea to play games with the police. 'Gina... or whatever her name is... moved in, full of enthusiasm for her room and the facilities. When I came back from a week away, she'd moved out. Initially, I wanted to find her to ask why she'd left so abruptly.'

'How long had she been living here?'

'A couple of weeks.' She knew the questions they'd ask so preempted them. 'I didn't know her well. She was the barista in a café I go to. When I heard she was looking for accommodation and was finding it hard to get anything she could afford I offered her my spare bedroom.' Hindsight was wonderful. As she spoke, all Leigh could think about was what a stupid idea it had been. 'It was a spontaneous gesture. I had the room; she had the need.' A few sips of her coffee gave her time to think before speaking again. 'She was bubbly, vivacious, full of what my mother would call joie de vivre. I suppose I thought it would be nice to have someone like that living with me.'

'You live here alone?' It was the other officer who spoke.

'Yes.' It was time to tell them about Matt. 'My ex-boyfriend, Matt—' It was her first time to use the term, not just think it. It made it more shockingly real. 'He used to come up for the weekend.' She got lost in her thoughts, letting the silence linger.

Too long. McLeod sat forward. 'You said *initially*.'

Leigh blinked. 'What?'

'You said initially you wanted to find her to ask why she'd left so abruptly. So what changed?'

Nothing. Everything. 'I had to go away unexpectedly. Matt and I were still together then. He had a week off, so he stayed here until the Tuesday.' *Stayed there and took the opportunity to shag the lodge* Wasn't it understandable to be a little bitter about it despite he acknowledgement their relationship had been over for a long time

'Ms Simon?'

She'd got lost in her thoughts again. 'Sorry. It's been a difficu time. What changed?' Maybe her long sad sigh said more tha words because she suddenly saw understanding in both officer eyes.

It was McLeod who put it into words. 'I'm guessing Matt an Gina had a liaison, am I right?'

'A liaison.' Such an innocuous word. So much better than th alternatives. 'Yes, they did. He said they got drunk together and or thing led to another.' She shook her head. 'Makes it all sound s inevitable, doesn't it? Maybe it was. She is very attractive. Me an Matt... we hadn't faced it, but really our relationship was on its la legs, had been for a while.' She dragged up a smile. 'Doesn't make any easier to accept though.'

'No, it wouldn't.' McLeod frowned. 'I'm still unsure why yo wanted to find her so desperately.'

'It wasn't for me. I would be happy never to see her again.' Sh reached for her coffee, took a sip and kept the mug cupped in he hands. 'It seems this woman, whoever she is, likes to make troubl She told a friend who called around that she and I were lovers.'

'And you weren't?' McLeod asked, reaching for his coffee again.

'No, we weren't. It was an odd thing to say but not troubl some. However, when she wrote to Matt's boss and said Matt ha raped her, that was different. He's a teacher. The principal had n choice but to immediately suspend him.' Leigh had wondere why Gina hadn't wanted to go to the police; now she understoo Not to protect the school as she'd intimated, but to protect herse But it didn't matter, she'd caused enough damage without. 'Ma might be a cheating prick, but he would never force himself on woman, drunk or sober. I'd like to find Gina and help clear his name.'

Riley put his empty mug down and looked at her. 'Sounds like this woman was out to cause trouble for you but I don't understand why. You were extraordinarily kind to have offered her accommodation.'

'I don't understand either. The more I find out about her, the more I realise I was totally misled by the shiny, glittery wrapper she wore like a second skin. Underneath, it seems there was something rotten. And if she was involved in the death of that woman in Glasgow, maybe even something evil.'

The two detectives exchanged glances before McLeod spoke again. 'Neighbours said there had been a woman living with the real Gina Henderson for a few weeks before she died but there was no sign of her. Our forensic people pulled some fingerprints from the spare bedroom but we'd no luck with them.'

'So you've no idea who she is, or where she is.'

'No, but thanks to you, we've broadened our net and our colleagues in the Met will be looking for her too. Now, if you could tell us everything you can remember, any detail, no matter how small.'

Leigh told them about Isobel and what she'd learned about Gina's previous accommodation. 'Isobel works in a café called The Coffee Cup. It's not far from King's Cross station, on St Chad's Street.'

'Great.' McLeod took a note of the name. 'Anything else?'

'Not that I can think of. I really didn't know her that well.' She frowned suddenly.

'Something?'

'Probably nothing, but something I thought was odd at the time. She'd cooked extra food and had it frozen in portions. It was still in the freezer. Plus, it looked as if she'd recently done a shop in our local deli; there were packets of food left in the fridge. I couldn't understand why she'd do that, then leave, taking none of it with her.'

McLeod tapped the pen he was using on his notebook and gave her a sharp look. 'Is that why you thought she hadn't?'

41

Leigh had foolishly assumed they hadn't known about her dealings with the Kentish Road police. McLeod and Riley had lulled her into thinking they were sympathetic. How stupid she'd been. She saw their sharp eyes watch her, waiting for her reaction.

'You obviously know all about my dealings with the local police. That hand sticking from the soil was realistic and scary. Gina had vanished. It seemed a logical step to ring the police. I don't think I was wrong in putting two and two together. It was a relief when they didn't add up to four.'

'There's no criticism intended, Ms Simon. Did you ever discover who played the trick on you?'

'No, I thought it might have been Matt; he has an odd sense of humour at times, but he insists he didn't.'

'Pity. It's good to get things cleared up. Strings neatly knotted and all that.'

She'd so many strings, they were strangling her. 'It's fairly far down my list of worries.' She shuffled to the edge of her seat, hoping they'd get the hint, finish up and leave. 'It was a joke in poor taste, that's all. Probably neighbourhood kids thinking it was a hilarious thing to do.'

'We'll need to talk to Mr... what's Matt's surname?'

'Gibbs.' She gave his address and phone number. Matt was going to be thrilled to have the police descend on him. Another restless shuffle. 'If that's all.'

'Yes, we've taken up enough of your time. Thank you, that's all been very helpful.' McLeod reached into his inside pocket and withdrew a business card. 'If you remember anything else, or if you hear from Gina, you can get me on this number, okay?' He put the card on the table next to his empty mug.

Leigh looked at the card and frowned. 'She has no reason to contact me.' She got to her feet, followed in succession by the detectives. At the front door, her hand on the catch, she turned to them as a thought struck her. 'What about the tracing agent; is it okay to keep employing her?'

'We've no proof this woman is guilty of any crime, Ms Simon, she's merely a person of interest in our investigation so it's difficult to insist you keep out of it. I think you're wasting your money but that's up to you. I know Spring Dooley, she's a well-regarded tracing agent and no fool. She won't get involved in anything illegal.' He met his partner's raised eyebrow with a smile. 'Perhaps I should say anything *too* illegal.'

Leigh stood in the doorway, watching as they walked down the street. She'd have liked to have asked if they were going to Kentish Town Police Station, but she supposed it was logical that they'd do so. Everything she'd said would be shared. They'd know she'd hired a tracing agent... and why. They'd know all about Matt cheating on her. They would, Philip would. She could imagine him sneering when he heard.

She slammed the front door shut. The detectives would hear,

aybe they'd look back and wonder why she was so annoyed. Why as she? She didn't care what Philip or any of them thought of her.

The thought of talking to Matt didn't appeal, but she needed to t him know what was happening. Back in the living room, she cked up her phone and dialled his number. It was answered on e first ring.

'Have you found her?'

She pictured his face creased in lines of worry. For his job, his osition in the school. Was one of those lines caused by worry for er... for cheating on her, for sending her to search for a maniac... were they all for himself? 'And hello to you too.'

'Sorry, sorry, Leigh. The stress is getting to me.'

Had he always been so self-centred? So obsessed with all things att? And had she been so infatuated with him that she'd never oticed? 'It's not exactly a picnic for me either.'

'I said I was sorry.'

Yes, he had, and, as always, he thought that one useless word ade everything okay. 'Fine, anyway listen. I have good news and d news. The good news is the tracing agent I hired found Gina. ne bad news, unfortunately, is she's dead.'

'Dead! Well, that's a relief.'

Leigh gripped the phone tighter. 'What?'

'Come on, it makes it much easier for me. I can persuade the incipal it was a story made up to discredit me.'

Leigh had told him Gina was dead and all he could think of was mself. She felt as though she'd been going around with her eyes ut for the last year. They were wide open now. What a pig!

'Unfortunately, that wasn't my only bad news. The second bit is e woman they found dead in Glasgow is the real Gina Henderson. e no idea who the woman you screwed is, but the police are oking for her in connection with the death of the real Gina.'

An indrawn gasp was followed by silence before the breath was released in a long hiss. 'This is a joke, yes? Tell me you're kidding.'

Leigh enjoyed telling him it was all true. 'I had two detectives from the Strathclyde police here today asking me about her. No doubt they'll want to talk to you at some stage; after all, you were intimate with her, weren't you?' Leigh took a ridiculous amount of pleasure in rubbing it in. 'I gave them your address and phone number. No doubt they'll call.'

'You're enjoying this, aren't you?'

'Only a little. Mostly I'm finding it all skin-crawlingly awful. I must go, I'm off out for dinner. Take care of yourself, Matt, although you don't need me to tell you that, you always do. Always did.'

She hung up, trembling. *Bastard!*

42

Leigh swung her legs up onto the sofa and plumped a cushion behind her head. How had she never realised Matt was such a shit? A year wasted. She supposed it could have been worse; there was a time when she'd hoped to marry him. The thought now made her nauseous. Or maybe the incredible weariness was to blame. She felt the weight of it pushing her into the sofa and reaching into her brain, then, as if helium balloons had been attached to every worry, they floated away, leaving a huge void she fell into with a sigh of relief.

It was still light when she woke and a glance at her watch told her she'd not been asleep long enough to do much good. In fact, she felt worse, groggy and disorientated, until all the balloons burst, and the worries came slamming painfully back.

Worries and reality. They worked together to make her head pound. She stayed where she was, her eyes shut. Reality. Going back to work wasn't possible. How could she face them, the many who would judge and blame, the ones who would pity? Her job was stressful enough, adding to it was bound to lead to mistakes and whereas leaving after three months would raise questions at future interviews, at least she'd be going with a spotless work record.

Leigh swung her feet to the floor and stood, her expression grim but resolute. It was the best thing to do. She had no doubt that the human resources manager would agree, almost smiling as she imagined Janet Collins' relief.

The decision made the future suddenly clearer. The idea to rent out the house and travel was solidifying from the vapours of the vague idea she'd had before. From *she couldn't possibly*, she'd come almost 180 degrees to *it was the perfect solution*. A little scary perhaps, but no scarier than what she'd had to face during the last couple of weeks.

She found herself humming as she opened the fridge, drifting to silence when she viewed the empty shelves. The following day, she'd go out and shop. That night, it would be a takeaway. Even the idea made her mouth water and she pulled open a drawer to search for the menu. It wasn't difficult to decide, she generally... in fact always... ordered the same thing. Matt, who chose something different each time, found it amusing that her taste was so narrow.

Luckily, she no longer had to be concerned with Matt's criticism. She rang and placed her order. Twenty minutes later, with the prawn poncho khana keeping warm in the oven, she sat and tucked into the chicken chot potti starter. It was as good as ever. Why choose anything else?

Her decision to leave her job put her in a celebratory mood. It was as good an excuse as any to open a bottle. The wine was good, the food delicious and Leigh felt her mood lift with every minute.

She'd told the police all she knew about Gina. If the tracing agent found out any more information, Leigh would ask her to pass it on to the police. Perhaps too, she'd ask her to communicate whatever she knew with Matt. Then she wouldn't have to speak to him again which would be better for them both.

The following day, she'd pack up the few things he'd left behind and send it to him with a message telling him to give anything she'd left in his place to charity. And that would be it. A clean break. Her only regret was it hadn't happened months before.

When she'd finished the meal, wiping up the last of the sauce with the final piece of naan bread, she filled her glass, left the dirty plates to be sorted the next day, and went back to the living room.

There was only one niggling worry remaining. Bernard Ledbetter. Was his body going to turn up somewhere? Hanging from a tree in the depths of some woodland? Washed up on some beach? And how would she feel if it did?

If he had been emotionally fragile and her allegations the last straw, was she to blame?

It had been he who'd gone racing to the HR office; did he really think Leigh wasn't going to explain why she'd tried to punch him? Or had he not realised how offensive his behaviour was? Because it was. *Wasn't it?*

Leigh sipped her wine. She remembered the first few times, the accidental brushing against her, the slightly off remark, the lingering glances. Did he think she didn't notice? Worse, did he think because she didn't complain that she liked his creepy attention? In retrospect, ignoring it was the wrong thing to do. If she hadn't, if she'd dealt with it there and then, things might have been different.

Too late now.

She was still mulling over how it would have gone if she'd taken a step to deal with it earlier when the doorbell rang. Her head jerked towards the door, heart immediately racing. Matt? Unlikely. The last time she'd had an unannounced caller it had been Philip.

She put her glass on the table and got to her feet. The bell chimed again. Impatient, same as last time.

Unlocking the door, she opened it a chink to peer through.

'You should have a safety chain, Leigh, and check who it is before you open the door. Any thug worth his salt could push inside.'

She glared at him. 'I guessed it was you. Go away, Philip.'

'No wait, please, I really need to talk to you.'

She didn't want to talk to him but found herself widening the gap another few inches. 'You can have a minute.'

Philip laughed. 'Can't I come in? I swear I'll only stay a few minutes.' He looked around. 'It's not the best place for a conversation.'

Leigh hesitated. After all, what harm could it do? 'Right, you can come into the hallway.'

It wasn't her wisest move. The hallway was narrow. Philip's broad frame took up more space than it should. She took a step backwards, then, determined not to appear intimidated or scared, she folded her arms and lifted her chin to meet his gaze. 'What do you want?'

He ran a hand through his hair, his eyes flicking to the open doorway to the living room. 'I think you'd better sit, Leigh. You're not going to like what I have to say.'

43

—————

igh tried to read his expression, but unlike the easily read rtatious one he'd given her in the clinic or the worried one in the ab, that night the shutters were down. There was something about s eyes that made her nervous, even a little scared. It was safer to knowledge that. It would help keep her wits about her.

He was right about one thing; it would be better to sit. Safer o... Her mobile phone was on the sofa.

'Right, you can come in, but this better not be a wind-up.' She d the way, taking her seat, her hand covering her mobile, fingers eling their way. Her safety net.

Philip sat on the sofa opposite. 'Seriously, you need to up your curity. New locks were a good start, but take my advice and get an arm that works and a safety chain. You shouldn't be so lax.'

Leigh froze. How did he know she'd had the locks replaced? e'd never mentioned doing so. Never. The only way he could ow was if he'd tried the old keys. The only spare set had been ven to Gina.

Only then did Leigh realise what she'd forgotten to tell the rathclyde police. The name of the last person to have seen Gina before she'd left. *Philip*. What had he said about the day he'd calle with her Kindle? That Gina had taken a long time to open the doc so long he'd almost given up. Had being kept waiting stirred up h temper? Had it exploded then when it wasn't Leigh but Gina who answered the door? He was a big man, she was a tiny woman, wouldn't have taken much.

He'd have tried to hide his tracks then. Bundled her clothes in bags, hangers and all, and taken them and poor Gina's body dispose of somewhere. He was a policeman; he'd know the best wa to do it without leaving a trace. It explained why all her food ha been left behind. Poor Gina.

It didn't explain everything, but Leigh was convinced she wa right. This was why she was so uneasy in his company. Her finge felt for the key she needed.

'How did you know I'd changed my locks?'

Philip looked confused. 'What?'

She folded her arms, her mobile resting in the crook of h elbow. 'I think you heard me... how did you know?'

'You must have told me?'

'No, I definitely didn't.' When he didn't answer, she screwed u her nose. 'It was you, wasn't it? You let yourself in with Gina's key You tried again last night and discovered your keys didn't fit. Tha why you came around this evening, isn't it?' She felt a dart triumph when she saw his eyes narrow.

'I've no idea what you're talking about.'

'You spun that tale about Gina telling you we were lovers. I ha to admit, that was clever, put me completely off the track.'

Philip got to his feet, startling her. 'I really have no idea wh you're on about.' He pointed at the wine glass. 'Sounds to me li you've been hitting the booze a bit heavily. I'd lay off it, if I we you.'

Leigh stood and glared at him. 'You killed Gina! Killed her, kept the house keys and let yourself in here to keep an eye on me.'

'What?' He ran a hand through his hair and looked towards the door as if marking his escape route. 'Okay, this was obviously a huge mistake. I think you must be having a breakdown. You're in some sort of paranoid delusional state. You need to get help.' He turned for the door.

'No!' Leigh put a hand out to stop him. 'You were the last person to see her. You might as well admit it!'

'You're off your head.' He looked back at the glass again. 'I don't know what you're drinking but you need to get help.'

'You can't go.' She held up her mobile. 'I rang the police when I sat down, they should be here soon.'

Philip looked at her in stunned silence. 'You did what?'

'You heard me!' She was right, she knew she was. 'You have keys to my home, Gina's keys. You got rid of her body somehow. You're a police officer. You'd know how to do these things.' To her surprise, he grunted in frustration, turned and sat back on the sofa.

'This is what I get for trying to help you. I need my head examined.' He looked up at her. 'Oh, for goodness' sake, sit down; you're wrong about me.' When she stayed on her feet he shrugged. 'Suit yourself.' He sat back and linked his hands behind his head. 'You were right. You didn't tell me about getting your locks changed. That was very sloppy of me.'

'I knew it!' Shouldn't she be feeling elated? Not a chill of disappointment to have been right. She regarded Philip's casual posture. Shouldn't he be looking a little worried?

He met her gaze and smiled. 'You didn't tell me, Kentish Road police did. They've been keeping an eye on you following your recent dealings with them. When they saw the locksmith standing on your doorstep they added the information to the file they have on you.'

'I don't believe you!'

He laughed. 'When they arrive you can ask them, can't you? They might even find it amusing.'

Leigh felt suddenly weak. Shaky feet took her to the sofa. She sank onto it and glared across the room to where Philip was looking annoyedly amused. 'I was sure...' She shook her head. So sure, of so many things. 'I heard someone at the door last night, someone who didn't know I'd changed the locks.' She had heard someone, hadn't she? It hadn't been a dream.

44
––––––––––

Leigh didn't know what Philip told the uniformed constables who pulled up outside her house ten minutes later. No sirens blaring. That, she thought sadly, said it all. They'd not taken her call seriously. Just as well as it turned out. She'd been a fool. Yet again.

She heard deep voices; a bark of laughter making her cringe. Then the clunk of the front door shutting. She looked up when Philip reappeared in the living room doorway, a satisfied expression on his face, his thumb raised. *Everything was okay.* She'd have liked to have taken that damn thumb and stuck it in his eye.

When he vanished, she stayed seated, too numb to argue, to insist he leave. Sounds drifted from the kitchen: the kettle being filled, the opening and shutting of cupboard doors as he searched for what he needed. Comfortable familiar sounds. They should have reassured her. But all she wanted to do was scream at him to let her be miserable in peace.

When he returned, he had a mug in each hand. 'Tea.' He put one on the table in front of her.

Leigh picked it up, cradling it between her hands. She didn't want it, but the heat was helping to thaw the numbness. 'I suppose it's filled with sugar for the shock?'

'No.' He smiled. 'I couldn't find any.'

She took a sip. It was too strong and tannic. 'You squeezed the teabag.'

This drew a laugh. 'You accused me of having killed your lodger, and now you're complaining about how I make the tea?'

She could feel her lower lip begin to tremble and pressed the mug to it. It was seconds before she was able to speak. 'I'm sorry, okay. I was wrong. Seems I can't help putting two and two together and coming up with a ridiculous answer.'

'You've had your trust in people dented.'

'Dented!' She put the tea down. 'You heard about Matt, I assume?'

He shrugged. 'Strathclyde police are keen to ensure cooperation by exchanging information. I read their report.'

What looked like genuine sympathy in his eyes made Leigh hurriedly pick up the mug and press it to her lips again. No more tears were going to be wasted on Matt or any other man. 'Our relationship had fizzled out anyway. We just hadn't said the words.'

'I'm sorry, Leigh.'

She didn't want his sympathy. 'Why are you here? Didn't you say it was better to keep your distance?' There was bitterness in her words, his eyebrows rising at her rude reaction to his expression of sympathy. She didn't care. She was so tired of caring. 'Please, go away.'

'I need...' He put his mug down and leaned forward, conflicting emotions crossing his face. 'You may find it hard to believe given the situation, but I care about you. I've liked you from the first time we met. When you turned down my invitation to go for a drink that last day in the clinic, I was gutted.'

Leigh frowned. She remembered the strange expression she'd

en flit across his face. Had she misread it? Had it been something
simple as disappointment? 'You know why I was at the clinic;
ny were you?'

He looked at her in silence, the struggle obvious in the suddenly
rrowed eyes, lips pressing together as if trying to keep the words
om escaping.

'Fair's fair,' she said when the silence continued.

That made him laugh. A short cynical burst of sound. He
oked at her again, his eyes softening, lips returning to their well-
fined sensuous curves. 'I've said it before, but you're something
se.' He sighed. 'I was there as part of a plea-bargain. No charges
ould be brought against me for criminal damage if I paid compen-
tion and did that anger management course.'

He seemed to think that was sufficient explanation. Leigh
anted more. 'Criminal damage?'

'You want blood, do you?' He sighed again, a loud huff that
emed to be part exasperation, part resignation. 'Right. Mr
thetic here arrived home early to surprise his wife, only to
scover, while he'd been working his ass off to ensure she had
erything her little avaricious heart could possibly desire, she was
tertaining someone else in our bed.' He reached up to loosen his
e and undo the top button of his shirt. 'It seems the affair had
en going on for a few months. After the guy left, mumbling
ologies, I lost my cool and smashed the place up.' He smiled
arily. 'It was her apartment; I'd moved in when we married. Her
ace, ergo the compensation and anger management course.'

Leigh was taken aback. She'd enjoyed his company at the clinic
t had taken his good looks and sexy smile at face-value and
smissed him as a player. She'd been wrong. The hurt and betrayal
her face were real.

'I'm sorry,' she said. 'I'd made assumptions.' She didn't elabo-
te. 'I seem to have been doing that a lot recently.'

Philip seemed relieved she'd brought the conversation back Gina, his hunched shoulders relaxing. 'You were taken in someone who appears to be a skilled con artist; you're not to blam for that.'

'Perhaps,' she conceded. She eyed him curiously. 'Why did yc come here tonight?'

'Ah.' He ran a hand through his hair again, loosened his tie little more. 'I shouldn't have—'

'But you did,' she interrupted him. She could tell from h expression he was having second thoughts about telling her wha ever he'd originally come to say. 'Please, Philip, whatever it is, isn't better I hear from you than from someone else?'

'Okay, promise you won't get upset.'

Words designed to send fingers of fear around her. She cou feel them grip. Wondered how tight they were going to becom 'Get on with it, please.'

'Right.' A final wrench had the tie off completely. He shoved into his jacket pocket. 'It's about Matt.' He held a hand up when I saw she was going to interrupt again. 'Let me tell you. He's going be picked up by the Hampshire police in the morning and que tioned about his involvement in the disappearance of your lodger.

Leigh laughed. 'That's simply ridiculous! She hasn't *disappear* disappeared. She sent that horrible letter to the principal of t school on Monday.'

'A typed letter. No signature. It could have been sent by anyone

'But...' A furrow appeared between Leigh's eyes as she tried sort it out in her head. 'You're saying Matt sent it himself, is that To give himself an alibi of some sort. That's the craziest thing I' ever heard. It could destroy his career.'

Philip shook his head. 'No. The principal says they've decided treat it as a malicious attempt to discredit a valued member of sta It might hamper Matt's chances of promotion, but he'll be kept (

as a teacher. The same wouldn't be the case if he was accused of Gina's murder.'

'Murder!' Leigh gulped then held her hand up. 'No, that's not right. Matt left to go back to Salisbury on Tuesday. He said he'd spoken to her then and she was okay with' – she screwed her face up and waved a hand – 'you know what I mean.'

'*He* says she was happy... maybe she wasn't. And maybe, contrary to what he told you, it hadn't been consensual at all, and she threatened to report him to the police.'

'She wouldn't have done; she would have known the police were looking for her.'

'Yes, but Matt wouldn't have known it was an empty threat, would he?'

Leigh stared. No, he wouldn't have. He'd have believed her. If Matt had been arrested for sexual assault, his career would be over. Being a teacher was all he'd ever wanted to be. What would he do to make sure it wasn't destroyed? Pretty much anything... but murder?

'No!' She let out a relieved sigh. 'You're forgetting, he wasn't the last person to see her, you probably were when you delivered my Kindle. I was with Matt all that weekend – I'm his alibi.'

Philip suddenly reached across and took hold of her hand. She looked at his strong fingers, then up to where his warm eyes were looking at her with pity. 'There's one slight problem with that,' he said. 'I'm fairly sure it wasn't your lodger I saw.'

45

Leigh pulled her hand away. 'What the hell are you talking about? You told me—'

'I told you I handed the package to a woman. We both assumed it was your lodger. It wasn't until you mentioned her being butterfly-like and ethereal that I realised we'd been speaking of two different people.'

'What?' Leigh clamped her hands over her ears and glared at him. 'You're talking rubbish!'

'I told you I'd waited a long time for the door to be answered, and what she said when I asked if she knew you, but I never thought to describe the woman I saw. The medium-height solid woman I saw, Leigh. Not petite or in any way ethereal. She said she'd been in the shower when I rang the doorbell which is why she'd taken so long. It also explained the long terry-towelling robe she wore and why her hair was wrapped in a towel balanced precariously on her head. And she had' – he waved a hand around his face – 'a what do you call it on her face, green gungy stuff.'

'A face pack.' Leigh was staggered by this new information. 'It wasn't Gina?'

'Not unless she's a shape shifter.' He sat back with a sigh. 'I don't suppose I could have a drink, could I?'

Leigh guessed he wasn't talking about more tea, or water. She pointed to a cupboard.

He didn't need to be told twice. Getting to his feet, he pulled the door open, bending to peer inside. He pulled out the bottle of whisky, put it on the table and went to the kitchen for glasses.

Making himself at home. Leigh hadn't the energy to care. Nor to refuse when he put a glass in her hand. The first sip made her cough, the second made her cry. 'I'm not sure I can take much more.'

Philip moved to sit beside her. He didn't take her hand this time, but she took comfort from his nearness. 'Because of the robe, etc., I don't have a clear idea of what she looked like or even if it was a woman.'

'It can't have been Matt; he was in Salisbury with me.'

Philip nodded to where a framed photograph of Leigh and Matt sat on a shelf. 'No, I wouldn't have mistaken his bulk for a woman's figure. The person I saw, male or female, was slimmer but definitely not petite.'

'Maybe Gina had a friend staying?'

'It's possible.'

'And whoever it was, they killed her. Nothing to do with Matt.' He might be her ex-boyfriend, but they'd spent a year together. Much as she'd have liked to, she couldn't dismiss all her feelings for him that easily. She remembered his self-centred response when she told him Gina had been murdered and frowned. She met Philip's eyes. 'You're thinking he might have hired someone else to get rid of her, aren't you?'

He nudged her slightly. 'There's no point in worrying yourself about it.' He caught her raised eyebrow and smiled. 'Right, yes, it is one of the scenarios we're considering. But it's what the police do, Leigh, think of all the possibilities, then see if anything fits.'

'Make things fit?'

His expression became shuttered again. Full policeman mode. 'That's not how it works at all. If Matt is innocent, the evidence will point that way. Meanwhile, until we have evidence to the contrary, your ex-lodger is simply a missing person.'

'Missing now that the Strathclyde police want her. Classified as a lost contact when I tried to get the police involved!'

'That's the way things go sometimes. Contrary to your fair's fair attitude, often it isn't.'

'No, it isn't. A simple gesture of kindness landed me in all this, as if I hadn't enough woes of my own.'

His police persona slipped off as fast as it had slotted into place. 'Speaking of which, are you going back to work tomorrow?'

'No.' The blunt word hung in the air. She gave him a brief smile. 'To prove I can make the occasional good decision, I've decided to quit. I'll ring the HR manager in the morning. I have no doubt she'll be relieved.'

'So what are you going to do, look for another job?'

Philip wasn't a friend. She didn't want to discuss her future with him, tentative secret plans she needed to give more thought to before taking the next step. She didn't want his input, his needs or his damn attractiveness to colour that decision. 'I'm not sure yet.'

He seemed disappointed in her answer, his eyes darkening. 'Fine.' He checked his watch and got to his feet. 'You're up to speed now with what's going on with Matt. I'll be off.'

She wanted to say, *what about me?* The noises she'd heard at her door. The intrusions. That awful latex hand. Bernard bloody Ledbetter. Instead, she got to her feet and trailed behind him to the front door.

'Stay safe, Leigh.' Philip didn't attempt to kiss her cheek this
ne or touch her in any way. Except with his eyes. They lingered.

Stay safe. It felt like goodbye. Leigh felt her eyes fill as she stood
d watched him walk down the street. Brisk strides taking him
ay as quickly as he could go.

It was for the best.

Way too complicated.

She was still trying to convince herself as she shut and locked
e door.

46

Leigh cleared away the empty glasses, put away the bottle of whisky and switched out the lights. A wave of loneliness swept over her. So much to be thankful for: her own home, loving parents, good friends, no money problems... at least not yet.

Giving up her job, ending a relationship that had suddenly turned toxic, both had been good decisions. She didn't need to rush into making another. It might even be a good idea to go home to Yorkshire for a while, nestle into her parents' unconditional love.

Go home, put her recent problems behind her.

It was shocking to think perhaps both Gina and Ledbetter were dead, easier to feel sorrow for the bubbly woman she'd thought she'd known, harder for the man who'd made her skin crawl. Not only hers... She remembered Janet Collins' admission. The HR manager had been right; it did make Leigh feel a little better, less isolated.

A sigh took her up the stairs. Weary, but not sleepy, she spent time on the routine of cleansing and moisturising she'd been skipping recently. All done, she slipped under the duvet and willed sleep to come.

She thought her worries would cascade around her again once the external distractions of light and sound were gone. It wasn't Ledbetter's face, Gina's or even Matt's who appeared full colour behind her eyelids, instead it was Philip who appeared, his smile warm and caring.

She woke hours later, ears straining in the silence to listen for anything amiss, drifting back to sleep within minutes when reassured by the silence. And so it went for the rest of the night, long periods of sleep, short breaks of instant awareness.

At seven she woke again. The heating clicking on. Traffic outside her window. The twittering of sparrows in a neighbour's unpruned garden hedge. It was good to lie there, letting the everyday sounds lull her, settling her thoughts.

That day was going to be the first day of the rest of her life. Psychobabble sometimes was exactly what she needed. Smiling, she slipped from the bed, had a shower and dressed. Over coffee, she jotted down her plan for the day. Nothing could be done yet, since most of the world was still asleep. She spent the waiting time catching up on social media she'd been neglecting, tweeting to say she was making changes in her life, posting something similar but more elaborate on her Facebook page. Over the following hour, she read the encouraging comments that wished her well, some wishing they had the courage to do the same.

Leigh hadn't needed the validation; it didn't mean she didn't like it.

By nine, she'd had enough. Having waited so long, she found herself reluctant to address the first item on her list. The phone call to Lancaster International. Putting it off, she stood to make more coffee, spending minutes searching the cupboard to see if she could find anything to eat. Dried pasta didn't seem to fit the bill.

It was ten minutes past the hour before she finally rang, the flood of caffeine joining forces with anxiety to beat a loud painful drumroll in her chest. The call was answered almost immediately, the receptionist's falsely cheerful voice grating. 'Good morning, Lancaster International.'

'Good morning, may I speak to Janet Collins? It's Leigh Simon.'

'Hold, please, and I'll see if she's free.'

The company didn't believe in wasted opportunity. Instead of hold music, Leigh was bombarded with marketing promotions. She tuned out, tapping her fingers on the table, reading over her to-do list, wondering if she was making a mistake, if she couldn't still change her mind, tell the HR manager she'd overslept and would be in within the hour.

Leigh could rush to change, pull on her work clothes, get herself into the office, keep her head down and get on with the job of earning a living, saving her career. Ignore the barbs, the comments, the nasty glances. The guilt.

'Ms Simon, you're not coming in today?' Collins' voice. Dispensing with formalities, cutting to the bottom line.

'Hi, no.' Leigh took a deep breath and let it out. This was the right thing to do. 'I'm not coming back. I'm sorry if that's letting you down, but I think you and I both know my position there is untenable as long as Bernard Ledbetter is missing.'

'Are you sure this is the right thing to do? It won't do your career prospects much good, I'm afraid.'

Appreciating the honesty, Leigh smiled. 'I know. I had intended to go back for that reason.'

'But?'

'There's always a but isn't there. Okay, here's the truth. I decided the job isn't right for me.' It sounded better than saying she hated it. 'I'm going to take some time off, maybe travel, see what it is I really want to do. Something with less stress, a job that allows me some personal time.'

'I understand.' Collins sighed. 'I wish you well wherever you go and whatever you do. If you need a reference, get in touch. I'd have to admit the anger issues but will temper that with your willingness to do that anger management course, and your ability to self-reflect. Mostly,' she said, a smile obvious in her voice, 'I'll make it as good as possible because I like you.'

Stunned, Leigh managed a bleated *thank you* before the line died. Well, that was a surprise. Who'd have thought the strange human resources manager would turn out to be a fan.

The positive outcome of her first call of the day energised her. She spent the next hour ringing security companies whose details she'd seen online. Finally, she settled on one who promised they could fulfil all her security needs. They agreed to come out to do an assessment that Wednesday. Satisfied, she hung up.

She stood and stretched, pleased with her progress.

The next couple of things to do were ones to be done in person. First, to speak to a local rental agent about the possibility of renting the house out for a year or so, and the likely income she'd receive. Getting her finances in order would allow her to give more consideration to her next step.

Her next step. Her future. For the first time in a long time, she was looking forward to seeing what it would bring.

47

The estate agent was on Kentish Town Road, not far from the delicatessen where Leigh planned to do most, if not all, of her food shopping. It was more expensive than driving to the supermarket, but the quality of food was better, and she liked to support independent shops when she could.

The estate agent, however, was a branch of a chain. She could have gone further, found another independent agent, but proximity seemed important when it came to renting out her house. Maybe she was being naive to think it would encourage them to keep a closer eye on it, but she liked to think they would.

She pushed open the door and was immediately greeted with beaming smiles from the two agents sitting behind desks. They were trying so hard to be sincere she wondered if it hurt, if at the end of the day their cheeks ached.

There were no other customers to claim their attention. Leigh returned both smiles, then, forced to choose between the agent on the left and the one on the right, chose the woman over the man and moved to take the seat opposite.

She decided she'd chosen well when the agent immediately

opped the fake smile and got down to business, asking succinct
estions, taking notes, frowning and asking for clarification when
e didn't understand. 'Okay,' she said finally. 'I'll need to call
ound to get a better idea of the décor, etc., but from what you've
id I think it would be very easy to rent. There are a number of
tions to consider.' She tilted her head to one side. 'It depends on
at you want really. You could rent it out on a multiple occupancy
sis where you could have upward of six people living there; to a
uple of young professionals who'd like more space; or to a fami-
' She leaned a little closer. 'If your house is in good repair, and
u have decent furniture, I wouldn't recommend multiple occu-
ncy; it tends to be harder on wear and tear.'

'No, I would prefer a couple, or even a small family. There's a
ce garden so it would be good for children.'

'Excellent.' The agent looked at her computer screen and
cked a few buttons. 'I'm free on Friday to come and have a look
er it if that suits?'

'That'd be great but as I said, I've not decided when I'm going as
t.'

The agent held a hand up. 'No worries. I can have a look, then
'll be good to go whenever you're ready.' She tapped a few more
ys then gave Leigh a figure that had her widen her eyes.

'That much, really?'

'Maybe more, sometimes we have very eager customers.' The
ent grinned. 'More money for you means more commission for
. It's a win, win.' They settled on a time for the Friday visit, the
ent flicking to the correct page on a leather-bound diary and
ncilling it in. 'Right, that's sorted. Here's my card, in case
ything turns up and you want to reschedule.'

'No, that should be perfect.' Leigh put the card into her purse.
l see you then.'

* * *

The news that the rental would give her a huge amount of financi
freedom had Leigh buzzing with ideas as she left the estate agen
and walked the short distance to the delicatessen on the same sid
of the street. A crazy idea came to her. She needed to get home an
give it more consideration.

There were a number of popular shops on this stretch
Kentish Town Road. Distracted pedestrians crossed backwards an
forwards, entering and exiting the various businesses with som
times little thought for passers-by.

A man, his face creased into lines of despair, exited the bettin
office and walked directly into Leigh. 'Careful!' He glared at he
'You should watch where you're going.'

She should watch where she was going! It hadn't been her who
barged out of the betting office as if she'd lost the clothes off her bac
if he hadn't stormed away at speed, she'd have shouted the comme
at him. She was forced to settle for glaring as he crossed through th
traffic, cars braking with a squeal of tyres and a blast of a horn.

He went from her head when she noticed two things simultane
ously. Someone staring at her from the street opposite, and
walking explosion of colour a little further on.

Trying to identify the person opposite, she swore under h
breath as a bus and a flurry of pedestrians blocked her view. By th
time she'd pushed through the crowd to the edge of the path, th
staring person had disappeared. She glanced up and down th
street, but there were too many places for someone to hide.

The walking flash of colour, though, was easier to locate. It wa
moving slowly. As Leigh watched, it vanished around the corner
Regis Road.

Unwilling to risk crossing through the traffic, Leigh stayed o the same side of the street, half running, half speed-walking to the pedestrian crossing at the junction, pressing the button rapidly the way she used to do as a child, believing that each was counted and made the lights change faster.

She shuffled restlessly from foot to foot, eager to be off in pursuit before whoever it was had vanished. The flamboyant colours were typical of Gina, but Leigh had been wrong before. It could be Beatrix or some other equally colourful character.

At last, the traffic came to a halt, Leigh flying across the junction before the lights changed in her favour. Down Regis Road she went, eyes scanning left and right. Never having had reason to travel along the road before, she was surprised to find it lined with businesses and small factories. Grey utilitarian buildings. No flashes of colour. She slowed as she passed some apartment blocks, moving on quickly when there was nothing to be seen. Finally, to her surprise, she reached the end of the road. She stood and spun around. Where had she gone? Into one of the businesses or factories. Did she live in one of the apartments?

Frustrated, Leigh walked slowly back to the junction. Perhaps the colourfully clad individual was completely innocent. This was Camden Town, after all; eccentric was more common than conservative.

She'd have liked if it had been Beatrix; she could have dragged her into a pub and got steaming drunk.

Leigh started to retrace her steps. She might have been wrong about seeing Gina, but she was certain there had been someone staring at her from across the street. At the junction with Kentish Town Road, she hammered impatiently on the crossing button again. More anxious this time, she didn't wait for the signal, seeing a gap in the traffic and rushing across. Her eyes kept up a constant scan of the faces approaching, those walking, others standing still.

Every few feet, she turned to look behind, startling the odd innocent pedestrian.

It was tempting to bypass the delicatessen, get home, lock the door and stay safe inside. But if she did, she'd be forced out again. She needed food.

Usually, the big, slightly eccentric deli was a pleasure to shop in and she'd take her time, try some of the samples that were always available, choose new things to try. That day, she picked up a wicker basket, threw an assortment of food inside and left as quickly as she could. With a sigh, she trudged home, heavy bags banging against her legs. She continued to scan the passers-by, seeing nobody she knew. Nobody staring in her direction. No strange explosion of colour.

Nothing... but the sensation she was being watched continued.

48

Leigh should have felt safer when she was home, but she didn't. She dropped her bags on the kitchen counter and stood listening, her head tilted. Had she heard the creak of a floorboard? Was there someone upstairs?

When her mobile rang, she yelped, then giggled nervously. Seriously, she was losing it. She frowned; hadn't Philip said the same thing not too many hours before? Perhaps he'd been right.

Her mobile was still ringing. She pulled it out, groaning when she saw Matt's name. The police had probably been in contact, and he was desperate to talk to someone who'd understand. She pulled a chair from under the table and sat. 'Hi.'

'Leigh, I thought you were going to ignore me.' He huffed a sigh. 'Not sure I'd blame you if you did, I've been so self-obsessed since this all has happened. And I don't think I even apologised for... you know, everything with Gina. I am, you know, really sorry.'

Sadly, she didn't care. Not about his apology, or his cheating. It was over. 'That's okay, forget about it.'

'Whew!' He gave a short laugh. 'That's great. We can put it behind us. Get back to the way things were.'

Leigh shut her eyes. He was kidding, wasn't he? 'Matt, it's over. It's been over for a while; we simply hadn't noticed.' When there was no reply, she thought the connection had been lost. 'Matt?'

'I'm here. You said it was okay. I thought that meant you'd forgiven me.'

'It's more a case of, it's okay because I realise I don't care. I'm sorry, I thought you felt the same.'

'Of course I don't! I love you.'

He loved the doormat she'd allowed herself to become. 'When you think about it, you'll realise it's for the best. We both deserve better. Someone we'd move closer to be with despite the obstacles.'

'So that's what this is about!' There was a sneer in his voice. 'Is this a desperate attempt to make me move to London? It's not going to work.'

This wasn't going anywhere; it'd be better to hang up. She made one more attempt. 'That's not what this is about. I'm sorry. It's simpler than that. I don't love you any more.' She wasn't sure she ever had, but there was no point in having that conversation, better to change to another. 'Have the police been in touch with you?'

'Yes.' His voice was sullen. 'They want me to come down to the station; some questions about my relationship with Gina. Nonsense waste of time but I might learn something to make the principal sweet.'

Leigh could have told him the school were ready to reinstate him and treat the episode as a vexatious attempt to discredit him. She might have done, except he'd want to know how she knew, and she'd have to tell him about Philip, how she'd met him, and what he was doing telling her police business.

How complicated her life had become. 'Good luck with it,' she said. There was no reason to tell him the police were looking at him as a person of interest in Gina's disappearance; he'd find that out soon enough.

'Do you want me to let you know how it goes, or is that it?'

Leigh heard the bitterness in his voice. Was he really annoyed e'd ended their relationship, or irritated he hadn't got in first? She d no doubt, when the story was told, he'd be the one to have ne so. 'Of course I'd like to hear how things go; we can still be ends, can't we?'

'I suppose.' Still sullen.

'Right, well good luck, I'd better go.'

'Rushing off, are you? Meeting a man friend, I suppose. That ln't take you long.' Sullen *and* sneering.

'Goodbye, Matt.'

She sat for a minute, trying to remember the good times they'd d. There had been some. But not for a while.

The food she'd bought was sitting in bags on the floor. Getting her feet, she unpacked, stopping every few items to listen, still nvinced she was hearing something. Finally, with everything ay, she couldn't put off going to investigate any longer and with r phone gripped tightly in one hand, she headed upstairs.

49

There was nobody in the bedrooms or bathroom. Leigh had know
there wouldn't be. Whoever had keys would no longer be able
use them on the newly installed locks. Before she complete
discounted her fears though, she checked each of the wardrob
With a shake of her head at how ridiculous she was being, she ev
bent to look under the beds.

Paranoia. Thinking she was hearing things, that people we
creeping around her house, following her, spying on her. Pu
stupidity. She needed to get a grip. There was nobody hidi
anywhere. No bogeyman waiting to jump out and scare her, or wor
grab her by the ankles and drag her into his monstrous swamp. T
idea made her laugh and put her worries into perspective. She had
wandered into a Stephen King novel. There were no monsters.

Or was she dismissing Gina too easily – if she had killed th
woman in Glasgow, didn't that make her monstrous? But wh
reason would she have for coming into Leigh's house so surrep
tiously? Apart from that glass of wine, nothing had been taken.

So many unanswered questions.

Maybe she was being paranoid but she was sure someone had been following her. *Almost sure.* There had been someone staring at her from across the street. It had been the stillness surrounding them that had attracted Leigh's attention. They'd stood out against the fast-flowing pedestrians. If only people hadn't got in her way, she might have had a clearer look; now all she could recall was a sinister-looking figure in a coat and hat, their face in shadow but definitely looking her way.

The thought brought her to the mystery of exactly who Philip had met the day he'd called around with her Kindle. He'd said it was impossible to describe the person, dressed as they were, their face obscured by a face pack. But he had described a mid-height, solid person, not a description that suited the delicate Gina. A friend was the best bet. Someone Gina had invited to stay. A boyfriend even? It was a reasonable explanation, but it didn't explain why this person, whoever they were, told Philip a tall tale about Leigh being their lover.

Was this unknown person the same one who'd been staring at her? The thought made her shiver. Maybe they were responsible for Gina's disappearance. Had her keys. Was the one who'd been letting themself into Leigh's home.

Her thoughts were a tangle. Talking it over with someone would help. Not Matt. Her girlfriends would offer oohs and aahs of sympathy but little effective advice or help. The only person who might understand was Philip. Would he look at her with a raised eyebrow and a shuttered stare and call her paranoid, or with that soft caring look that offered more. She wished she could be sure it was right to trust him.

It struck her that she hadn't heard from Spring since Saturday. Perhaps it was simply because the tracing agent had nothing to report. No harm in ringing her to check. With her contacts, Spring might also be able to allay Leigh's continuing doubt as to whether to trust Philip or not.

Half expecting to have to leave a message, she was relieved when the tracing agent answered on the first ring. 'It's Leigh Simon. I was wondering if you'd learned anything more about Gina.'

'Hang on there one tick.'

Leigh heard shuffling of papers before the agent's voice came again. 'Sorry. Right, Gina Henderson. Afraid not. As yet, I've no idea who your ex-lodger is. Still working on it, but it might be that the police find her first. You do know they're actively looking for her now, I assume.'

'Yes, I do thanks. I'd like you to keep looking; as you said, you can go places they can't.'

'Sure, no problem.'

There was less enthusiasm in her voice though. Leigh guessed Spring would put little time into the search now she'd discovered how unlikely it was she'd be able to find Gina or whatever her name was. 'Can I ask you about something else?'

'Sure.'

'I've recently had dealings with a police officer. Philip Dunstable. Do you know anything about him?'

When the agent replied, there was a trace of puzzlement in her voice. 'Dunstable, sure, yes, I know of him.'

Leigh wondered if she was crossing some kind of unwritten line, then she thought *what the hell* and asked, 'What can you tell me about him?'

'I'm not sure why you're asking, but as I only know a little, I'm happy to share. Dunstable currently works for the Missing Persons Bureau. Before that he worked homicide which is where I came across him. He was married. I heard his wife died earlier this year.'

'Died?'

'Yeah, some accident I gather. I don't know much more, I'm

afraid.' There was noise in the background. 'Listen, I have to go. I'll be in touch if I hear anything about your Gina, okay?'

'Yes, thanks.' The phone went dead before Leigh had a chance to ask more. Like, whether she was sure about Philip's wife. The woman he'd said was having an affair, whose home he'd smashed up in anger. Why wouldn't he have mentioned she'd died in an accident?

Sins of omission.

Why would he leave such an important detail out?

She'd wanted to hear something positive to prove she could trust Philip. If she could, then she could lean on him. Because she was a weak stupid woman with no backbone. She thumped the heel of her hand against her forehead. Stupid, stupid, stupid! It was time to have a bit of gumption. Get her life in order.

Ending her relationship with Matt had been a good start. So had quitting her job. The plan to go travelling was also a good step, but now it would be for a short time. The idea that had struck her earlier had taken root.

To put her primary degree in mathematics to a different, better use. Funnily, it was remembering Matt enthusing over his pupils, the challenge and satisfaction of his job, that put the notion of training to be a teacher into her head. She could do it. Rent out the house. Live with her parents while she trained. The idea excited her far more than travelling the world without a long-term plan.

She needed to concentrate on her future and put Philip out of her head.

50

Making a proactive decision about her future seemed to reset Leigh's brain. It allowed her to dismiss the person she'd seen staring as a product of her overactive imagination. She even accepted she was being a little paranoid. In view of all she'd been through recently, it was, she decided, a perfectly normal response.

She'd liked to have consigned her belief that someone had been in her home to the same waste bin... except for that missing glass of wine. Imaginations didn't drink.

It was easy to fill in the rest of the day. With an A4 pad beside her, she spent hours checking out relevant universities, scribbling down entry requirements, distance from her parents' house. On a separate page she jotted down cost per semester. Tuition, living costs, transport costs. To her surprise, she discovered she was entitled to a bursary to help with fees.

After a few hours, she had several pages covered in neat handwriting. She picked up the page relating to finance and nodded. With the bursary, it was going to be easy. Her parents would be delighted to put her up for the year; they wouldn't want or expect payment, but she'd insist on the going rate.

It was almost seven before she picked up her mobile and dialled
r parents' landline.

'Hi, Mum.'

'Leigh, how lovely to hear from you.' Her mother's voice, always
eerful. 'Neil, it's Leigh.'

She heard her father hollering a hello. He'd be in his favourite
at. A venerable, ancient leather chair that her mother had
tched because he swore it was the most comfortable seat ever
ade and nothing could replace it. When Leigh thought of him,
'd be in it, their large tabby, Catkins, curled up on his lap. 'I
ought I'd come for a visit next week; is that okay?'

'A visit! That's fantastic! Did you hear that Neil, she's coming for
isit.'

'A few days; I've some news for you.'

Her mother's squeal was ear-piercing. 'You're getting married!'

Leigh laughed. 'No, better news than that, I promise, but you'll
ve to wait till I'm up next week.' They chatted for a while longer
fore she hung up with a smile. Her mother, she knew, would start
eparing the following day, and would drive her father crazy fuss-
g. It would be good to be home.

Humming, Leigh opened the fridge, took out one of the
iches she'd bought and put it in the oven. It would take twenty
nutes.

She was still humming as she went upstairs, deciding to have a
ick shower and change into pyjamas for an evening of chilling in
nt of the TV. Once in the shower, she changed her mind and took
r time, using a loofah to give her skin a good scrub. Washing all
r problems away.

Mindful of the twenty minutes quickly ticking away, she dried
rself, pulled on a pair of brushed-cotton pyjamas and with
nger giving her a nudge, ran barefooted down the stairs. She set
late on a tray and opened the oven door, using a towel to pull out

the top rack. Wrong one. She shoved it back and stooped to pull o the lower one.

Her mouth was suddenly dry. She bent down to peer inside t oven. Apart from a few burnt crumbs, there was nothing. Straigl ening, she looked around to where the tray sat on the counter. T plate was there, shiny clean. No quiche. She took both racks o and dropped them, hot as they were, on the counter, then got dow on her knees, her head almost inside the oven, searching for t quiche.

It wasn't there.

Frantic, her hands shaking, Leigh pressed her foot to the ped of the rubbish bin. The quiche had been packed in one of the del distinctive brown paper bags. She'd scrunched it up and thrown into the bin.

It should have been on top. It wasn't. Leigh stared into the bi then, desperate, she upended it, sending rubbish tumbling to t floor: wrappers, used teabags, old dried-out slices of toast. She g down on her knees again, her hands spreading the mess o searching for that one distinctive piece that would prove she was going crazy.

With a sob of disbelief, she sat back on her haunches.

What was happening to her?

She stayed there for several minutes, pushing her hand throu the waste now and then in the faint hope that this time she'd fi the bag. Finally, she struggled to her feet, pins and needles in bo legs making her unsteady.

Using the countertop for balance, she made her way across to chair and sank onto it. Resting her elbow on the table, she dropp her forehead onto her sticky hand. This was ridiculous... she'd p the quiche into the oven. She lifted her head, frowning in puzzl ment. Hadn't she smelled it cooking?

Getting to her feet, she went to the fridge. All the food she bought from the deli was there, neatly piled up. She shut the door, crossed back to pick up her bag and searched inside for her purse. The receipt from the deli was shoved into the coin section. She pulled it out and ran her eyes down it. Every item was itemised. There should be three quiches.

She stood with her hand on the fridge door for a few seconds. Afraid of what she'd find, terrified of what she wouldn't.

Checking, double checking, she turned away from the fridge with wide eyes.

There were only two. She'd been right, she had put one in the oven. Only, someone else had taken it out.

51

Leigh had experienced fear before, but she'd never felt a gut-wrenching terror. It froze her in place, scrambled her thoughts, rendered her incapable of decision.

Minutes passed. It wasn't till the light faded, and terror became a living breathing force bubbling up from somewhere deep inside that she moved with short jerky steps to a chair, dropping heavily onto it, its feet screeching eerily on the wooden floor.

Leigh's eyes were fixed on the back door. Stupidly, she'd had the front door locks replaced without giving any thought to the back. Why would she? The spare bunch she'd given to both Matt and Gina had only included keys to the front.

Had her intruder guessed she might have the locks changed and had a copy of the back door key made? She'd assumed her intruder had come in only twice; now she realised how terribly pathetically stupid she'd been. Whoever it was, had come and gone as they'd pleased.

Her fingers closed over her mobile. She should ring the police. *And tell them someone had come in and stolen a quiche from her oven.* Even in her terror, she had to admit it was funny. Not only had someone broken in and taken the blasted thing, but they'd also taken the bag it had been wrapped in to make her doubt her sanity.

Had she not had the receipt to check, she'd have believed she was going crazy.

Was that their aim... whoever was responsible... to make her doubt her sanity? The police already did.

She crossed her arms on the table and lay her head down, tears falling. Sobbing and snuffling noisily. When the doorbell rang her head jerked up and she looked towards the door to the hallway with eyes wide in fear.

Pulling up the end of her pyjama top, she wiped the cotton over her face and listened. When the bell went again, she got to her feet, moved to the open doorway and stared at the front door. She should have asked the security company to come out and fix a chain to it as an emergency. Too bloody late now.

The mobile was in her hand. It wasn't too late to ring the police. Instead, she took a few steps towards the door, jumping when the bell went again. Whoever it was, they were persistent. Knew she was there.

It might be the person who'd come in the back door. Maybe they wanted to give her the quiche back. Her giggle was verging on hysteria. She slapped a hand over her mouth, pressing painfully against her teeth. If she stayed quiet, whoever it was would get tired trying and leave. Wouldn't they?

Perhaps a normal person would. The bell went again, then in the following silence, she heard someone calling her name.

'Leigh, answer the damn door. I know you're in there.'

A voice she instantly recognised. *Philip.* For a man who didn't want to be seen with her, he certainly spent a lot of time turning up uninvited.

Leigh didn't want to see him, didn't want to let him inside. But neither had she wanted someone to sneak in through her back door and steal her damn dinner.

Philip was a police officer. Perhaps telling him was the sensible thing to do. Before she'd time to change her mind again, she unlocked the door and pulled it open. 'One of these days, you'll ring and see if it's convenient.'

'If it isn't I can go away.' He stood frowning at her, hands jammed into his pockets, tie slightly askew.

'You look like you've had a rough day.' She stood back, waved him inside. 'Before the neighbours ring the police. I've had my fill of them.'

He grinned. 'Present company excluded, I'm assuming.'

She didn't reply, leading the way into the kitchen and sitting on the chair she'd vacated only moments before. 'What are you doing here? For a man who doesn't think it's safe to be seen with me, you're sure spending a lot of time in my company.'

He took the seat opposite. 'You look like you've been crying.'

'It's not illegal, as far as I know.'

'No.' He nodded towards the mess on the floor. 'You going to tell me what happened?'

She wanted to. Wanted to share her worries. Was it so wrong? It didn't mean she was a pushover, a doormat. 'We're not friends, Philip; if I tell you what happened, I'm telling you as a police officer.'

A shadow passed over his face, narrowing his eyes and lips. The transformation was remarkable. And unnerving. Suddenly it was important for Leigh to know the truth. To know if this man was one of the good guys, or someone she should be afraid of, distrust, throw out of her home. 'You told me you did that anger management course because you trashed your wife's apartment?'

He regarded her silently.

'I assume that was before she was killed in an accident?' She

d heavy emphasis on the last word, almost tempted to do that
ful finger curling in the air. 'Seems strange you'd tell me one
ng but not the other.'

'Does it?'

'More than a little.'

He looked around the room. 'Is there any of that whisky left?'

She hesitated then shrugged. They weren't friends, but they
uld be drinking buddies. She went to the living room, returning
oments later with the bottle. Putting it on the table, she opened a
pboard for two glasses.

He had the bottle open, waiting.

She put the glasses down. 'Only a little drop for me.'

He kept his eyes on her face and poured a generous measure
o both. 'I don't like drinking alone.' Half his glass was gone in
e gulp. 'I didn't lie to you, Leigh. You asked why I was doing that
ger management class.'

True, she had. 'And the accident, were you involved in that?'

His face tightened. 'What, you think I caused it?'

It was Leigh's turn to knock back half her whisky. 'A few weeks
o, I thought I knew everything, now I'm doing cartwheels simply
keep up with the twists and turns in my life. Truth seems to have
come an optional extra.'

'I've never lied to you,' he insisted. 'I was doing that blasted
urse because I trashed the apartment. I was supposed to do it last
ar. It was deferred twice due to work commitments.' He smiled
efly. 'I may have exaggerated my own importance, but I knew I
d to do it eventually or be held in contempt.' He swirled the
isky, holding it to his nose without drinking. 'Good stuff this.' He
ok a sip.

'My wife and I split up after I discovered her infidelity, and I
oved into the apartment in Hornsey. Divorce proceedings had
mmenced... we didn't have children, the apartment was already

hers, so it wasn't going to be difficult... then in March, she and h
new partner were killed in a freak accident while on holiday
Marbella when the roof of a venue collapsed trapping sever
people. Six people died, Sadie and her partner included.' He too
another sip of his drink. 'Sadie was beautiful. Bright, bubbly, alwa
ready for fun. We married too quickly. And soon discovered th
marrying in haste, repenting at leisure, was more than a cliché
think we both realised after a couple of months, we'd made
mistake. We wanted different things. She hated being married to
man who spent his days dealing with the dregs of society and wh
didn't always want to party when he got home.'

'And you?' Leigh was fascinated by what he'd told her. The
were so many layers to this complex man. 'What had you wanted?'

'Me?' He threw back the last of his drink. 'I wanted someone
share my day, to laugh with over the silly things life threw at us,
plan a future together. A partner, not a playmate.'

He reached for the whisky bottle and refilled his glass.

Leigh held her hand over hers. 'I don't want any more.' Whe
he put the bottle down, she screwed the lid back on and stretch
to put the bottle on the counter behind.

The action made him smile. 'Not subtle, are you?'

There didn't seem to be any point in answering. 'What are y
doing here, Philip?'

52

Philip frowned, then stared into his drink and swirled the honey-coloured liquid around the glass again. 'I could make up a story, tell you I've come to update you on the search for Ledbetter and Gina.'

When he lifted his eyes and met Leigh's gaze her breath caught. Danger sirens whooped in her head. Physical attraction was a fool's game. She didn't need this. His explanation of his wife's accident seemed to exonerate him... he'd have known it would be easy to check up on. But she refused to trust him completely. 'I think it would be better if that was why you were here. I don't need more complications in my life.'

It looked as if he was going to argue, then he smiled and nodded. 'Timing might be a bit off; I grant you that. Right, I'm back in police mode. Tell me what made you cry.'

She didn't answer immediately. Pushing her barely touched glass away, she stood and crossed to the kitchen, stepping around the mess on the floor. 'I'm going to make some tea; would you like some?'

He lifted his glass. 'I'll stick to the hard stuff, thanks.'

She took her time. Reaching for her favourite mug, taking the box of camomile tea from the cupboard, peeling one bag from the packet. She popped it into the mug, poured the boiling water on top and stood staring into it while she wondered if she was right to tell him about what had happened. He might think she'd lost it. The receipt she'd been depending on to prove she was right, didn't really prove anything. She could have heated and eaten the quiche earlier and forgotten. Was that what had happened?

'Whatever you tell me will be in confidence.'

She turned to look at him. 'This isn't a confessional. You're not a priest, you're a policeman. If I told you something pertaining to a crime, wouldn't you have to do something?'

'Why don't you tell me and let me decide.'

Fishing the teabag out, she dropped it into the sink and took the mug back to the table. 'It's a weird tale; you probably won't believe it.' When he said nothing, she took a sip of her tea and, haltingly, told him the story of her missing quiche. She didn't realise how desperate she was for him to believe her until she looked up to see a frown on his face. A frown... He wasn't laughing in disbelief.

'I thought you had the locks changed.'

'I did, but only the front door ones. I never included the back door key when I gave Gina and Matt keys to the house.' He needed to know the rest. 'I know you read the reports the Kentish Road police wrote. They were convinced I left the front door open.' She kept her eyes fixed on his. 'I didn't. Someone opened the door. Two days later, I left half a glass of wine on the table; in the morning, the glass was empty.' She lifted the mug of tea, took a sip and put it down. 'So many strange things. And now this.'

'Get the back door lock changed tomorrow.' He stood and walked to the window. 'You need to get some security lights too.' He turned to look at her. 'Have you thought any more about getting a working alarm, upping your security?'

'There's someone coming around on Wednesday. Security

lighting is a good idea; I'll get them to install some too.' She indicated the back door with a jerk of her head. 'Tomorrow, I'll ring the locksmith and get the lock changed.' She waited till he'd sat again before saying, 'There's more.'

'Go on.'

'This morning, I was on Kentish Town Road, and I swear someone was staring at me. I couldn't make out who it was, nor whether they were male or female. Of course, that made me think of the person you handed my Kindle to.' He'd described a taller, bigger figure than the dainty Gina. Suddenly, Leigh frowned.

Philip looked at her intently. 'What is it?'

'Wait,' she said, trying to work out the idea that had come to her. She was remembering a conversation she'd had with Gina shortly after she'd moved in. Leigh had made some comment about liking the pink streaks in her hair.

'They're extensions.' Gina had reached up and unclipped one, holding it out. 'I like to change how I look sometimes; it keeps people on their toes.'

Change how she looks. With startling clarity she knew who Philip had spoken to. She knew she was right. But could she convince him?

'When Gina, or whatever her name was, wasn't working, she wore the most outrageously flamboyant clothes. But whether she was working or not, one thing she always wore was full make-up.' Leigh rubbed her index finger along her eyebrows. 'She had these ridiculously big dark brows. You couldn't take your eyes off them. I often wondered if she'd bad skin because she wore unusually heavy foundation too, and splashes of blusher across her cheek. Even her lips... she used heavy outliner to change the shape of them, adding a cupid's bow where there wasn't one.'

Leigh looked at Philip intently. Did he understand what she was getting at? She willed him to believe her. It made sense.

'It suited her personality. All larger than life.' She put the mug down, pushed it aside and picked up the abandoned whisky. 'But what if it was all one big disguise. I described her as being ethereal which is why you decided it couldn't have been her you met. But' – she sipped her drink, feeling the alcohol burn; the more she thought of it the more she knew she was right – 'you said she was wearing a robe, had her hair wrapped up in a towel. What if, under the robe, she was wearing more clothes, giving the impression she was bigger. And maybe she was wearing high heels too. With her hair up in a towel, the overall impression would be of a taller person. Taller and bigger. Not the ethereal Gina, but another disguise.'

Philip frowned, then nodded slowly. 'It's possible.'

'And the person I saw today, staring at me from across the road. I didn't think it odd at the time, but it was warm today and they were wearing a big heavy coat. And a hat, like a trilby. Again, adding bulk and height.' Leigh clasped her hands together. 'I know I'm right. It was Gina.'

igh took another sip of her whisky and waited for Philip to mment.

'It's possible.'

She let out a sigh of relief and trembled on the edge of tears. e'd never realised the power of being believed. 'More than possi-; it explains so many things.'

'Not the important one though. The *why*.'

Leigh raised a hand in defeat. 'I can't think of any reason why e'd want to repay me by stalking me, invading my house. After , I never asked her to leave, that was her own decision. Okay, we'd it of a disagreement when I told her Matt was staying—'

Philip held a hand up to stop her. 'You never mentioned this fore?' His voice was sharp. 'What kind of disagreement?'

Hadn't she told the police? Leigh couldn't remember. 'I was ving to attend that course; Matt was staying to go to some of the ibitions he wanted to see. I mentioned it to her that he'd be staying hout me; she didn't like the idea. Moaned because she hadn't a lock her door, as if she was at risk.' Leigh pressed her lips together, willing to tell Philip she'd been so angry she couldn't remember

exactly what she'd said in response. 'We had words. I told her if s
didn't like it, she could leave... or words to that effect anyway.'

'Instead, she stayed, slept with Gibbs, reported him to t
school for having forced himself on her and then started to st
you.'

Leigh's mouth opened and closed. Stunned, she sat witho
blinking as new thoughts cascaded through her mind. Finally, ir
voice she barely recognised, she said, 'You think this is all reven
for me telling her basically to like it or lump it?'

'You're talking about someone who's been using a dead woma
name for months... a woman she may have killed... I think sh
probably capable of anything. We don't know who she is, or wh
she's done before. The fact she can seemingly sail along witho
being caught shows she's not stupid. She may have some form
antisocial personality disorder—'

'A psychopath?'

'It's possible. They tend to be cold and calculating and this Gi
certainly fits that description.' He drained his glass. 'Until we fil
her, we're second guessing ourselves.'

Leigh was struggling to absorb all she'd heard. 'If revenge
what she's after, she's doing a good job. Finished my relationsh
with Matt, ruined his career prospects, has me looking over r
shoulder.' Getting to her feet, she crossed to the window and star
out into the darkness, wondering if she could persuade her neig
bours to leave their lights on all night long. 'She could be out the
waiting for an opportunity to come inside again. And maybe th
time, she won't be satisfied with taking my dinner.'

Philip pointed to the lock. 'Put the key in and turn it a little, th
it won't be possible to open it from the outside.' He checked I
watch, then looked at her. 'It's almost midnight. I can ring t
station and ask them to send a car by every few hours, but that's r

going to stop someone coming through the back. The report stated there's a vulnerable spot at the end of the garden.'

'Yes, there's accessibility from the gardens behind. It's on my list of things to sort out.'

'Sooner rather than later.'

'Yes.' She'd contact the landscape gardener and ask him to do it as soon as possible. 'It'll be like Fort Knox soon.' She'd be safe inside then, but what about when she went out? What was to stop Gina accosting her? She hadn't that day, but maybe the plan had been simply to unnerve her. If it was, it had worked.

'I'll stay tonight; it would be for the best.'

Leigh, lost in worries of Gina creeping up behind her, thought she must have misheard. 'What did you say?'

Philip smiled. The sexy attractive one that she finally admitted made her slightly weak. 'I'll stay here tonight. It would be safer. I'm a police officer. To protect and to serve is our motto.'

She wanted to argue against it, wanted to insist she didn't need him to stay, but with relief hurtling along her veins, she couldn't tell the lie. Instead, she picked him up on his. 'I know that's wrong. To protect and to serve is the motto of the Los Angeles Police Department.'

'I borrowed it,' he said easily. 'I don't think they'll mind.'

Her shoulders slumped. 'No, I'm sure they wouldn't, and I'd be extremely grateful if you stayed.' She got to her feet. 'I'll make up the spare bed for you.'

She was conscious of him following her as she climbed the stairs. Very aware of him standing behind her when she opened the airing cupboard for bed linen. His masculine scent enveloped her. She found it oddly comforting and the simple domesticity of dressing the spare bed was definitely reassuring. She went back for towels, reaching for the newer, softer ones she'd bought in M&S not long before. 'Here you go. The bathroom is next door. I have an en suite, so it's all yours.'

He dropped the towels on the bed. 'Great, thank you.'

'Right.' She stood in the doorway. 'Sleep well.'

'I usually do.' He tilted his head, raised an eyebrow and smiled. 'But I also wake easily, so if you need me, just shout and I'll be there.'

If she needed him. Leigh looked at his mouth, wondering what it would feel like pressed to hers. It had been too long since she'd felt this level of desire. Matt had been selfish in bed. She didn't think Philip would be.

She took a step backwards, appalled at where her thoughts were going. Seriously, what kind of an idiot was she? 'Thank you; hopefully it'll be a quiet night. If you're up early, help yourself to whatever you like in the kitchen. You'll find bread in the freezer.' Nothing dampened growing passion like a conversation about mundanities. With a final nod and muttered goodnight, she shut the door behind her, scarpered across to her room, shut that door too and leaned against it, stupidly breathless.

How old was she? Sixteen? Embarrassed at her reaction, she stayed leaning against the door for a while. She could hear the faint sound of his voice and wondered who he was speaking to so late at night. A girlfriend, lover, colleague? Whoever it was, the conversation was short. Leigh listened to the sound of his bedroom door opening, the faint creak of the bathroom door, the gurgle of pipes as he used the toilet and handbasin. Only when he'd returned to the bedroom and silence crept over the house, did she push away from the door and crawl under the duvet.

54

If someone tried to enter through the back door during the night, Leigh wasn't aware of it. She woke only when she heard the distinct sound of the front door shutting. Leaping from the bed without thought, she hurried to the window and pulled the curtain back, her hand gripping the material as she peered out to see Philip at the front gate. He turned then, too quickly for her to hide, and smiled to see her standing there.

She raised a hand in farewell.

He did the same, then tapped his watch. With a final wave, he headed up Gaisford Street, long strides eating the pavement until he disappeared around the corner onto Kentish Town Road. Leigh stayed staring, wishing he'd waited, or she'd woken earlier.

Showered and dressed, she crossed to the spare bedroom. Half-expecting to find the duvet thrown back, she smiled to see her unexpected guest was a particularly tidy man. The duvet was neatly spread, the pillows plumped. In the bathroom, she found the towels folded across the side of the bath.

About to strip the bed, she picked up the pillow, then without thinking, held it against her face and took a deep breath. Horrified, she dropped it as if it was on fire. She had to stop this; it was becoming an obsession. She pulled the linen from the bed, carried the bundle down and shoved it into the washing machine. Soon it was chugging away. She wished she could wash thoughts of Philip away as easily.

He'd left a note. A line scribbled along the margin of a newspaper he'd taken from the living room.

Thank you. I'll be in touch.

She looked at it for longer than the words warranted, then folded the paper and tossed it onto the counter to be dumped into the recycling bin later. The mess on the floor needed to be sorted; she couldn't spend the day stepping around it. She certainly couldn't ask the locksmith to come before it was cleared away.

Her nose crinkled at the smell coming from it. Wishing she had something as mundane as a pair of Marigolds, she ripped a refuse bag from the roll, shook it open and started to scoop up the rubbish.

Old teabags had stained the creamy tiled floor. With a sigh, she took the mop out. It took a few minutes, then everything was as good as it had been.

It was after nine. Time to ring the locksmith. 'As soon as possible,' she said when asked when she wanted the work done. 'In fact, it's rather urgent.'

'No problem,' the calm voice answered, 'we can have someone out within the hour.'

Pleased with the success of her first call, Leigh was optimistic ringing the landscape gardener. 'It's Leigh Simon, I was wondering if it was possible to do the work on the back boundary as a matter of urgency.'

'Give me a sec and I'll check.'

Leigh crossed her fingers.

'Okay, the first day we have free is three weeks tomorrow.'

Three weeks! 'I'm having a problem with someone entering the
rden through a gap in the hedge and I don't want to wait that
ng. Is there anyone you could recommend who could do the job
oner?' Her voice broke. 'I'm desperate.'

'Okay, hang on a second.'

It was a lot longer than a second before a different voice spoke.
s Simon, I hear you've been having problems.'

'A few. Someone got into the house. The police have advised me
make the place secure.'

'I see. Give me a second.'

How many more seconds did she need to give? Leigh let her
eath out in a gust of frustration.

'We'll have a team out to you on Thursday.'

'That's fantastic!' She felt tears well at this unexpected kindness.
n so grateful.'

A new lock on the back door that day, the end of her garden
ade secure on Thursday. It was all going to be okay.

Philip wouldn't need to provide security any longer.

She was still digesting this thought when the doorbell rang.
ecking her watch, she was surprised to see it had been almost
enty minutes since she'd rung the locksmith. That was probably
em now.

She stood by the front door, shaking her head at her hesitation.
geymen didn't tend to come in daylight. It was probably an erro-
ous belief, but it did allow her to open the front door. She broke
o a smile when she saw the hideous uniform of Larry the Lock-
ith. 'Hello.' She stood back and waved him in. 'It's the back door
s time. I should have had it changed when you were here.'

'No problem, I'll have it done in two ticks.'

'Would you like a drink?'

'Coffee would be great, thanks. Milk and four sugars.' H
grinned. 'I've a sweet tooth.'

Probably what made him a little on the roly-poly side. But h
was pleasant, and as chatty as he'd been the last time when Leig
hadn't the energy or desire to speak to him. This time, rested fro
the good night's sleep, she made them both coffee and stoo
sipping hers and chatting as he replaced the lock. He had a host
stories about places he'd worked, all of which were amusi
enough to have Leigh chuckling.

Then he was gone, and the house was quiet. She switched
the radio, turning the volume up so the beat of the music was hea
wherever she went. Hours vanished on internet searches. Looki
at schools in London, checking the vacancies, wondering whe
she'd end up teaching. Concentrating on her future made t
present less worrying.

Before it was dark, she pulled the curtains in the living roo
and kitchen. Then, hungry, she took out another of the quich
she'd bought. Despite the new lock on the backdoor, she sat a
watched the cooker, holding her breath until she opened the ov
twenty minutes later and saw the quiche sitting on the rack.

Maybe that was the end of the strange goings-on. Gina wou
realise she'd done all she could and move on to some more gullib
idiot to play her tricks on. Leigh ate, wondering where the wom
was living, what poor fool she'd managed to sucker this time.

For a change, Gina didn't linger in her thoughts. Instead, Phi
pushed his way in with his usual persistence. Better than Ledbet
or Matt... but equally as unsettling.

55

Leigh refused to admit to disappointment when she didn't hear anything from Philip on Tuesday night. The new locks on both doors gave her a certain amount of confidence in her safety, but she didn't sleep as well, waking several times to listen for sounds. And while she was awake, she stared into the darkness and wondered what Philip was doing.

She woke early and lay for a long time, forcing her thoughts to the new, exciting future she'd planned, anticipating with a smile her parents' reaction when she told them her news the following week.

Pleasant thoughts chased the minutes away and suddenly it was eight thirty and she was forced to rush, skipping a shower and pulling clothes on willy-nilly. The alarm assessor was coming at nine; she needed to have coffee and something to eat before that, wanting to be alert for everything he said.

On the dot of nine, just as she was swallowing the last of her toast, the doorbell rang.

'Hello,' she said, opening the door.

A tall thin man with a prominent nose and thickly gelled hair stood on the doorstep. He gave an oddly formal bow and held a business card forward. 'JJ Lake. Corrigan Alarms. We have an appointment.'

'Yes, come in.'

A minute later, she was missing Larry the Locksmith. JJ Lake was a man with absolutely no sense of humour, who responded to her quips with a blank stare. But he seemed to know what he was talking about, and that, she supposed, was what mattered.

He was there an hour, checking every window, each access door, scribbling notes on a pad, nodding and hmming until Leigh wanted to scream at him to stop. Instead, she checked her watch every few minutes, wondering if time had actually stopped and she was locked in a vacuum with the most boring man in existence.

Finally, he was done. 'Right, this should be pretty straightforward. Internal sensors on doors and windows, twenty-four seven alarm monitoring. I'll get this written up and a quotation out to you by the end of the week.'

'That's not necessary. I want to proceed, whatever the price.' She'd never asked how much it would cost to secure the rear boundary. Getting everything done would probably use up all her meagre savings and her overdraft facility. If necessary, she'd take out a loan. 'When can you install it?'

Lake frowned at this change in protocol. Perhaps he saw the determination on her face because instead of arguing, he shrugged. 'I'll have to ring the office to see when the team will be available.'

'Good.' Leigh folded her arms and stayed standing in front of him as if to prevent him from leaving before he'd rung. She thought she saw a flash of humour cross his face, but it was too brief to be sure.

'I'll ring and find out, shall I?' He didn't wait for an answer. Pulling out his phone, he rang and had a quick conversation with someone on the other end, then hung up and looked at Leigh. 'Saturday. It'll take a few hours but by the end of the day you'll have an alarm installed and working. And a safety chain on your front door.'

'That's wonderful. Thank you so much. It'll be a relief.'

'I can't believe you didn't already have a working alarm. Odd for living in the city, if you don't mind me saying.' He glared at her as if she'd been guilty of some awful social taboo.

But his crotchetiness couldn't dent Leigh's pleasure in knowing her security issues would all be sorted within the next few days, and she escorted him to the door, still smiling.

Over the next couple of hours, she phoned friends she hadn't chatted to in a while, starting with one of her oldest friends, Maria, a woman she'd known since junior school days. 'I've some news for you,' Leigh said after initial hellos. 'Well, lots of news actually. The most uninteresting being that Matt and I have split up, much more interesting is I decided being a trader didn't float my boat, so I've chucked the job.'

'What! Well, do y'know, I'm glad... about both actually... I never thought he was good enough for you, and never thought you were tough enough to be a commodity trader. Now, being totally selfish, you'll have more time to meet me for lunch.'

Leigh laughed. 'I will for a while, but I have plans. I've decided to rent out the house and live with my parents while I train to be a teacher.'

There was silence as her friend digested this. 'Yes, I could see you as a teacher. But Yorkshire?'

Leigh was amused at her friend being more surprised by the move to Yorkshire, even for a short period, than her break-up with Matt. 'You forget; unlike you, I love my home county. I'll have to wait and see what happens after I qualify. I may choose to come back here and get a position in a local school or sell up and buy something closer to my parents.'

'It's the first time in months I've heard you so excited, Leigh. I'm happy for you.'

They arranged to meet for lunch the following week, and Leigh hung up and dialled the next friend. The reaction from each was the same, all expressing relief she was leaving her job as a commodity trader. 'Did I look so unhappy?'

'Not unhappy as such,' her friend Andrea said. 'More as if a light had been switched off. Or maybe that was due to Matt. I have to admit, I wasn't keen on him. You don't seem too upset about the break-up so you've probably realised you were totally unsuited.'

Leigh shook her head. It was nice, if a little scary, to be known so well. 'It took me a while to realise the truth about both.' A final few minutes of chat about Andrea's twin boys and the conversation ended with arrangements to meet for coffee the following week.

Surprised to see how late it was, Leigh did as she'd done the previous night and pulled the downstairs curtains. Both front and back doors were checked twice before she was sure they were locked tight. She stared out across the back garden, lit up by her neighbours' lights. With all that was going on, she'd forgotten her idea to ask them to leave them on overnight. It didn't matter; by tomorrow evening, access to her garden through the shrubbery at the end would be impossible, and by Saturday, her home security would be complete.

She celebrated what had been a successful day with a glass of wine over dinner – this time a beef and beer pie from the deli. She resisted the paranoid need to sit and watch it as it heated, instead going into the living room and sipping her wine as she scrolled through TV channels to find something suitably cheerful to watch. It came down to a toss-up between reruns of *Friends* or *Frasier*. Settling for the latter, she was already chuckling a minute later.

When it was time, she put it on hold, loaded her tray with everything she needed and took it back to the living room. Episode

er episode of *Frasier* was a good accompaniment to a pie, so good
e ran a finger through the miniscule amount of sauce left on the
te and licked it clean.

Not even the continued silence from Philip managed to destroy
r hard-earned good mood but every now and then, she picked up
r mobile and checked. No messages from Matt, none from Philip.
e refused to feel disappointed or relieved about either.

56

The team from the landscape gardeners was due to arrive at eig[ht]
thirty. After another good night's sleep, Leigh was up and ready a[nd]
drinking the last of her coffee when the doorbell rang.

'Hi,' she said, smiling at the two men who stood on her doorst[ep]
in T-shirts, worn jeans and rugged work boots. Ready for busines[s.]

'Gerry and Stephen,' the older of the two said, indicating the tal[l]
younger man a step behind. 'Here to sort out your back boundary.'

'Thank you, I know it was short notice.'

'No problem.' He pointed to where their van was illega[lly]
parked. 'If we can unload quickly, Stephen can find somewhere [to]
park it for the day.'

'Yes, of course.' She pointed through the house towards the re[ar]
door. 'Everything has to come through, I'm afraid.'

He indicated the roll he was holding. 'No problem, we'll lay t[he]
floor protector and it'll keep it clean.'

Leigh smiled in satisfaction. They weren't cutting corners to [start]
the job early. Promising them a cuppa after they'd unpacked, s[he]
left them to roll out the protector and went to put on the kettle.

They had everything through to the garden in ten minutes, including, to Leigh's surprise, a big golden retriever.

'Is it okay if Camelot stays in the garden?' Stephen asked, rubbing a big hand over the dog's head. 'I was going to leave him in the van, but he started to whine. He'll be no problem. Honest.'

Leigh looked at the beautiful creature and held a hand towards him. Once he'd given his approval, she ran a hand over his soft ears. 'He's gorgeous. Yes, it's no problem.'

'I'll tie him up, otherwise he'll dig holes in your flower beds.'

Leigh ruffled the dog's ears again. 'No, there's no need, honestly, there's nothing in those beds yet, let him dig away.'

The two men wasted no time, taking their tea with them as they stood discussing the best way to proceed. Leigh watched for a few minutes, then, confident she could trust them to do what was needed, she left them to it.

Less than an hour later, a yell drew her attention from her laptop to the kitchen window. When it came again, she got to her feet to peer out. Stephen was pulling at Camelot's collar, trying to drag him away from where he was digging in the flower bed.

Leigh smiled. The poor lad probably thought he was making too much of a mess. She was happy for the gorgeous creature to dig all he wanted. Tidying up would give her something to do over the weekend.

She stepped outside and headed down the garden towards them. 'It's okay,' she said, holding a hand up. 'He won't do any harm and I honestly don't mind if he makes a mess.'

Camelot, paws muddy and tongue lolling, was struggling to get away but Stephen held tight. He was frowning, staring into the hole the dog had dug. He looked up at Leigh's words and pointed. 'There's something... I think it's a hand!'

'Another one!' She almost laughed at his look of horror. 'It's okay, honest, it's a fake one, it's happened before. Kids playing tricks. It's one of the reasons I want the boundary secured.'

'But it's a hand!'

Leigh was surprised to see the colour leech from the young man's face. She took a step towards him, stopping as Camelot growled at her, teeth bared.

Stephen shushed the dog, bending down to run a hand over him. 'He's scared.'

'There's no need. It'll be a pair to the one I found last week,' she said, shaking her head and moving closer to the hole the dog had dug. 'I'll take it away.'

Stephen looked to where the older man was working. 'Gerry, you'd better get over here.'

Leigh tried again to reassure him. 'Seriously, it's okay.' She remembered how horrified she'd been when she'd seen the latex hand. It wasn't the kind of thing you expected to see buried in the garden. She certainly hadn't, nor had she thought to expect a second. Perhaps whoever had planted the first, had buried the second deeper, hoping it would rise to the surface after heavy rain. Some people had a warped sense of humour.

She smiled and held a hand up as Gerry came hurrying over. 'It's okay, honestly, it's just a joke-shop hand. I found the same last week.' With a final smile of reassurance for Stephen, she crossed to the hole, her shoes sinking into the soft soil the dog had thrown up. The hole he'd dug was about a foot deep. Leigh stood at the edge, her confident smile fading as she noticed this hand was dramatically different from the pink latex fake. This one... the fingers were curled in a fist, the skin a dirty grey.

'Stay back,' Gerry shouted.

Ignoring him, she bent closer. It was a scarier fake than the last. A tear in the skin over the knuckles looked so real. And then she noticed something that shouldn't be happening. A wriggling movement on the back of the hand. She screamed when a shower of maggots erupted through the tear and scattered onto the dark soil, and she shrieked when a plume of noxious stink rose to send her stumbling backwards, a hand over her mouth, her stomach contracting. She fell against Stephen who yelled and lurched backwards as he tried to keep them both on their feet. Camelot, released in the melee, howled, raced to the edge of the hole and growled at the contorting maggots.

'Fuck!' Gerry said. Turning his back on the awful mess, he put a hand on Stephen's shoulder. 'Take Camelot inside, lad. Go!' He waited till the younger man had caught hold of the dog's collar and hauled him away before turning to the visibly shaking Leigh. 'We need to ring the police.' He jerked a thumb behind him. 'That's no fake.'

Leigh pressed her hand more firmly to her mouth and nodded. It was her garden. Her responsibility. But she couldn't do this alone. 'I'll ring a friend; he's a police officer.' Even in her distress, she acknowledged the irony of calling Philip a friend now, when she was in need. She looked back to the hole, relieved she couldn't see inside. It didn't matter, she would remember that sight forever. Trembling, she headed back to the house.

Stephen was sitting on the floor, his face buried in his dog's thick coat. It wasn't obvious who was comforting whom. Leigh guessed it was mutual. She wished she could join in.

Instead, she picked up her phone and scrolled through for Philip's number.

'Dunstable.'

Leigh swallowed the lump in her throat. 'It's me. I need help.'

'Leigh? What is it? Are you okay?'

'Yes, no...' She took a deep breath, trying to stay in control. For a little longer. 'The men came to sort out the garden boundary... they have a dog; he was digging in the flower bed. He found a body part,

Philip. In almost the same place the fake hand was found. But this time, it's a real one.'

'Leigh, are you sure it's not another good fake?'

'Do maggots hatch out in latex hands? Lots of maggots, squirming out from the skin. And there's a smell of something rotten.'

'Shit! Okay, listen don't touch anything. I'll get the local police to attend. They'll be there quickly, and I'll be there as soon as I can.'

'Hurry. Please.'

She dropped the phone on the table, then joined Stephen and Camelot on the floor to wait. As the icy fingers of shock began to thaw, she felt the first wave of sorrow. Poor Gina.

melot was happy to sit between Stephen and Leigh, offering nfort to both; only the sound of a police siren made Leigh reluc- tly leave the dog's side and get to her feet.

A glance through the window showed her Gerry, spade in hand, nding guard over the garden. Perhaps he expected an influx oss the back boundary, or the rest of the body to rise, maggots pping from every aperture.

She heaved, swallowing frantically as she went to open the front or. PC Sharp and Carter stood on her front step. They looked less n impressed.

'Here we are again,' Carter said, sounding resigned rather than noyed.

Leigh didn't bother with words. They'd see soon enough.

In the kitchen, the two officers eyed Stephen and Camelot with ld curiosity before exiting through the back door. Leigh didn't low. She'd seen enough, and the content of the hole didn't need planation.

Carter wasn't going to come back to her swinging a fake latex

hand. It would be as she'd expected last time. Scenes of crime o
cers, homicide detectives. The whole shebang. She hoped Phi
would get there first. Her mind had gone into shock; she could
think past staying on the floor, her fingers kneading Camelot's thi
coat.

It was Gerry coming inside a few minutes later, who told her t
officers had rung the station to set the process rolling. 'They want
take a statement from me and Stephen, then they said we could g
He looked back to the garden, then down to where she sat. 'D'y
have someone who can be with you? This has been a shock.'

Leigh struggled to her feet. 'Thank you. I have a friend on t
way.' She glanced through the window. 'Looks like the garden
going to be out of bounds for a while.'

'Afraid so. Don't worry, as soon as they allow us, we'll be back
sort it out.' He shuffled uncertainly, then, unable to help himself,
asked, 'Have you any idea who it might be?'

Leigh was looking through the window at the two officers, bc
on their radios. Even at a distance, she could see their serio
expressions. 'My lodger went missing over a week ago; I
assuming it's her.' Leigh remembered how horrified she'd be
imagining the colourful bubbly Gina trying to claw her way fro
her grave. Since then, more information had come to light to ta
the shine from her butterfly wings, but Leigh still felt saddened
the loss.

And worried.

A dead body, buried in her garden, didn't get there on its ow
She saw the question in Gerry's eyes and shook her head. 'I've
idea who could have done such a thing.' She was sudder
appalled. 'It wasn't me; you know that, don't you?'

'You were hardly going to encourage Camelot to be digging
the garden if you were responsible,' he said philosophically.

Leigh hoped the police would be equally sensible.

Carter and Sharp took statements from both men, using the living room after Leigh nodded her permission. It didn't take long; neither had much to say and soon they were taking their leave. She was sorry to see them go, sorrier still to see the golden retriever trotting off with his owner.

'You don't want a statement from me?' Leigh asked when the two officers returned. She filled the kettle, took down mugs, the jar of coffee and tin of teabags. 'Can I get you a drink?'

Both accepted coffee and it wasn't until they had mugs in hand that Carter answered her question. 'There'll be a homicide detective here shortly. He'll want to talk to you and take your statement. With it being your house, and garden, there'll be more questions.'

'Plus, of course, I know the victim, don't I? Gina, my lodger.'

'Identification will be done in due course,' Carter said, unwilling to be drawn into a discussion regarding the identity of the body.

Leigh hid a smile when she saw Sharp raise her eyes to the ceiling, glad she wasn't the only one who thought Carter a pompous prick.

More personnel started to arrive, officious types with severe expressions and an abrupt way of speaking as if too busy to waste time or energy with extra words. They carried equipment through the house with scant regard for the paintwork.

Perhaps Leigh should have been less concerned with such trivialities, or relieved the floor was still covered and protected from the heavy, often muddy, feet trundling back and forth. Sometimes, it was the mundane things that anchored.

'You should sit in the living room,' PC Sharp said to her when Leigh had to, yet again, move out of the way.

It was a suggestion, not an order, Sharp's expression kind and sympathetic enough to bring easy tears to Leigh's eyes. 'Yes, I think I will.'

She shut the door behind her and sank onto the sofa, dropping her head back and heaving a sigh as the memory of that hideous hand came barrelling back to make her shudder. Voices drifted through, some loud and authoritative, others raised in question, yet others in complaint. None were familiar.

It was silly to be expecting Philip's arrival to make everything all right. There was a dead body in her garden. Someone had to be held accountable.

The numbness of shock was fading further, curiosity creeping in to take over. With Gina dead, Leigh's theory about her ex-lodger being responsible for creeping around her house, following her, staring at her from across the street, was shot to pieces.

The person Philip handed her Kindle to, had to be the same one who had been following her, and the same one who'd used keys to come inside... they had to be the same person. Had to be Gina's killer. It was the only thing that made sense.

She shut her eyes, refusing to face up to the truth screaming from the sidelines. Leigh was no expert, but for the hand to have been so deteriorated as to have maggots crawling from it... she shivered again... Gina had to have been dead for a while. And it didn't take a rocket scientist to know that dead people didn't send letters to school principles. A dead woman wasn't likely to be accusing Matt of rape.

Matt... he'd insisted the sex was consensual. What if it hadn't been? Philip had suggested as much, and hadn't she had her own doubts? What if Gina had cried rape, told Matt she was going to report it... Was he capable of murder to keep his career? He knew Leigh had planned to have flowers in that bed, knew it wouldn't need to be dug again, the flower seeds were to be sown on top.

Leigh groaned, got to her feet and crossed to the window. Was she seriously believing Matt was capable of murder? She shook her head. It had to be the mystery person... the one Philip had met, the one who'd been following her.

Gina was obviously no saint; perhaps there were any number of people who wanted her dead.

But if it wasn't her following Leigh, who was it? And why?

58

An hour later Leigh heard a voice she recognised. She sat perched on the edge of the seat, eyes fixed on the door. When it opened, she held her breath. It was Philip, his head turned to speak to someone out of sight. Unable to see his face, she couldn't tell if his expression was police officer cold or male-friend sympathetic.

When he came in, closing the door behind him, she saw his expression. One hundred per cent police.

She opted for formal as a result. 'Thank you for coming. I couldn't think who else to call.'

He merely nodded and took the seat opposite. 'You were right, not a fake this time.' He jerked his head towards the door. 'It's a slow process. You'll need to find somewhere else to stay for a few days.'

She slumped against the cushion behind. 'Why? Can't I stay here? I'll keep out of the way.' His expression gave nothing away and she felt fingers of dread creeping around her. 'I don't understand.'

'Your garden, and your house are a crime scene, Leigh. Whoever

s who's buried in your garden was probably killed here. The
m will be searching every inch of every room for signs of
lence. You need to go elsewhere; an officer will go upstairs with
u and wait while you pack a bag.'

She stared. 'I'm a suspect?'

A slight smile appeared. 'If you were involved, it's highly
likely you'd have encouraged some big dog to dig freely in the
den.' He leaned forward, closing the distance between them, and
pped his voice. 'But you're not out of the woods yet. I'm not a
micide detective, but the senior investigating officer is a friend;
s allowing me to be involved since it's likely that the body is of a
man we're looking for.'

'Poor Gina.' Leigh sighed. 'So much for my theory she was
eping around the house and following me.'

Philip reached out to run a finger across the back of her clasped
ids. 'It's more likely the person you saw is to blame for her
ith.'

'But why are they following me? Why come into my house?' Her
ce trembled. 'I'm not in danger, am I?'

'Until we know what's going on, we'll keep a close eye on you,
i't worry.' This time he laid a hand on top of hers. 'We'll find
n.'

'Or her? Couldn't it be another woman?' Leigh remembered her
iversation with Isobel. 'She owed money to a waitress in the café
ere she'd worked. And I bet there were other women she
ined.'

'We'll be looking at every angle. Talking to everyone.' He took
hand away and sat back. 'Including Matt Gibbs.'

She wasn't surprised. Gina's death would raise a lot of questions.
ie letter to the principal wasn't signed. It could have been sent by
one.'

He got to his feet without commenting. 'Where will you go?'

'I'll have to think. Can I have a few minutes?'

'There's no hurry. Before you do anything, the SIO D[a]
Newton wants a word. When he's finished, there'll be an officer
the hallway. When you're ready she'll go upstairs with you.'

'Right.' She wanted to ask him to stay, thoughts of being qu
tioned by this unknown detective worrying her. A childish thoug
She wasn't a child and she'd done nothing wrong. None of t
strange things that had happened recently had been her fault.

Detective Chief Inspector Newton proved to be a big bear-li
man with a pleasant, unthreatening manner, and a kind way
speaking to her that made her eyes water. With an odd word
encouragement from him, she gave an account of everything th
had happened from the day she'd invited Gina to move into h
home.

The detective took notes in a neat notebook with a startli
shiny pink cover. 'From my daughter,' he said, waving it. 'She dar
me to use it.'

'And, of course, you had to.'

'I like to show how brave I am.' He turned the pages, stopping
peer at what he'd written. 'You sure you never told this wom
about inheriting the house?'

'Definitely. It's not the sort of thing I'd bring up in conversati
Not even all my friends know about it. I have no idea how she fou
out.'

'Con artists have their ways.' He shut the notebook and dropp
it into his jacket pocket, the edge of it poking out, pink and proud

Colourful, like Gina had been.

A con artist. Leigh hadn't thought of her as one, but s
supposed it fit. If Gina was a con artist... it was likely Leigh wou
eventually have been a victim. Not a pleasant thought.

'We'll have more questions later,' Newton said and stood. '

Dunstable has told you about finding somewhere else to live for a few days, yes?'

'Yes. I haven't decided where to go as yet, but I will.'

'When you're ready, PC Sharp is outside. She needs to be with you, check what it is you're taking away, okay?'

What? In case Leigh would try to smuggle the murder weapon out of the house? She wanted to say she was as much of a victim as the dead woman... but it wasn't true, was it? Leigh would eventually be able to put all this behind her. Gina would never be able to play her tricks on anyone again. Never float down the street in a haze of colour, dance across the café in sheer pleasure. It would be nice to remember her that way, forget about her part in the death of the woman in Glasgow, forget about those hideous squirming maggots.

Pushing thoughts of her away, Leigh considered where to stay. Any of her friends, she knew, would happily put her up for a few days. But she'd have to explain so much... and accept their silent critically raised eyebrows without comment.

They'd know all the details eventually, but for now, she couldn't face it. Instead, she did an internet search for a phone number, and rang it. Seconds later, she hung up, nodding in satisfaction.

There was no point in putting it off any longer. Opening the door a crack, she peered out and saw PC Sharp propped against the wall opposite. Her bored expression vanished when she saw Leigh.

'I need to pack some things.' Leigh looked up the stairway. Were there officers up there already? Searching through her belongings? She felt Sharp's eyes on her. 'Is there someone up there?'

'No, not yet.'

'That's something, I suppose.'

'You know I need to check everything you take?' Sharp's voice was sympathetic. 'It's procedure. Nothing personal.'

'It's okay. I'm not sure anything is going to be worse than what I saw this morning.'

It wasn't worse, but it was intrusive and toe-curlingly demeaning to have someone running their fingers along the seams of her knickers. Leigh didn't know how long she'd be expected to stay away. Unfortunately, when she asked Sharp, the answer was less than helpful.

'It takes as long as it takes. Depends on what they find.'

Frustrated, Leigh took a large holdall from the top of the wardrobe and filled it with the underwear, adding T-shirts, jumpers and jeans when the officer had cleared them. A few books from the pile on the bedside table were carefully flicked through. Her toilet bag was checked and added on top.

The only item Sharp refused to allow her to take was a hairbrush. The officer took a careful look at the rounded wooden handle and shook her head. 'Not this, I'm afraid. Is there something smaller you could bring?'

Leigh stared at the offending item. Did Sharp think she, or someone else, had clobbered Gina over the head with the handle of the brush? No point in complaining; the officer was merely following instructions. 'I have a folding one in my handbag; it'll do.'

A last look around, and she was done, the holdall pulling on her hand as she made her way back downstairs. 'DI Dunstable said I was to leave my new address with you.'

Sharp nodded and took out her notebook, an expectant expression on her face, pen poised.

'It's Gaisford B&B. Two doors up.'

'Convenient.' Sharp scribbled the name and put the notebook away. 'If you go elsewhere, make sure you let us know.'

'I'm planning to visit my parents next week. That'll be okay, won't it?'

Sharp shrugged non-committedly.

'Right,' Leigh said with the first glimmer of irritation. She picked up her holdall and handbag and walked out the open front door. Police vehicles lined the road either side. A police constable she didn't recognise was directing traffic, another was posted at her garden gate. A small group of people stood staring but after a curious glance in Leigh's direction, with nothing more interesting to see, they moved on.

59

Gaisford B&B's landlady, Sylvia, who Leigh knew well enough to stop for a chat if they passed on the street, glanced at her with sympathy, then peered along the street in horror. 'You poor lamb,' she said, pulling Leigh into a hug. 'What an awful thing! You know I used to tell your aunt she was crazy not getting that back boundary sorted. Something like this was going to happen one day. I bet they were drug dealers or something.'

She babbled on with her theory of a falling out among thieves. It saved Leigh having to talk, and since she wasn't asked any questions, she didn't have to lie.

Sylvia insisted on making tea and serving it in her comfortable lounge. 'Here you go,' she said, putting a tray on a low table. 'Tea and cake.' She patted Leigh on the shoulder. 'Stay here for as long as you want. Switch on the TV if you like or' – she pointed to a pile of magazines – 'you might find something there to take your mind off things.' She handed over a key attached to a small wooden globe. 'You're in room 2, first floor. It's to the front; I didn't think you'd like to be looking out on what's happening out back.'

Leigh was touched by her kindness and thoughtfulness. oosing the B&B had been a good choice. She was relieved ugh, when the landlady left her with a promise to be there if she eded her.

What she needed was peace but that wasn't going to happen. e drank the cup of tea, but the cake was an unfortunate choice, ped as it was with coconut flakes, reminding Leigh instantly of se damn maggots. It was enough to push her to her feet with a mace of distaste. She took the key, picked up her bags and went stairs.

The room was spacious, the furniture luxurious, the en suite cked with everything she could need. A tray on a dresser held a iety of herbal teas, and an upmarket coffee maker she guessed 'd use a lot over the next few days.

It took only minutes to unpack her bag and put everything ay. There was a comfortable armchair near the window. Leigh sat it with one of the books she'd chosen at random, groaning when saw it was a crime novel. She tossed it aside and picked up the er. It was marginally better, although she wasn't sure she was in mood for a romance novel. Especially, she decided a few pages er, when it wasn't very good. Why hadn't she thought to bring her sted Kindle? She was sure to have found something to suit her od on it. Too late, she couldn't face going back to ask for it.

The TV didn't provide any distraction either. Her large room ldenly felt small, claustrophobic. What was happening in her den? Had they removed Gina's body? The B&B was only two rs away, but it was set further back from the road, allowing only estricted view of the front of Leigh's home, and there was nothing opening on the road outside. She could walk up to Kentish Town ad, peer in as she passed. Or she could ask Sylvia if she could k through one of the back bedroom windows.

She was still mulling over her choices when she heard a tap
her door. Expecting it to be Sylvia, she opened the door with
smile on her face. It died instantly when she saw Philip and D
Newton outside.

'Can we come in?' Philip asked. He looked over her should
taking in the room. 'Or we could use the lounge downstairs if you
prefer.'

Should she go all Victorian coy and say she couldn't invite t
such handsome strangers into her boudoir? Maybe flutter l
eyelashes for added effect? What was it in the eyes of both det
tives that made her want to delay? She wasn't sure she wanted
find out, but it didn't look as if she had much choice. 'Here is fir
she said.

She sat back on the armchair, crossing her legs, trying to lo
unconcerned. Newton took the only other chair, leaving Philip
choose between standing or perching on the end of the be
Looking uncomfortable, he chose the latter.

'This is a nice place,' Newton said, looking around the roo
'Convenient for you too.'

If he was trying to put her at ease, it wasn't working. Leigh
rigidly, shoulders tense, jaw locked. All the various parts of her ke
together by strings of tension. If they let go, she'd collapse.

'It will be a couple of days before you'll be able to go home, I
afraid, but if you need anything, you just need to ask.' He shuffl
uncomfortably, and the chair, far too small for his bulk, creaked
protest.

She felt Philip's eyes on her and refused to look his directic
Sympathy would be her undoing. 'I assume you've more questic
for me.'

Newton sniffed, took a balled-up handkerchief from his pock
rubbed his nose energetically and shoved it back. 'Hay fever,'
explained. 'Questions... yes, we have a few, I'm afraid.'

Leigh had one of her own. 'Can I ask, first, have you removed Gina's body?'

Newton glanced at Philip before looking back to her. 'It was a slow process. Although the hand you saw was relatively close to the surface, the rest of the body was buried deeper.'

Leigh felt a jolt of nausea. Had she been right; had Gina been buried alive and tried to claw her way from her grave? She met Newton's gaze. 'She was buried alive?'

He looked taken aback. 'Buried alive? Why would you think that?'

'I think Ms Simon is thinking the hand was extended because they were trying to claw their way from the grave,' Philip said, drawing their attention. 'I think a more reasonable explanation is that rigor mortis had set in before the body was buried. They'd probably tried to push it down but were unable.' He shrugged. 'Despite previous violence leading to the death, the perpetrator was obviously too squeamish to break the arm.'

Previous violence. 'Poor Gina, what kind of a monster would do such a thing?'

'Ah well, now there's the thing,' Newton said. 'It's not Gina.'

Leigh thought she must have misheard. 'Sorry, what did you say?'

'I said it's not Gina. We all made the obvious assumption, but it quickly became clear we'd made a mistake. The body is that of a man.'

'A man?' Leigh felt her head was going to implode. 'Then where's Gina?'

'As yet, that's still a bit of a mystery. The one we're more concerned with though, is how this particular man came to be buried in your garden.'

'This particular man...' She looked from Newton to Philip in a daze. 'I don't understand.'

It was Philip who took pity on her. 'Luckily, I was here. I was able to identify the man immediately.' He waited a beat. 'It's Bernard Ledbetter, Leigh.'

60

Leigh stared at Philip. Any moment now, he'd laugh and say it was some bizarre tasteless joke because what he'd said couldn't possibly be true. Ledbetter couldn't be buried in her garden. When the detective continued to look at her with sympathetic eyes... not the shuttered police expression she'd come to dread... her shoulders slumped in disbelief. 'But that's impossible.'

'When was the last time you saw Mr Ledbetter?' Newton asked, drawing her attention.

It was all too much; she wanted to bury her head in her arms and bawl. Tell them both to go away and leave her to her misery. Ledbetter, the man she'd accused of being sexually inappropriate and tried to punch, a man who'd turned most of her work colleagues against her, was dead. *Buried in her garden*. Leigh wasn't a fan of crime shows but she'd watched enough in her day to know the police would be looking for means, motive and opportunity. She'd definitely had a motive. It seemed the bawling would have to wait. 'On the Friday before I did that course. Three weeks ago.'

'And not since?'

'No. When I went back to work, he hadn't shown up.' She

braced herself for Newton to say *convenient* and when he didn't, she felt tears gather. 'I may have disliked him, but I wouldn't have wished him any harm.'

'Although you did try to punch him.'

'It was a reaction. Plus, I missed.' She could almost see the wheels turning behind his eyes. She'd missed, but didn't it show her tendency for violence... how far would she have gone?

Newton scribbled a note in his notebook, then looked up at her. 'He's never been to your home?' When she shook her head, he asked, 'Or maybe he walked you home after an office party one night?'

'No!' Too loud. She saw his eyes narrow. Was he thinking she'd somehow lured Ledbetter to her house, lost her temper and succeeded this time in hitting him? Hit him, killed him and buried him in her damn garden!

'I'm simply trying to figure out how he ended up here. In the garden of a woman who'd accused him of impropriety.'

She took a steadying breath and forced herself to speak calmly. 'He's never been here or walked me home after a party. I've not been with the company that long; there's been no parties or nights out since I joined, or at least, none that I've been invited to.'

'Sounds like you didn't get on with your workmates.'

It wasn't a question, but Leigh picked him up on it anyway. 'I got on with them fine but they're a cliquey lot and it takes time to get through that. Since I made the allegation about Ledbetter, it's been harder.'

'Nobody else had made any allegation?'

'No.' She wanted to shout that it didn't mean she was lying, didn't mean Ledbetter wasn't a misogynistic lecherous bastard. But it all seemed so useless. The man was dead. Nobody would want to hear a bad word against him now.

Dead and buried in her garden. She'd been so convinced it had

en Gina, it was hard to make the adjustment. She felt Newton's
es on her and looked up. 'Ledbetter was management; it would
ve been easy for him to have accessed my file to get my home
dress.'

'But why would he want to?' Newton lifted a hand and batted
own question away. 'We'll find out eventually.' He scribbled in
notebook before looking back to her. 'You had work done on the
den recently.'

Leigh frowned. She wished he'd stop making statements and
a damn question. The flash of irritation vanished as fast as it
appeared. 'Yes, a few months ago. It's not finished yet; they've to
ne back next month to do the planting.'

'And it was your idea to spread the work out.'

Leigh saw where he was going. Had she organised it so that the
ds would be ready with nice soft soil it would be easy for her to
a deep hole in? Then they'd come back and plant flowers and
ubs and nobody would ever know there was a body feeding the
ts. It would have worked too, if she'd not let Camelot plough a
ldy great hole. 'As we've already discussed, I'd hardly have
wed that dog to dig holes if I'd buried a body there.'

'No, you wouldn't,' he said calmly. 'Did Mr Gibbs help in the
den?'

The question puzzled her. Matt didn't have a motive to kill
dbetter; he'd never even met the man. 'No, he didn't. The land-
pe gardener had his own team; they did all the work.'

'Did Mr Gibbs know about your problem with Mr Ledbetter?'

'No. I didn't tell him.'

'Why not? Did you think he'd be angry?'

Leigh shook her head. 'No, not angry as such.' Could she
lain what she didn't really understand? 'He'd have criticised me
not pulling Ledbetter up on his behaviour the first time it
ppened, and Matt would've gone on and on about what I should

do, and he'd have brought it up every single time we spoke. It w
easier to keep my mouth shut.'

'The same as you did when Mr Ledbetter behaved inapp
priately?'

She was startled by his insight. 'Yes, I suppose you're right.'

'I often am.' He put his notebook back into the baggy pocket
his jacket and got to his feet. 'That's it for now.'

Leigh held a hand up to stop him. 'Matt wouldn't have h
anything to do with it. He's not the violent type. Phil—' S
stopped. 'DI Dunstable will have told you about the strange pers
who was here when he called around. And about the person w
was following me.' She dropped her hand to her lap. 'I w
convinced it was Gina in some sort of a crazy disguise. Since t
body isn't hers... and she's not dead... maybe it was her.' She w
getting herself in a tangle. 'Ledbetter was tall, she is tiny, there's
way she could have killed him. So perhaps, the person
Dunstable saw, the one who was following me, was someone el
and it was this person who killed Ledbetter.'

'Dunstable has told me all the details,' Newton said. 'They do
account for Mr Ledbetter's presence in your home though.'
tapped his thumbnail against the top of the pink notebook sticki
from his pocket. 'As yet, all we have are questions, but we'll
answers eventually.' He indicated the door with a tilt of his he
'We'll head.'

Leigh half expected Philip to wait behind but he left withou
glance in her direction. She got to her feet and watched from t
window as they walked up the street. They were deep in conver
tion, heads together, Philip gesticulating emphatically with
index finger. Then they were lost to view, and she was on her ov
And scared. It was good to admit it. And sensible to be scared.

Why had Ledbetter been in her house?

61

Leigh was afraid the story would make it onto the nine o'clock news... the only one her parents listened to... but she was in luck as yet another gaffe by the prime minister ensured focus in his direction. There might be a reference in the newspapers the following day, but her parents only read the *Yorkshire Post* during the week. They read *The Guardian* on a Sunday; Leigh would buy it and check to see if she'd made its pages.

Hopefully, they'd be kept in the dark until she visited; she didn't want them worrying needlessly. Once she was home, she'd tell them everything.

She wondered about ringing Matt to warn him, deciding in the end to send him a message.

I need to talk to you. Ring me when you can.

A few minutes later, she saw he'd read it, but he didn't ring, didn't reply. She was saddened, but not completely surprised. He was probably thinking *what's left to say...* he'd soon find out.

He'd blame her. It was Leigh who'd indirectly embroiled him in the lives of both Gina and Ledbetter. He was a suspect by association. Luckily Leigh wouldn't have to listen to his complaints.

Foolishly, she'd expected to hear from Philip. It wasn't until the light began to fade that she decided he was keeping his distance.

Restless, and hungry, she pulled a jacket on, shoved her purse and keys into a pocket and went to get something to eat. The nearest place for good food was the pub on the corner, but she was known there; there would be sideways glances, perhaps even questions. Instead, taking the long way around to avoid passing her home, she walked to a little Italian pizzeria she and Matt used on occasion.

A table in the corner, a half carafe of house red, and a mushroom and artichoke pizza. It was almost normal. Eating on her own wasn't but at least she could let her mind wander where it willed, drifting from thought to thought, theory to theory, few of them making sense.

Afterwards, she walked home, this time choosing the shorter route, slowing as she came to her house. They were still working, if the lights shining from every window was an indication, but there were fewer police vehicles parked along the road and no bored constable guarded her gateway.

Leigh slowed almost to a stop as she passed, staring at the door, almost willing it to open. It didn't, of course; those things happened in movies and books, not real life. With a sigh, she moved on to the B&B, trudged up the stairs to her room and locked the door behind her.

* * *

The following day passed. That was all Leigh could say in its favour. Breakfast in the B&B dining room was a pleasant if short-lived diversion, her lack of appetite doing it little justice. When she'd delayed as long as she could over a cafetière of excellent coffee, she returned to her room to stare out the window and watch as police vehicles pulled up outside. It was mid-morning before she saw Newton arrive. He glanced in the direction of the B&B, making her pull back, although there was no way he could have seen her.

There was no sign of Philip. Probably back doing his own job, searching for missing people. Gina perhaps.

Leigh was tired of trying to understand where Gina fit into the story with Bernard Ledbetter, or even if she did. Only finding her would answer that question, and despite the detectives' confidence, there was no guarantee they could. The Strathclyde police hadn't, after all. They still didn't know who she was, so how *could* they find her?

She was a chameleon woman; she could be anywhere.

For lunch, Leigh ate some of the biscuits supplied with the tea and coffee. She was sitting watching an episode of *Escape to the Country* when she heard a knock on the door.

Not the landlady. Leigh had told her over breakfast she didn't need the room made up, promising to ask if she needed anything. If it wasn't Sylvia, it had to be the police.

Leigh wasn't consciously hoping it would be Philip, but when she opened the door and saw him standing there, she couldn't help giving a relieved smile. 'Hi.'

'Hi, can I come in?'

She stood back. 'Of course.'

He took the chair Newton had taken the day before.

'I can make coffee or tea, if you'd like.' She pointed to the hospitality tray. 'The landlady keeps me well supplied.'

'No, that's okay, thanks.' He looked at her. 'I have some news for you, and some more questions.'

She sat on the armchair. 'Where's your pal, DCI Newton?'

'He's gone to interview a suspect.' Philip held a hand up to stop the question on her lips. 'I've been temporarily assigned to his team because of my familiarity with the case so Newton asked me to get some information for him.'

'Okay.' Leigh couldn't make sense of this new twist. 'You may as well fire ahead then.'

'DCI Newton has friends in all the right places, so we've had some results back already.'

Leigh wasn't sure whether to be pleased or not that Philip seemed to be less policeman, more friend that morning. There was sympathy in his eyes that made her wonder what the results were. 'Okay,' she said again for want of anything more intelligent to say.

'The post-mortem showed Bernard Ledbetter died as a result of a blow to his head. Traces of his blood were found on your kitchen floor. It had been scrubbed clean, but the team found traces in the grouting between the tiles. They also found traces of semen.' Philip linked his fingers together, rested his clasped hands between his knees and leaned closer to her.

Leigh had wondered where the sordid tryst with Gina had occurred. 'Matt admitted to having had sex with Gina, now I guess I know where it happened.'

Philip sighed. 'The semen samples were from two males, Ledbetter and one other. Other samples taken proved to be saliva from a third person, a female this time, and these were a match to tissue taken from under Ledbetter's nails.'

This time, Leigh couldn't even manage an *okay*. Dazed, she was grateful when Philip reached for her hand. The sensation she was falling away receded. She saw the sympathy on his face and knew it wasn't over yet. 'Go on, please.'

He gave her hand a final squeeze and let it go. 'Other forensic evidence proves the woman and Ledbetter had engaged in sexual intercourse.'

gh was stunned. In all her theorising, this wasn't something ?'d considered. 'Gina was in a relationship with Ledbetter?'

'All we know is they had sex shortly before he was killed. No ?re. We're still trying to join the dots.' He nodded to the hospi- ty tray. 'Maybe coffee would be good after all.'

Leigh was relieved to have something to do to allow her racing ?ughts to calm. 'Here you go.' She handed him a mug and a plas- wrapped packet of biscuits.

She stood with her coffee, looking out the window at the police ?icles. 'Any idea when they'll be finished?'

Philip tore the packet open with his teeth. The two biscuits were all; he popped both into his mouth and shoved the wrapper into jacket pocket. 'They're hoping to be done sometime tomorrow.' swallowed some coffee. 'There's more to tell you, Leigh, and it's ? good.'

She turned to look at him. 'Every day I hope things are going to better and they get worse; why should today be any different?' ? sat and gave him a quick smile. 'Get it over with, Philip.'

'First, a question. Did Matt ever help with the work on yc garden?'

'No, never. DCI Newton already asked me this. The landscap had a great team, they did everything. Matt has never been int ested in the garden.'

'Okay, now think carefully before answering. Would he ha helped to put any of the tools away when they were finished?'

She frowned. 'No, they didn't use mine, they had their own.'

'And when was the last time you used any of your ov equipment?'

'Not since last year. I had thought I could do the work myse After an hour, when I'd achieved very little, I gave up. I put t spade away in the tool shed and I'd swear that was the last tim saw it.'

'And Matt would have had no reason to open the shed remove any of the equipment?'

There was only one reason for Philip to be asking these qu tions. 'You think Matt buried Ledbetter?' Appalled, Leigh shook h head. 'No, that couldn't be!'

'They found epithelial cells on the handle of the spade. The a match with the second seminal fluid sample. Traces of blood the blade of the spade, match Ledbetter's.' Philip ran a hand ov his hair and rubbed the back of his neck tiredly. 'I'm telling you more than I should, you know.'

'Yes, I know, and I appreciate it. I'm just...' Sick, numb, a mess emotions she couldn't even begin to unravel. 'It looks like I did know Matt at all, doesn't it? What happened, did he and Ledbet have a falling out over Gina, got into a fight or something?'

'We should know more after DCI Newton talks to Mr Gibl Philip drank more of his coffee. 'Ledbetter didn't appear to have a defensive injuries but we're not ruling anything out.'

Leigh thought for a moment. 'Matt could have taken out a spa when I wasn't in the garden. There isn't a lock on the tool shed. All your evidence might be' – her forehead creased as she tried to think of the correct word – 'what's the word… circumstantial?'

'If that was all we had to go on, the defence would have a field day, but there is a final piece of evidence that's more conclusive.' He reached into his pocket for his mobile. 'See if you recognise this?' He held it forward.

Leigh took it from him, peering at the photograph on the screen. She knew it immediately. How many hours had she pored over details of various designs before choosing this for Matt's Christmas present? A multi-stranded dark brown leather bracelet with a magnetic clasp. 'If you turn over the clasp, there should be an *M* on one side, an *L* on the other. I had it engraved specially.'

Philip took his phone back and slid his finger across the screen. 'Like this?'

Just like that. Leigh stared at the image, remembering when she'd had it done, hoping he'd like it. 'Where did you find it?' She didn't really need to ask; she knew the answer, but it gave her seconds to gather her thoughts.

'In the grave under Ledbetter's body. I'd guess it got caught when Matt was pulling him into the hole he'd dug. By the time he'd noticed it was missing, it was probably too late. Anyway, he'd assumed the body would never be discovered.'

'You can't prove he killed Ledbetter though, can you?' She knew she was right when she saw Philip's frown.

'We can't prove he killed him, but there's enough evidence to make a strong case. The bracelet is more than circumstantial. There's only one way it could have found its way into the grave that was dug for disposing of the body.' Philip pushed the cuff of his jacket back to check the time. 'DCI Newton is talking to Matt now. A confession would be good but we're fairly confident we'll get a conviction without. Meanwhile, we're still searching for Gina.'

'You've still no idea who she is, do you?'

'Not yet.'

'Strathclyde police were never able to find her; seems to me she's like a silverfish slinking away to disappear into the cracks.' And if they couldn't find her, it would be Matt's word against the evidence piling up against him. Despite it, Leigh still struggled to believe he was responsible for Ledbetter's murder. 'If you can't find her and hear her side of the story, her version of what happened that night, it's going to be Matt's word against the evidence, isn't it?'

'I'm sorry, yes, I'm afraid that's the way it will go.'

63

Leigh sat for a long time after Philip left, thinking about Matt, the months they'd been together, the future she'd once planned with him, the dramatically different prospect that now seemed to be facing him. Even if he could prove he didn't kill Ledbetter, it seemed clear he was involved in burying him. With a criminal record, he'd find it hard to get a good teaching position; his career at Bishopdown Senior School would certainly be over.

The hours dragged by. Some were spent staring out the window daydreaming, more watching the TV: films and documentaries and even reruns of old comedy series. She'd planned to go for a walk, but it seemed even the weather was against her, a light rain growing heavier as the afternoon crept on, the day turning dark and grim.

Leigh thought of Matt being questioned by Newton and hoped the change in the weather wasn't an ominous omen. By four, the heavy low cloud and deluge of rain made it dark enough to turn on lights. She sat in the armchair and listened as rain pelted off the windowpane.

She checked her phone regularly and answered messages from friends who were still oblivious to what was going on. Leigh had never been so grateful for an incompetent prime minister whose antics had filled the newspapers recently.

* * *

That night, monsters prowled the edges of her dreams... a vividly colourful one with ghastly fangs dripping blood, one with a long writhing tentacle where a moustache should be. It wasn't hard to see where her subconscious was going; it was a shame real life wasn't as easily understood. During the many periods of wakefulness, she reviewed everything that had happened over the previous weeks.

She'd wondered if her stupid spontaneous offer of accommodation to Gina had been the catalyst for everything that had happened, but that was before Leigh had discovered her ex-lodger had been in a relationship with her nemesis, Ledbetter. How long had it been going on?

Ledbetter and Gina. Had they been in cahoots? And for what reason?

* * *

At breakfast, Sylvia thoughtfully provided a selection of Sunday newspapers. First down, Leigh had her choice and picked up *The Guardian*. Usually, she began with the more entertaining supplements. That morning, she worked in reverse, scanning the news pages for any mention of Matt.

It came on the third page. A small article.

Teacher arrested for the murder of city trader

Teacher Matt Gibbs has been charged with the murder and unlawful burial of Bernard Ledbetter who was found buried in a garden in Camden Town on Thursday. The police have refused to comment on an ongoing investigation.

A small article. But big enough.

Leaving the remains of the paper on the table with her barely iched breakfast, she took the news section with her and went k to her room to make several phone calls. She picked up her bile, sighing loudly to see the series of missed calls. The first was m her parents. They'd be worried sick.

'Mum, hi,' she said when the phone was answered on the first g.

'Why didn't you tell us!'

'I didn't want to worry you. Honestly, it's okay. I'm staying with a nd.' The lie was essential; if her mother knew she was staying ne in a B&B, no matter how good it was, she'd be on the next n south from Yorkshire. 'I was going to tell you next week. Matt I I had already split up before all this came out.'

'But he buried a body in your garden! What kind of a man does nething like that? And who's this man he killed anyway?'

'I promise, when I'm home next week, I'll tell you all I know. n't worry, everything is okay. I'll be able to go home later today or iorrow.'

'You must be devastated. I'll come down. You shouldn't be ne.'

'No, please, Mum. Honestly, I have a lot to do to keep me busy. en I'll be home, and you can spoil me rotten.'

'Well, if you're sure.' Her mother didn't sound convinced.

'I am. I might stay longer when I come up next week though, if t suits.'

Her mother seemed to be more than happy with that resolution I Leigh hung up with a smile. It would be good to go home.

There was no reason she couldn't stay there for as long as s
needed to reset her brain.

An hour later, she put the phone down with a weary sigh. All
her friends wanted to rush over to support her. She put them off
telling them her mother was coming down. A white lie needed
her sanity, and with promises to each that she'd tell them t
details the following week, she hung up.

She folded up the news section of *The Guardian* without readi
the rest. It would be polite to return the paper to the dining roo
but lethargy kept her pressed to the chair.

Her eyelids were drooping, sleep sneaking up on her, when h
phone rang, startling her. An unknown number. 'Hello?'

'Leigh, it's Philip.'

'I saw it in the newspaper.' She couldn't hide the hint of rese
ment in her voice that she'd had to read it, that he hadn't rung
tell her. To warn her. 'You've arrested Matt for Ledbetter's murder

'Shit! I'm so sorry, that wasn't meant to be released. I te
Newton these things always get out.'

'It's only a small piece in *The Guardian*,' she relented. 'It does
give a lot of detail, but it does mention Matt's name, and Camd
Town. Not hard for people, including my parents and friends, to p
things together.'

'I'm sorry.' His sigh was audible. 'I do have some good news
you. They're finished in your house; you can go home wheneve
you want.'

He was right; it was good news. 'Thank you. It will be a relief
be home.'

'I'm swamped with work but perhaps, later in the week, I cou
call around?'

Leigh hesitated. Would she ever be able to separate the attr
tive man with the sexy smile, from the police officer who w
involved in such a convoluted part of her life? Was it better to pu

all behind her? 'I don't know. I'm going home to Yorkshire late next week and have promised to meet other friends so it's going to be busy.'

'Fine.' One short word that said it all. 'Take care, Leigh. I'll be back in my role with the MPB on Monday. I'm sure DCI Newton will be in touch regarding the case.'

The line went dead.

Immediately, she wanted to ring him back and beg for time. She didn't – if she had, she'd have begged him to come over as soon as he could, that she'd be waiting.

When she got back from Yorkshire, with her sanity restored – she'd ring him then and explain her hesitancy.

She knew he'd understand.

64

An hour later, with her few belongings thrown willy-nilly into her holdall, and her stay paid for, she thanked Sylvia and made the short trip between the B&B and her home.

Luckily, the rain had stopped. A temporary lull, Leigh guessed, eyeing the dark clouds. She'd have been better keeping a closer watch on where she was walking. Her foot sank into a puddle of rainwater on the uneven footpath, making her swear loudly.

Typical. You look one way for danger, and it comes from a different direction.

She reached her front door without further mishap and slipped the key into the lock. It was only then she remembered the alarm that was supposed to have been installed the previous day and swore again. Louder and more colourfully. She guessed the police had sent the company away. First thing Monday, she'd ring and explain.

Half expecting the house to be left in a state of disorder, she was relieved to see it was much as she'd left it. Maybe things weren't exactly where they should be, but they'd made an obvious effort to leave things as tidy as possible.

She stood in the kitchen doorway for a long time, her eyes drifting over the floor tiles, trying to see the slightest spec of the blood and other bodily fluids the police had found. Her vivid imagination conjured up what it must have looked like when Ledbetter had been murdered and she shivered.

In that second, she made a decision. It was impossible to stay living there knowing what had happened. She'd forgotten to cancel the visit by the estate agent on Friday. That very efficient woman would have called around and doubtless knew all the facts by now. Leigh would talk to her and see how easy it would be to sell the house. The agent may advise her to wait for a few months till memories had faded.

Her parents would be happy for her to move home for as long as she wanted. Her future lay elsewhere. Perhaps she'd stay in Yorkshire, get a job there. She was going to get on with her life, not wait around. What had that wonderful Beatrix Austin said? *Don't wait. Not for anything.* Leigh was going to wear purple now, not wait till she was seventy.

Shutting the kitchen door, she picked up her holdall and headed upstairs. Here too there was little indication her home had been searched. Little indication, but the idea that strangers had gone through her personal items made her squirm. She stood, her holdall hanging from one hand, and wondered about going back to the B&B.

It was a silly idea, quickly dismissed. She couldn't, however, put the image of fingers fumbling through her underwear out of her mind. There seemed to be only one solution. She emptied her drawers into the laundry basket and brought it downstairs. It took two trips. And two runs of the machine to get everything washed.

She hung half the clothes on an airer in the kitchen, the rest went into the tumble dryer. She hummed as she worked. After the laundry, she went around the rooms, adjusting furniture, ornaments, photo frames. Even when they didn't need anything done. Reclaiming her space.

It was nearly eight before she'd run out of things to do and she stood feeling a little lost. She could eat; she had no appetite but it was something to do to pass the time.

The food she'd bought from the delicatessen was still in date. A steak and mushroom pie mildly tempting. She took it out and slipped in onto a rack in the oven.

While she waited for it to heat, she opened a bottle of Merlot and sat sipping it, trying to keep her thoughts fixed in the groove marked *numb*. A glass of wine would help. A bottle might almost guarantee it, but that was probably a step too far.

The pie was probably delicious. Certainly, the few mouthfuls she managed to swallow were very tasty. She pushed the rest away and refilled her wine glass. Tomorrow would be soon enough to get back into good habits. Anyway, when she was home with her parents, the strongest they drank was the tea her father made.

Tired, she was contemplating going to bed, early as it was, when the doorbell rang, making her instantly alert. *Philip!* He'd said he was busy. Had her rejection made him more determined? She should ignore it; pretend she was out. Shouldn't she?

The doubt irritated her, and she knocked back the remnant of the wine in her glass. When the doorbell pealed again, she got to her feet. Who was she trying to kid; she was pleased he'd come round.

But when she opened the door, words of greeting ready on her lips, it wasn't Philip who stood there.

65

gh was startled by the vision on her doorstep. The woman had impossibly towering bee-hive hairdo and an unnaturally pale e with dark, cat eye make-up and purple lipstick. In contrast, the ther jacket, tight-fitting mini dress, tights and Doc Martins, all in ck, looked unremarkable.

'Can I help you?' When the painted lips curved in a smile, Leigh ped. 'Gina?'

'Not any more, she's outlived her usefulness. It's Flavia now.'

Leigh held fast to the door with one hand, the door frame with other. As a pose, it wasn't welcoming and reflected how she felt.

e police are looking for you.'

'Yes, but they won't be looking here, will they?' She looked over gh's shoulder. 'I know you're alone, so why you don't invite in?'

Was she a vampire? Was she unable to cross Leigh's threshold hout that precious worded invitation? Just then, as if to prove wasn't, Flavia opened her mouth and laughed. Leigh didn't see pointed incisors. Such a stupid thing to think. For a moment wondered if she was lost in one of her crazy dreams.

'Sorry,' Flavia said. 'It's just that you look so damn worrie(
promise I mean you no harm.'

'Did you say the same thing to the woman in Glasgow bef(
you killed her and stole her identity?'

'Oh please,' Flavia said, irritation in her voice and in the furr
appearing between her eyes. 'I didn't kill Gina. She was doing tl
all by herself; it was only a matter of time before she bought doc
drugs from an even dodgier supplier. I tried to warn her, but sh
gone past the stage of listening.' She looked behind her as footst(
alerted her to people approaching. 'Listen, there's something y
need to know, but I'm not standing here on the doorstep to tell y(
so either let me in or I'll keep my secrets.'

Secrets? Perhaps Leigh would learn what had happened tl
night. It might help free Matt from any suspicion in the death
Ledbetter. Gina... Flavia... whatever her name was, she might
the key. Releasing her grip on the door frame, Leigh stood back a
waved her visitor through.

Flavia smiled and headed straight for the kitchen. She eyed
red wine with satisfaction. 'Exactly what I need.' Without wait
for an invitation, she opened a cupboard, took down a glass a
poured.

'Do help yourself,' Leigh said, sitting and reaching for her gl
'Is Flavia really your name?'

'Why, don't you like it? I thought it suited me. I can change
something else, if you'd prefer.'

Leigh slammed her glass on the table, sending the w
swirling. 'I'm not playing games with you, whatever your name
Say what you've come to say and go away.'

'That's not being very friendly,' Flavia said, taking the ch
opposite. 'Especially considering I've come to help get your un(
serving boyfriend off the hook for murder.'

Leigh wanted to punch the air. She knew Matt hadn't be

responsible for Ledbetter's death, knew he wasn't capable of *that* level of violence. This woman... she'd somehow embroiled him in her schemes. Maybe she'd blackmailed him into burying the body. Her lips curled in a sneer. 'I knew he wasn't responsible. He's not that kind of man. His only crime was allowing you to seduce him!'

'Seduce him?' Flavia's laugh was short, harsh, lacking any humour. 'Is that what he told you? My dear, your eyes are going to be well and truly opened.' She lifted her glass and tilted it to take a large mouthful heedless of the excess running from the corners of her mouth.

Leigh stared in horror at the red stains on her unwanted visitor's chin. Fear had long sharp nails. It jabbed, concentrating all her thoughts. She glanced towards where her phone sat on the counter.

'Yes, get your phone,' Flavia said. She must have seen Leigh's surprise. 'I think it'll be better if you record this conversation. You've had trouble getting the police to believe you, haven't you? With your strange tales of people invading your home in the wee hours.'

'That was you?'

'It was. Believe it or not, it wasn't done to scare you. I'd have come in during the day, but I was trying to be inconspicuous. I left the front door open, the first time, for a quick escape.' She shook her head. 'Silly decision. Those damn cops turned up. I was lucky, I had time to hide behind the sofa when they did a cursory sweep of the living room with their torches. As soon as they went upstairs, I scarpered.' She grinned. 'It was quite fun.'

'Why?' Leigh shook her head. 'You really scared me. And it was you who took the quiche from the oven too, I suppose.'

Flavia laughed. 'I'd been in and out of the house a few times by then. That day, the quiche smelt so damn good I couldn't resist taking it. Anyway, I reckoned it was one of the ones I'd left behind.

You'd kindly left the wrapper in the bin, so I helped myself. Very nice it was too.'

Leigh stared at her, wanting to cry, to scream, settling for repeating her pathetic question. 'Why? What did I do to deserve what you did?'

'You think it's about you?' Flavia refilled her glass and took a sip, looking into the wine with a frown. 'Yes, I suppose it is, really. You invited me to move in; you went on that blasted management training, leaving Matt here; you had a falling out with that man whose name I didn't know until this morning. These things... all so inoffensive in themselves... had such a disastrous outcome.'

Struggling to understand, Leigh latched onto the one puzzling item. 'Bernard Ledbetter. You weren't in a relationship with him?'

'No.' Flavia shuddered. 'I'd never met him before that night.' She nodded to the phone. 'Turn on the recorder; let me tell you exactly what happened that Friday.'

66

Gina was ready to leave to meet her friends. She was wearing a new dress, this one a vision in white gauze with a fitted bodice and layered skirt floating to mid-calf. It made her feel like the fairy from the top of a Christmas tree. Of all the personas she'd adopted over the years, this fey fairy one might be her favourite. There would come a time, no doubt, when she'd be forced to cast it off. Till then, she was determined to enjoy it.

Another minute and she'd have left. This thought pierced her for days, weeks, months afterwards. To have been so close to escaping all that followed.

But she was still there when the doorbell rang.

Stupidly, she had no reservations, dancing to answer with no expectation of the violence that was going to explode.

'Hi,' she said.

The strawberry-blond man rubbed a thumb and first finger over his weedy moustache. 'Where's Leigh?'

'She's not back till Sunday; can I take a message for her?' Gina was trying to be pleasant, but she was suddenly sorry she'd answered the door. There was something in this man's expression she didn't like, something she'd seen before. She went to close the door, squealing when he shot a hand out to stop her.

'I had something to give her,' he said, pushing his way inside. 'Seems I'll have to give it to you instead.'

Gina ran then, making it to the kitchen before he rammed into her from behind. His hands were on her, tearing at her precious fairy dress, tearing at her. Then a sweet moment's release when he moved away and she thought he'd gone, only for his weight to return, pressing her back into the edge of the counter, pushing inside her dry resisting body. Pounding her.

Neither of them heard the front door open. It wasn't until Gina saw Matt's horrified face that she managed to scream for help. At the same time, Ledbetter turned, his face red and sweaty.

Matt's fist connected and sent Ledbetter stumbling across the floor. Gina, stunned, shocked, reached for the nearest weapon, her hand closing over the cast-iron pot kept on the counter. It was a heavy weight in her hand, the first swing of it making her stumble, the second swing hitting Ledbetter's head with a satisfying crack. He looked startled before collapsing, first to his knees, then flat on his face.

Gina threw the pot to one side and sank to the floor gathering her torn dress around her body.

'He's dead,' Matt said, feeling the fallen man's neck for a pulse. 'Shit; we'd better ring the police.'

'No, no police.'

Matt crossed to her side. 'It was self-defence. I can testify to that.'

Gina shook her head. Then she made her second mistake of the evening. 'No, I can't have the police involved.'

'You can't.' He looked back to the body. 'Do you know him?'

'No, I've never seen him before.'

Matt walked to the window and stared out. 'I know where we

put him.' He turned to her and grinned. 'We can bury him in
bottom of the garden.'

Gina was still on her knees. She'd have liked to have gone
stairs, got into the shower and turned the water on, hot as it
uld come. But she wasn't sure she could stand. When she saw
tt approaching, she thought she'd misunderstood his words and
ked up. He was standing too close.

'I said I'll do it, but you have to do some work for me first.'

She still didn't understand. Not until Matt undid the zipper of
jeans. Then she shook her head and tried to get to her feet. The
n-handed slap across her face sent her reeling. The hand in her
r pulling her up was agonising. But nothing compared to what
owed.

67

Leigh had grown more rigid as Flavia's story progressed until s
was sitting still on her chair, the stem of her glass pressed painfu
between her fingers. 'I don't believe you.' But there was no con
dence in the words. 'Matt said he'd gone back to Salisbury on t
Tuesday.'

'Matt said, Matt said,' Flavia sneered. 'He lied to you. He stay
here all week. Barely spoke to me, but I could feel his eyes on n
weighing me up, wondering if I'd be game. I ignored him, hopi
he'd get the message.' She took a mouthful of wine and wiped
hand over her mouth. 'Some men don't like being ignored. T
night, maybe punching Ledbetter gave his testosterone a boost
maybe he believed in "to the victor the spoils".' She shrugged. 'A
know is, he no longer cared if I was game or not. I was his. A sex t
A blow-up doll with holes for his pleasure.' She drained her gla
'And he used them all.'

'Stop!' Leigh got to her feet and walked away. Reaching the
wall, she rested her forehead against it.

'When he came back in from burying the body, I was still on t
floor. He looked at me as if I was a piece of filth and told me to

gone before you got back. He said my secret would be safe if I simply vanished. I'd no choice but to agree.' She reached for the bottle and filled her glass again. 'I lay there for a long time, planning my revenge. I wanted to destroy him.'

Leigh turned around. 'You sent the letter to the school.'

Flavia lifted her glass in a mock toast. 'Yes, I was hoping they'd fire him.'

'They probably would have, except I told Matt you were wanted by the police for the death of that woman in Glasgow. It threw enough doubt about your credibility to allow them to reinstate him. His confession that he'd cheated on me, to be honest, probably did him more harm in the eyes of the principal. At least it would have done until he was arrested for murder. That,' she snorted inelegantly, 'trumps all else.'

'Now you know it wasn't him.' Flavia nodded to where the oversized cast-iron pot sat on the counter. 'It was the perfect weapon.'

Leigh shivered. 'You didn't mean to kill him...'

'Didn't I?'

'He'd raped you; you were defending yourself.'

'No, I was getting revenge. Matt had already pushed him away at that stage. What I did was payback.'

'The legal system would have taken the situation into account. You wouldn't have gone to prison—'

'Not for that, perhaps,' Flavia interrupted her. 'I didn't kill that woman in Glasgow, but that doesn't mean I haven't done some things the police would like to prosecute me for.'

Leigh was still struggling to believe everything she'd been told. There were still dangling strings. 'You said you didn't come into my home at night to scare me, so why did you?'

Flavia rolled wine around her glass. 'I'd barricaded myself into my bedroom that night. When I came out in the morning, Matt was gone. I was so angry, I stood on the landing and screamed until my throat was hoarse. I was determined to get revenge, but I didn't know where he lived. I looked everywhere in your too bloody tidy house but couldn't find an address for him. The only thing I found was his business card, so I knew where he worked, that he was a teacher. But Salisbury is a big place and, these days, hanging around outside a school is to invite the wrong sort of attention. I thought you'd have a diary or something in your handbag to tell me where the bastard lived.'

Leigh shook her head. 'I keep everything on my phone.'

'Yes, it didn't take me long to find that out.'

'But you kept coming back?'

Flavia sighed. 'I was having flashbacks to what happened that night. Not only to the rapes but to the dead body. The blood.' Her mouth twisted as she remembered. 'I had to clean it up. That Saturday morning. The blood. The spunk from both men. The tears, snot and spit from me.' Her hand shook when she lifted the wine to her mouth. She drank deeply, more wine spilling, dripping to her shirt. She put the empty glass down, nodding her thanks when Leigh reached over with the bottle to fill it again. 'I kept waking, thinking I'd missed a bit; my head wouldn't allow me rest till I came back to check.

'The way Matt treated me, the violence of it. It wasn't a one off, Leigh. Men like him keep that part of their lives separate. I'm guessing he has a sex life in Salisbury you know nothing about.'

'Probably.' Leigh held a hand over her eyes. She didn't want to let Flavia see the truth in them. The guilt. How many times had Leigh forgiven Matt when he'd hurt her? All the promises it would never happen again. The bouquets of flowers. And hadn't it grown worse recently? She still remembered the pain of that bite. Instead of dismissing it, forgiving him, she should have insisted he get help in dealing with it. If she had... She dragged her hand down her face.

There was nothing to be achieved by telling Flavia now. 'I'm so very sorry, I never thought him capable of such a thing.'

'Stop beating yourself up; you didn't make him rape me, that was his choice.' Flavia wiped a hand over her mouth, an eyebrow rising when it came away stained with wine. 'Seems I'm slobbering a bit.' She used the sleeve of her shirt to wipe her face. 'Tell me, who was that Ledbetter guy and why was he so mad at you?'

'Bernard Ledbetter.' Leigh explained what had gone on in Lancaster International. 'That's where I was the week I was away. On an anger management course.'

'Seems to me they'd have been better off sending him on that.'

Leigh felt a twisting twinge of guilt. 'If I hadn't reported him, none of this would have happened.'

'You were right to do what you did. Probably should have done it sooner.'

They sat in silence for a few minutes, each lost in their thoughts. It was Leigh who spoke first. 'You never did find out where Matt lived, did you?'

'No. I rang the school, but they wouldn't tell me. Then, of course, all hell had broken loose here.'

It was a good way of describing what had happened. Leigh shivered as she remembered the maggots oozing from that awful hand. Ledbetter's. She was still finding it hard to come to terms with that. 'I thought the hand was a fake at first, you know, like the first one.' She frowned at Flavia. 'Was that you?'

'Yes.' Flavia shrugged. 'Someone had left it behind in the café and hadn't returned to claim it, so I brought it home. When I was ready to leave that day, I went out and stuck it in the garden. I meant it as a signal to Matt. You know, like a wave to say I'm watching you.'

'I thought it was neighbours' kids playing a trick.' She didn't say she'd been so convinced it was Gina's body that she'd rung the police.

'It was a silly idea. I was simmering with anger that day. I think I scared the wits out of some guy who came around with a package for you.'

'Philip, a friend; you told him we were lovers.'

Flavia laughed. 'I'd just got out of the shower... I think it was my sixth or seventh... and I'd applied a face mask to try and reduce the bruising to my face. When he kept ringing the doorbell, I looked out your bedroom window and saw a well-dressed, very handsome man. I remember wondering what would happen if I answered the door. Would I be raped again?' She sighed, her shoulders slumping. 'That's when I knew I had to answer it, had to prove to myself that I could. So I pulled a heavy dressing gown on over the towel I'd wrapped myself in and went down.'

Her eyes lost focus, her voice barely a whisper when she continued. 'I felt sick with fear as I stood at the door, but I had it in my head that if I could do it, if I could open the door to a strange man, then the terror would fade.' She huffed another sigh, then with her voice a little stronger, added. 'When I did, there wasn't a monster on the other side and, I was right, it did help. Just a little.'

Seconds passed before she spoke again. 'I hope I didn't make things difficult for you. He looked so supremely self-confident and smug that I couldn't resist it when he asked me if I knew you.'

'No, he's a friend, that's all.' Leigh imagined the woman, layers of thick material giving her bulk, hair wrapped in another towel giving extra height, a face mask obscuring her features. Obviously traumatised... *her sixth or seventh shower*... yet filled with bravado. It no longer seemed important but, out of curiosity, she asked, 'How did you know I'd inherited this house? I'm sure I didn't tell you.'

'No, you didn't. I heard you talking to another customer, you were complaining about the cost of getting tradesmen to do work.

ly someone who owns a place does that. I followed you home
e evening.' Flavia smiled. 'I am what I am. A con artist, confi-
nce trickster, scam artist, whatever you want to call me. So I have
rned to use what I know. You wear M&S suits which told me you
n't have an awful lot of money. It wasn't a huge leap to guess
d inherited the house.'

Leigh couldn't help but be impressed. 'You'd never think of...'
e seesawed her hand.

'Going straight, you mean?' Flavia laughed. 'No, way too boring
me. This way, I get to be whomever I want, whenever I want.'
e tilted her head to one side. 'I wasn't following you that day
en you saw me on Kentish Town Road, by the way. It was simply
l luck we happened to be in the same place at the same time. It
n't happen again. By this time tomorrow, I'll be a long way from
e.'

Leigh reached for her glass. 'Why did you come here?'

'Two reasons, actually.' Flavia reached a hand over and laid it on
gh's. 'Offering me accommodation was a very kind thing to do
l you were poorly repaid for it. I wanted to explain so that you
n't be reluctant to be as kind again.' She grinned and winked.
ough perhaps next time, be a little more careful.'

'I think I might be,' Leigh said. 'What was the second thing?'

Flavia took her hand away. 'I didn't plan to kill that guy. It was
bad luck the first thing my hand found was that pot. I've always
ded to use my wit rather than violence to get revenge on those
o harm me. My letter to Matt's school principal was part of that.'

Flavia's expression hardened when she mentioned Matt's name.
denly she looked older. Leigh was tempted to apologise again
her part in the pain she'd been caused but before she could say
same useless words, Flavia spoke again.

'I wanted to make him suffer. To destroy his career.' She reached
her glass and took a sip of wine. 'His career, not his life, so now

I'm in a bit of a quandary... should I allow him to go to prison
something he didn't do, to get revenge for something he did?'

Surprised, Leigh shook her head. 'You're giving him m
consideration than he gave you.'

'I can't help thinking, if I'd rung the police after that Ledbe
guy had raped me, Matt wouldn't have been able to take advant
of the situation.'

'No!' Leigh reached for her hand and held it tightly. 'You c
blame yourself for what he did! He should have been offering
comfort, not taking advantage.' She gave the small-boned hand
held a squeeze, tears welling to think of what this butterfly-wor
had been put through by the two men. 'You wouldn't go to
police now? Tell them what happened?'

Flavia turned her hand to clasp Leigh's. 'It's too late. If I wen
the police now, it would be my word against his and, with
history, his legal team would tear my credibility apart.' She reac
across and tapped the phone. 'I can't be objective about this. C
decide what's the right thing to do. Still too caught up in the pain
what happened.'

Her fingers curled around the phone. She picked it up
placed it on the table between them. 'You know the full story, so
going to leave the decision of what to do up to you. If you give t
in to the police, it will help clear Matt of murder. They won't pro
cute on the rape allegation based on this, so he'll be safe from tl
All he'll be charged with is burying the body.' She tapped a sl
dull beat on the phone as she held Leigh's gaze. 'I'm leaving
choice to you. You can give it to the police or delete it.'

Leigh tried to pull her hand away, but what Flavia lacked in s
she made up for in strength and her hand was trapped. 'What?
can't put this on me!'

'You're a good woman. You'll do what's best.' Flavia relea
her grip, drained her glass and got to her feet. 'You'll never see

again. The police can look to their hearts' content, they won't find me.' She swung her jacket over her shoulders. 'Once I'm gone, I'll put what happened here out of my head, but I'll remember you and your kindness.' She leaned down and planted a kiss on Leigh's cheek. 'We could have been friends. Take care. Do the right thing.'

Then she was gone. Leigh didn't move, even when she heard the front door shut.

Do the right thing!

Two hours later, she was still wondering what that was. She'd listened to the recording on her phone three times, stopping and restarting several times. Gina had admitted she was a confidence trickster so why should Leigh believe her? She analysed every word, every phrase of the recording, checking for tone and believability. She wasn't sure if she was trying to convince herself she believed or she didn't. Believing Gina... Flavia... whoever the fuck she was... meant believing the man she'd loved was a monster.

Leigh had fast-forwarded over the details of what Matt had done to Gina because she couldn't bring herself to listen. Finally, she did... listened to every word, hearing the absolute sadness in Gina's voice as she explained every demeaning disgusting depraved detail of what Matt had done to her.

A self-confessed con artist. Liar. Chancer. Leigh shouldn't believe a word out of her mouth, shouldn't cringe at the painful truth in every shocking word. Shouldn't, but did.

Which meant Matt, the man she'd once hoped to marry, *was* a monster.

Sadness and horror formed a lump in her throat. She slid the mobile across the table, folded her arms and rested her head in the crook of her elbow as tears burned. Hot stinging tears for herself, for Gina, for the crazy situation Leigh found herself in.

Gina had said they could have been friends... but Leigh knew she'd meant before... before Ledbetter and Matt. Two men whose paths she'd never have crossed if she hadn't met Leigh.

Was this why she'd been given this horrific decision to make? A final act of revenge.

If she handed the recording over to the police, they'd be obliged to hand it over to Matt's defence team. They'd use it to get the murder conviction quashed. He might serve time for burying the body – he might not. His team could use the recording to prove he'd been the victim of a woman with a history of manipulating circumstances.

That was the right thing to do... the easiest... she'd hand it over, put it all behind her, forget about it and get on with the new life she'd planned. It was the *easiest option*... and she'd always taken that, hadn't she? If she hadn't done so in the past... with Ledbetter, with Matt... none of this mess would have occurred. The realisation made the tears overspill and trickle down her cheeks.

She sat up straighter and brushed the tears away. It was time to accept some responsibility for what had happened. If she handed the tape over, Gina was right, her story of being raped would be dismissed.

Leaving Matt free. He'd get a teaching job elsewhere. Carry on with his life. And maybe, in the distant future, he'd meet another vulnerable woman, and do it all again.

But if Leigh didn't hand it over...

If she deleted the recording and Matt went to prison for Ledbetter's murder, she would have to keep what she'd done a secret forever. She thought of Philip who so carefully separated the different parts of his life – if she deleted Gina's tale, she'd never be able to tell him what she'd done. Their relationship was doomed before ever beginning.

There was only one person she'd ever be able to talk to about it, and Leigh didn't know who she was.

Do the right thing... not the easiest. Almost of their own accord, her fingers crept across the table and curled around her mobile. She pressed play to listen one more time, Gina's sad words echoing around the room.

The decision wasn't difficult in the end. *Do the right thing.*

She deleted it.

ACKNOWLEDGMENTS

,ve a huge debt of gratitude to so many people for getting me to
s stage of what is the most wonderful career.

Firstly, I'd like to thank the Boldwood Books team – especially
brilliant and insightful editor, Emily Ruston, who has helped
pull this, my twenty-first book, into shape, my hawk-eyed copy
tor, Candida Bradford, for her hard work and wonderful
gestions and finally, my proofreader, Shirley Khan, for that last
ish.

The writing community is amazingly helpful and encouraging
I I've been lucky enough to have made many friends... other
ters, bloggers, reviewers and readers... all of whom make being a
ter less lonely. Thank you all.

Special thanks have to go to the long-suffering writer, Jenny
Brien, who is first to read my manuscript and who is generous
h her time and advice. It is Jenny I turn to when my writing isn't
ng too well – to my pathetic cry of 'this one is rubbish' she invari-
y offers an eye-roll and her usual come-back of, 'you always say
t!' Thanks for being there, Jenny.

Thanks, as usual, to my friends, sisters, brothers, nieces, neph-
s, grand-nieces, grand-nephews, and my husband, Robert.

And of course, thanks to you, readers, without which there'd be
point.

ve to hear from readers. You can find me here:

https://authorcentral.amazon.co.uk/gp/books
Facebook: https://www.facebook.com/valeriekeoghnovels
Twitter: https://twitter.com/ValerieKeogh1
Instagram: https://www.instagram.com/valeriekeogh2
https://www.bookbub.com/authors/valerie-keogh

MORE FROM VALERIE KEOGH

We hope you enjoyed reading *The Lodger*. If you did, please leave a review.

If you'd like to gift a copy, this book is also available as an ebook, digital audio download and audiobook CD.

Sign up to Valerie Keogh's mailing list for news, competitions and updates on future books.

https://bit.ly/ValerieKeoghNews

ABOUT THE AUTHOR

Valerie Keogh is the internationally bestselling author of several psychological thrillers and crime series, most recently published by Bloodhound. She originally comes from Dublin but now lives in Wiltshire and worked as a nurse for many years.

Follow Valerie on social media:

 twitter.com/ValerieKeogh1

 facebook.com/valeriekeoghnovels

instagram.com/valeriekeogh2

Boldwood

Boldwood Books is an award-winning fiction publishing company seeking out the best stories from around the world.

Find out more at www.boldwoodbooks.com

Join our reader community for brilliant books, competitions and offers!

Follow us
@BoldwoodBooks
@BookandTonic

Sign up to our weekly deals newsletter

https://bit.ly/BoldwoodBNewsletter